When I hired hit men, I had no idea what I was getting into. And now things were rapidly spinning out of control…

It seemed like lifetimes passed as the fire burned and Diane stared in my direction. "Tom, you out there?" Diane called. "Come on Tom, get back here." She paced back and forth, letting the axe swing by her knees. "Bardos is going to be okay. Bullet just nicked him. Can't say the same for you, unless you come back here."

I didn't move, barely breathed.

"You saw too much. Saw a man get chopped up. But if you don't get out here, I'm going to think you're getting scared. Getting cold feet. And if you're scared, then I don't think I can trust you. You might end up telling someone. This is why Bardos was right, and I messed up by bringing you here. You didn't need to see it happen. You just needed to know it did. But now you've looked, and I figure you can't look away. And I can't trust you're going to forget."

Diane stopped pacing and held the axe with both hands.

"Come out here, Tom, and let me finish this. This way you get to pick how it happens. Trust me, every person I've ever dealt with—at the end, they wish they could have controlled it. That's all they wish at the end."

I stayed still on the dark, hard, cold dirt.

"Be seeing you soon," Diane said, and she stomped out the fire. She took a long walk around the clearing, climbed back into the van, and drove off.

I tried to think about Renee again but I couldn't even remember what her face loc᠁

All I heard were my br

Tom Starks has spent the three years since his wife's murder struggling to single-handedly raise their daughter, Julie, while haunted by memories of his dead spouse. When he learns that the man accused of her murder, Chris Taylor, has been released from prison, Tom hires a pair of hit men to get his revenge. But when the hit men botch the assassination, Tom is inadvertently pulled into their violent world—And now those hit men are after him and his daughter.

KUDOS for *I'll Sleep When You're Dead*

I'll Sleep When You're Dead is a haunting tale of vengeance and its toll. It is both thrilling and tender. The domestic scenes are every bit as gripping as the action sequences. E.A. Aymar weaves a touching tapestry loaded with surprises. – *Michael Sears, author of* Black Fridays, *winner of the Shamus Award for Best First Novel*

A twisty, tightly-written thriller with jolts of unexpected humor and a deeply moving examination of human grief. A terrific read. – *Lou Berney, author of* Whiplash River *and* Gutshot Straight, *nominated for the Edgar and Barry awards*

In *I'LL SLEEP WHEN YOU'RE DEAD*, E.A. Aymar has crafted a brutal, harrowing tale of love, lust, loss, and the fool's gold promise of revenge. – *Chris F. Holm, author of the* Collector *series, winner of the Spinetingler Award*

The bereaved and vengeful hero of E.A. Aymar's new thriller *I'll Sleep When You're Dead* is a young widower who talks directly to the reader: "Wine, classical music, and architecture: the three big cultural gaps in the education of Tom Starks," he says of himself. "Coming in fourth—how to hire assassins." Don't miss the opportunity to follow Starks' chilling learning curve. In this tightly-wound novel, set in part on the streets of Crabtown, USA, the dead speak and those that speaketh too freely wind up dead as Tom Starks stalks the man who killed his wife while trying to raise an adolescent daughter. Along the way, he struggles mightily, stumbles, and keeps going. As the great Johnny Winter once sang at the end of a dark alley: "It serves me right to suffer…it serves me right to be alone…" – *Ralph Alvarez, author of* Tales from the Holy Land *and HBO's* The Wife

The plot was well thought out and completely unpredictable. Just when you think things are going to go right for Tom at last, they don't. – *Taylor Jones, Reviewer*

The book was refreshingly honest, the plot riveting. This one is hard to put down. – *Regan Murphy, Reviewer*

ACKNOWLEDGEMENTS

I owe a lot of thanks to a lot of people and I'm going to forget to include someone. I just know it.

Thanks to everyone at Black Opal Books for believing in me and this book, particularly Lauri, Cora, and Faith. I was lucky to end up with such a terrific publisher.

I had the privilege to work with a couple of superheroes in their fields: Angela Del Vecchio, who designed the cover, and Alice Peck, who edited the original version of this manuscript way back when.

Like most writers, I have a network of friends and other writers who read the early stages of my writing: Michele, Amy, Natalie, Jenny, Nancy, Sara, Carolyn and Lindsay. Thanks to all of you for your feedback and encouragement.

Thanks to the people I've worked with side-by-side for years, who have really become a family to me. In particular Marty, Ellen, Leslie, Christina and, of course, Molly.

There are a number of other writers and artists I've befriended over the years, and I'm lucky to know and be inspired by them: KD McCrite, Sarah Erdman, Ellie Ann Soderstram, Nina Cole, Michelle Davidson Argyle, Jenny Drummey, Sara Jones, Janet Bell, Kelly McCann, Ryan Schiewe, and Kristen Elise. Google these people and check out their work. You won't be disappointed.

I've had the fortune to study under some terrific teachers, like Alan Cheuse, Susan Shreve, Richard Goodwin, Holly Karapetkova and Marguerite Rippy.

Thanks to my agent, Jeanie Loiacono, for helping me read through contracts and always being available for questions.

A lot of people gave me advice when it came to marketing this book. If you've never met me and you're reading this line, then their advice worked! Thanks Peggy, Kathleen, Evin, Peter, Cleve, Howard, Laura, Rachel and Dana Kaye.

Of course, thanks to Mom and Dad.

And thanks to my wife for the most complete love ever. Aww.

Finally, thanks to you for buying this book and reading my work. If we ever meet, let's do one of those flying chest-bump things.

See you in the next book.

E.A.

I'LL SLEEP WHEN YOU'RE DEAD

BOOK 1 IN THE DEAD TRILOGY

E. A. AYMAR

A BLACK OPAL BOOKS PUBLICATION

Dear Mickey,
    Happy Reading!
        EA

GENRE: MYSTERY/SUSPENSE/MAINSTREAM/ROMANTIC   ELE-
MENTS

I'LL SLEEP WHEN YOU'RE DEAD
Copyright © 2013 by E. A. Aymar
Cover Design by Angela Del Vecchio
All cover art copyright © 2013
All Rights Reserved
Print ISBN: 9781626940857

First Publication: NOVEMBER 2013

Published by Black Opal Books **http://www.blackopalbooks.com**

DEDICATION

To Nancy

and

Coach Neil Shaefer (1953 – 2013)

"Mercedes lives, and not only lives, but remembers."
– Alexander Dumas, *The Count of Monte Cristo*

PROLOGUE

Just an hour before my wife was murdered, I pulled into a long line of vehicles waiting outside of our daughter's elementary school. I was tired. Today, teaching had drained me. I wasn't a particularly good student growing up, but I found myself irritated when my junior college students showed the same lack of motivation.

One paper clearly indicated the student hadn't even opened the book: *Hemingway's novel uses the symbolism of a man who lost his arms to illustrate the symbol of how helpless he feels.*

A bell rang and a group of children rushed through the doors, making beelines for our long line of cars and SUVs. Julie disengaged from the pack, trotted to my truck, and climbed into the passenger seat.

"How was school?" I asked as I guided my truck into the street.

"It was okay. I have to write a book report."

"Really?" I glanced at her, my curiosity piqued. "On what book?"

She shrugged. "I dunno. We have to pick one."

"What are the choices?"

"I dunno."

"You don't know?"

Julie sighed and crossed her arms. "She gave us a list."

"Can I see the list?"

Julie stared out her window and absent-mindedly played with her hair, the way an older woman would. "Later," she said.

I started to speak but caught myself. I wanted to tell her to talk nicer or say something that started with, "Young lady," but I wasn't sure how harsh I should be. I hated to admit it, but I didn't feel comfortable disciplining Renee's daughter, even if I had legally adopted her. Besides, Renee was better at this stuff than I was.

"I'm going to help you with this," I said defiantly.

Julie sighed and continued to look out the window. "I know you will."

When I worked out the calculations later, based on what the crime scene investigators reported, I realized Renee faced her murderer at some point during that argument with Julie.

He'd watched her for days, because he knew she liked to buy fruit and vegetables at the small market just off the Jones Fall Expressway. Somehow, he'd convinced her to walk around the store and, once there, forced her to the ground and pushed a rag deep in her mouth, too far for her to pull out. He dragged her into the trees that bordered the back of the store, just before the nature trail that wound through a small delicate forest. He threw her to the ground but Renee climbed to her feet and tried to run off, awkwardly pulling at the rag. He rushed after her and tackled her. They crashed into a tree. A deep cut on the side of her head left the bark bloody.

Renee sprawled on the ground, dazed. He picked up a metal baseball bat he had left leaning behind a tree.

She saw him approach, probably saw a glint of sunlight reflect off the metal, and tried to climb to her feet. That's when he swung the first time. The first blow hit her squarely on the side of her head and knocked her off her feet. She was barely conscious as she crawled away, as he kicked her in the ribs, knocking her to her back. Renee raised her hands to protect her face as the bat came down, and then her hands dropped as the bat came down again and again.

The medical examiner told me she wasn't raped, but her clothes were removed, probably because the murderer was worried about evidence.

The image of Renee's naked dead body made things worse. Nudity left her helpless. Even after death, the murderer took something from her.

I'll never understand how Julie and I were able to drive home, both of us stupidly irritated, while Renee was viciously murdered just miles away. There should have been some sign, a feeling, a premonitory sense that something terrible was happening. But there was nothing.

Until three years later…

CHAPTER 1

Just Fall

I was going to kill someone later in the afternoon, so I canceled classes that Monday and spent the morning on the couch, watching crappy television judge shows and trying to keep calm.

I took a long shower at eleven then, at noon, drove my truck out of Baltimore and toward D.C. The sky grayed as I headed around the curves of the Beltway and, eventually, thick rain splashed against the windshield. You could never tell what November weather was going to do. Neither Baltimore nor D.C. had real seasons. It was always too hot or too cold, buried in snow or heat, running back and forth between extremes like rats or people who believe in politics or religion.

I finally reached my destination, a neighborhood in Falls Church, Virginia. I slumped down in my truck and slipped on sunglasses and a black baseball cap. It was probably obvious that I was trying to disguise myself—

completely defeating the purpose—but I didn't want to take the chance of getting spotted.

I waited.

An hour passed, then another, and my nervousness rushed ahead of my impatience. Light rain bounced off my windshield. I reached over to my small gym bag on the passenger seat and touched the edge of my Glock 30. I touched it every few minutes to calm myself down, even if petting a loaded gun wasn't the smartest idea in the world.

Using it probably wasn't too bright, either, but Chris Taylor was out of prison. Three years ago, he'd been sentenced for killing my wife, Renee Starks.

"I haven't talked to her in years," Chris Taylor protested after his arrest.

I, myself, in a daze, was one of several people who'd even told the police that, to my knowledge, Renee and Chris hadn't spoken since their brief relationship in college—so brief that she barely ever mentioned him. But his initials were on the baseball bat found in the bushes near her naked body and so were his fingerprints. He was given a life sentence, but released in three years when a retrial cast enough doubt on his conviction to overturn it.

Renee was so palpable—even now, such a presence, that sometimes I lost myself in thoughts of her. Sometimes I felt her return, like she was sitting here in the passenger seat of my truck, looking at me with her wide brown eyes, one hand brushing her bangs away from her face.

'*What are you doing, Tom?*' she asked.

"Trying to kill this guy."

'*How are you going to do that?*'

"I'm going to wait until he's alone then shoot him." I paused. "That's not much of a plan, is it?"

Renee shook her head. '*You were never good at planning things. That was one of my complaints about you.*'

"You know," I said, "you're awfully critical for a dead chick."

A door slam startled me. I peered out my window and, through the hedges, watched an elderly woman emerge from the house with a man I didn't recognize. But I remembered the woman. Chris Taylor's mother had been tall and delicate with long, black hair—which was now short and gray. Throughout the trial, she bore a constant expression of determination on her face. Now her face was old and pained, droopy as a melted candle, all signs of her previous determination gone. She looked like a shrunken version of herself.

Chris Taylor came out of the house behind them.

He ducked into a black Lincoln Navigator with his mother and the man before I could get a good look at him. The SUV's red tail lights gleamed as they slowly drove down the street.

I started the truck and followed their vehicle down the neighborhood's narrow, winding roads, trying to distract myself by glancing at houses as we passed them. The homes here were humungous and brick, behind long circular driveways, and set apart from each other, not like the chains of row houses that ran through Baltimore. Tall trees were everywhere, stripped of leaves by the coming winter, their brown barren branches stretching plaintively toward the sky. Some of the homes were hidden on the tops of hills, finally visible and monumental when I rounded a curve. The entire suburb was pristine and aloof, with the type of tension a held breath holds, the suspense of a secret.

I had driven around this neighborhood so often during the past month that I could do it blindfolded. And I knew exactly where Chris, his mother, and the man with them were going. She went to a nearby church every weekday afternoon. I assumed she would take Chris with her —if not, then I would have snuck into her house and killed Chris there. I knew the path she took, what time she left, and when she returned.

I watched their car turn onto the curved road that led to the parking lot, then I pulled over to the shoulder. I took off my hat and sunglasses, pulled the small Glock 30 from my gym bag, shoved it into the back of my pants, and left my car, ducking my head from the rain. The wet, gray sky looked like a dirty tissue.

I crept into the thick trees and underbrush that lined the road. There was a place where the branches and bramble were so thick that I could crouch about ten feet from the parking lot and no one would be able to see me, especially with the darkness from the stormy afternoon. The poor weather was a surprise, but one I chalked up to good fortune.

St. Elizabeth Catholic Church was the kind of structure children draw, a small simple building with a high steeple and narrow cross above the front doors. Only four or five cars were in the parking lot, and I wondered how many people even knew this building was here. Churches were mixed into Baltimore—you could stand on the top of Federal Hill and see their crosses or golden domes dotting the city like punctuation marks spread through a long paragraph. But the churches were isolated from each other and everything else here in northern Virginia, hidden in neighborhoods or tucked back from sidewalks, as if they didn't want to intrude on the world around them.

Chris, his mother, and the other man emerged from the Navigator, and I watched Chris stand and stretch, his hands raised high. He was still long and lean and lanky, with the body of a swimmer, his blond hair shaved off, leaving him with just a haze on his head. His face was thinner than I remembered, and his eyes still held the same blue. But the blue was worn. His boyishness was gone.

The other man walked around the car, clapped Chris on the shoulder, and said something I couldn't hear. I wiped rain from my face and leaned forward, trying to listen. The man suddenly turned and I saw the flash of a gold cross over his chest. I thought he might be some type of minister, or maybe even a priest, but he wasn't wearing a collar. Then again, I wasn't sure if priests constantly wore collars the way that a policeman or federal agent always carried their guns. It had been years since I'd knelt in a church.

The man and Chris Taylor's mother headed toward the doors, but Chris stayed outside. Alone.

I reached around my back and took out the Glock. I held my breath as Chris walked toward me, stopped a few steps from the trees, and looked up, letting the rain splash his face. My eyes burned as I scanned the parking lot, trying to see if anyone was watching. But the cars were empty.

I pointed the gun at Chris. There was no mounted sight, so I looked down the v-shaped inlet at the tip and centered it on his chest. Branches were between us, but they weren't thick, and I assumed the bullet would tear through them on its path. If the shot to the chest didn't kill him, I would run out and shoot his fallen body in the head then rush to my car and drive away.

I didn't expect to escape. I wanted to, but I wasn't a professional killer. All the cop shows and news stories I'd watched suggested that the police would easily find an amateur criminal, especially one like me with such a strong motive. So going to prison was something I expected, but I was ready to sacrifice myself.

My hand, my entire arm, shook as I pointed the gun at him. Minutes seemed like they passed but, in actuality, it was only seconds.

I tried to remember the training from my stint in the Army—take a deep breath, exhale as I slowly squeeze the trigger. And I tried to remember my loss—Renee's love and touch, the simple easy joy whenever I saw her. I had lain in bed last night, thinking about my loneliness, and promised myself to remember that feeling in case I didn't think I could go through with it today.

It was nothing but a tug from one finger, a simple cross from circumstance to consequence.

A gigantic leap made with the tiniest effort.

I tried to tell myself that all I needed to do was pull that small metal crescent and I could deal with everything else later, the guilt and repentance and doubt, all of that would come afterward.

Just fall in.

Rain tapped on leaves, and the brown day darkened even more. My knees ached from my crouched position, and the pain was so intense that I thought about rushing Chris, dragging him into the woods, then shooting him. The thought formed into a plan—I could leave his body here and get a head start on the cops. I squeezed my eyes shut in pain, opened them, and Chris was gone.

For a brief moment I wondered if this was my imagination, a hallucination, grief spinning some elaborate fantasy. It wouldn't be the first time. But when I peered out of the underbrush, I saw Chris walking toward the church. I followed him, stepping through branches, not worried about noise because the rain was falling even harder. In fact, I realized the rain was so intense that the gunshot might even be muffled. I stayed about ten feet behind Chris, walking near the edge of the parking lot, the gun pointed straight ahead.

I was just waiting for the right moment. If he turned around, I promised myself, I would kill him immediately. It didn't seem right to shoot him in the back. Not because I considered it cowardly, but because I wanted Chris to know who murdered him. I realized that was something shooting from inside the underbrush wouldn't give me.

I wanted him to see me.

I stopped, aimed, and opened my mouth to call him.

Nothing came out.

Chris reached the church doors.

I tried to speak again and again. Nothing. He opened the doors.

"Renee." I desperately hoped her name would give me strength, even as the doors closed. But, at that moment, I couldn't even remember what her face looked like.

I closed my eyes and held the gun more tightly than I had ever held anything. Love, God, or hate.

CHAPTER 2

California Mist

I slept fitfully that night, waking tired the next morning. Sleepily, I climbed out of bed, staggered down the hall to Julie's bedroom, and banged on her door. There was no answer, and it took me a few moments to remember she wasn't here. And that was probably for the best, since my goal for the day was to hire a hit man. And also to grade some papers and go to the grocery store. But after that, get a hit man.

I headed to the kitchen, flicking on lights along the way.

Julie.

I remembered her anger when I asked her to move in with her aunt and uncle for a couple of months. I wanted to distance her from me, to distance her from Chris Taylor's murder and my arrest. I'd thought Julie would turn to me after Renee's death—her biological father had vanished when Renee was pregnant—but Julie had closed herself off after Renee was gone, short with her statements and dismissive with her attitude. I thought time would help, but now Julie was twelve and all time did was make her resentful.

I ate a couple of Eggos and walked on the treadmill, trying to ease the night aches out of my leg. I was a decent runner growing up, to the point where I earned a track scholarship at a Division III college. But I graduated with an English degree and no idea what to do with it, so I followed a couple of my teammates into the Army and a training injury promptly left me with shrapnel stuck in my leg. I received a medical discharge, a barely noticeable limp for life, and absolutely no chance of running again. Pacing on the treadmill was the best I could do.

I headed into work at Baltimore Community College and spent a restless morning teaching composition classes and grading papers. But impatience got the best of me, so I cancelled my afternoon classes and drove to Mack's Guns and Gifts in Towson, just outside of the city. I last drove here a month ago, when I bought the Glock.

It was one thing to lack the courage to kill someone, but I was nervous about just entering the store. I sat in my driver's seat and waited as day turned to evening, the sky turning purple like the flash of a king's robe as he walked away.

I picked up my mobile phone, entered a code to block my number, pressed REDIAL and waited for Chris Taylor to answer the phone at his mother's house.

"Hello?"

Definitely him.

"Hello?" he said again.

I hung up, opened my car door, and stepped outside.

A night chill knotted my guts. I walked across the parking lot, my eyes down. The same man that sold me my gun was standing behind the counter, an older man with features that reminded me of a giant bird. He had a hunched back, shoulders that dramatically rose to his collar, hooded eyes that darted rather than held their gaze, and a long nose that extended and hooked. A tall bald man examined a hunting vest near the back of the store.

I walked over to the counter. "I bought a gun here a few months ago."

The old man leaned forward. The nametag on his flannel shirt read MACK. "What?" he asked.

"I bought a gun from you," I told him.

"How's it been?"

I wasn't sure how to answer that. "Happy, I guess? It's hard to tell."

The bald man walked past the counter and called out, "All right, Mack. I'm out."

"Night, officer," Mack called back.

I watched the man leave the store. I had no idea he was a police officer. "I'm going to look around for a bit," I said.

"We close in twenty minutes."

I wandered away from the counter and headed down a row of duck decoys and coolers. Mack's Guns and Gifts wasn't big. It only held five rows of hunting gear and a small glass counter with shelves for pistols, rifles, and knives. I fingered the vinyl of a small model tent and waited, but I knew I couldn't take too long. There was the chance that someone might come inside. I walked back to the counter.

"I remember you, now," Mack said. "Glock, right? Never owned a gun before?"

His memory worried me. "That's right."

"And your name is…Tom. Tom Starks?"

"That's right," I said and swallowed, thinking it might be a good idea to leave. But I stood my ground. "I need to ask you a question."

"What?"

I glanced toward the door and raised my voice. "I need to ask a question!"

"I asked *what*!"

"If I needed to find someone who could shoot the gun for me, where would I look?"

Mack looked puzzled. "Someone to teach you how to shoot?"

I shook my head, leaned in closer, and said, slowly, "If I needed to find someone who would kill for me, do you know where I would look?"

"What?"

My throat was dry. I leaned in closer to Mack and he turned a large hairy gray ear toward me. Frantic thoughts bounced around my mind. *He has my name and address. He could report me to the police. I could end up in prison.* But I couldn't stop myself. "I was wondering if you knew of someone who I could hire to…kill a guy."

The old man stared at me, hard.

I looked back at him blankly.

"Get the hell out of my store," he said.

"What?"

"Get the hell out of my store!" he yelled. "Get the hell out of my store! Get the hell out..."

I backpedaled then turned and pushed through the door, flinching as the door's bell clanged above.

I got the hell out of his store, as well as the hell out of Towson. Just before I reached Baltimore, I pulled over to the side of the road and tried to calm down. My breathing slowed after a few minutes. I headed back into traffic and went to pick up my daughter.

I drove to Homeland, a ritzy Baltimore neighborhood, where houses were huge, single and separated from each other by manicured lawns, unlike the row houses that linked together every other neighborhood in the city. Trees filled the yards. Thick trees, the kind that look like they should be in children's books.

Houses here were made of colorful bricks, had unique windows and doors, and the aloof sense of privacy expensive areas always expressed. Homeland was different from much of the city, different than the neighborhoods mixed with houses and businesses and unpredictable energy and the occasional oasis of a historic building or warm community amidst poverty or depression. I liked the ugly prettiness. Baltimore was like an isle of grass or flowers littered with shiny bright beer cans. In that unreasonable beauty was the beautiful element of Baltimore.

It was a quick dark day—the middle of November. I savored summer, when women walked around in skirts and sandals and smiles, but winter's darkness brought a cozy intimacy to the city that, to me, no other season could.

I stood on the Wilsons' doorstep, rang their doorbell, and stared at my reflection in their glass door. My short dark hair needed a brush run through it, and my brown eyes were tired. I was getting a little paunchy. It may not have been noticeable to most people, but I noticed it, even if my height did hide a lot of sins.

My reflection was jerked away when Ruth Wilson opened the door. "Hey, Tom. Julie'll be out soon. She's just washing off makeup."

"Makeup?"

"She came home, wanting to try some on," Ruth said, a little defensively. "I didn't think it'd be a problem."

"It's no problem," I assured her, although the idea did make me uncomfortable. "It's probably better that you supervise something like that instead of me."

Ruth, Renee's sister, and her husband, Dave, did a lot to help with Julie, and I didn't have a right to complain.

"How are things with you?" Ruth asked.

"Oh, okay."

Ruth nodded like she expected this answer and leaned against the doorframe, her arms crossed and a small smile that painfully reminded me of Renee. She wore jeans that hung low on her hips and a small white T-shirt.

"How's Julie been?" I asked.

"She's good. You know we can keep her as long as you need. Longer than you said."

"I know."

"How's teaching?" Ruth asked.

"It's okay. I'm thinking about switching texts in my lit class."

"Yeah?"

"I figure the students will like it. Maybe pump some life back into them."

Ruth ran a hand through her brown hair and frowned. "Tom, stop."

"Sorry?"

She glanced back into her house. "*Pump some life?*"

"I wasn't—" I said, but Ruth lifted a finger to her lips and I let the matter drop.

Ruth always saw double-meanings in everything I said, especially since...

It happened a year after Renee's death, when we both finally felt like we were recovering. There had always been a closeness to my relationship with Ruth, and a harmless flirtation that, for some reason, seemed natural. One night, she and Dave came over for dinner. Julie was in bed and Dave was passed out on my couch, an empty bottle of wine sitting between his legs. Ruth and I were tipsy and laughing as we cleared the dishes, then somehow we were kissing in the kitchen.

And then her back was to the sink and her butt hoisted on the edge of the counter, legs wrapped around me, eyes on the doorway. It wasn't enough. I needed more and so did she. We pulled up our pants and hurried out the kitchen's backdoor and into the dark backyard. I lay on the mud and she settled herself slowly, squatting, sinking over me.

"I can't," I whispered.

"Yeah, right. My cunt."

"No, I said *I can't*."

She stopped. "Why not?"

"You're not Renee."

And that's when everything changed.

Ruth reached between our bodies and yanked my penis out of her. She was pulling her pants up by the time I stood. "Don't let Dave see you with all that mud," Ruth said, as she examined her own clothes.

"I'm sorry," I told her. "Also, I usually last longer than that."

Ruth nodded. That was the last time either of us ever directly spoke of it.

But I wondered if she thought about it, and if she felt the same sense of guilt I did.

I had known her relationship with Dave was unhappy. Renee used to tell me how depressed Ruth was about her marriage, and Julie told me about the fights she overheard when she stayed at their house. Ruth and Dave argued about money, about how much time he spent at work, and especially about children. Ruth couldn't have children naturally and wanted to try other methods, like insemination, using a surrogate, or adoption, but Dave dragged his feet until he eventually admitted that he wasn't sure if he wanted kids. He wasn't certain, he just wasn't sure. So they stayed together, but their foundation had already started to shake.

Maybe these were typical arguments between any couple, but they sounded explosive the way Julie described them. Smashed plates and punched walls. Dave was a reasonably nice guy, but there was a strong sense of "don't mess with me" about him. He was a former boxer and ferocious attorney, so he could ruin your life in multiple ways. Everything about him seemed carved in stone. A square jaw, thick-muscled build, and a small scar to the side of his right eye, a reminder of his boxing days. I often considered that scar when I remembered that night with Ruth. It was helpful in making sure that it never happened again. I spent a few nervous months expecting Dave to show up at my house, a subpoena in one hand and a boxing glove over the other. But Ruth kept our secret.

Julie appeared at the door and squeezed past Ruth, her cheeks red from scrubbing, faded blue over her eyes. "Hey," she said, unenthusiastically.

"Hi."

"I guess I'm ready."

"Not for makeup!" I exclaimed, trying to make Julie laugh, but she scowled instead. Ruth just looked puzzled.

"Sorry," I said.

"So I'm spending the night with you?" Julie asked.

"Yup. Last-minute change of plans."

Julie sighed. "Hate going back and forth."

I took her out to dinner. Julie barely spoke and sullenly picked at her food and then we went to a parent-teacher conference at her school.

She was too young to have total responsibility for her grades or behavior, and both needed improvement. I felt like I was going to be the one in trouble.

"Your daughter is doing poorly in my class, Mr. Starks," one of Julie's teachers, a short brunette, who looked like she was in her thirties, but carried a sternness that aged her twenty years, told me. "Do you need help?"

"Like, a tutor?"

"I meant, like, a *counselor*."

"Oh," I said. "Julie did see a child psychologist after her mother died, but she hated it so much that I promised her she'd never have to go back."

"You might consider talking to our school counselor," the woman said and nodded sagely. "She's *excellent*."

"I'll surely think about it," I offered, wondering why I had used the word *surely*, and looked toward the classroom door. I could see Julie through a small square window, standing across the hallway, staring at her shoes with her shoulders slumped. She was too old for a babysitter but sometimes, randomly, I felt uncomfortable leaving her alone in the house. "I'd better go," I said. "I don't want to keep her waiting too long. But I will make sure that she spends more time with her homework. I'm a teacher too, you know."

"But for a community college, correct?"

"That's correct."

"I see," the woman told me, but I noticed the look in her eyes. She looked thoroughly unimpressed.

"You're still getting D's," I told Julie as we walked through the school parking lot to my truck.

She attended Whitegate now, a private school in upscale Canton that Renee's life insurance was paying for. The night was cold and late. Not many cars were left in the lot.

"Guess so."

"Maybe we need to spend more time studying. I think I should start checking your homework after you finish it."

"I don't think so," Julie said.

"You don't think so?"

"I said *no!*" she shrieked.

I quickly looked around and saw an older couple staring at us. "Okay, okay. Chill. We'll talk later."

Julie glowered at me. "No one says chill anymore, *Dad*."

We went home and quietly watched television until she fell asleep.

I looked at Julie on the couch, her face still tense. The child psychologist told me, after Julie had angrily stormed out of his office, that she was going through a period where she would push away everyone who was close to her because she was scared of losing someone else. Renee's abrupt death terrified her. The doctor told me that, if I pushed back, if I let myself snap and give into anger, Julie might decide it was easier to abandon me altogether than risk getting hurt.

"You could lose her for good," he ominously warned me. I had to be careful punishing her and, despite her anger, any boundaries I established needed to be positive.

I really didn't know how to do that.

I hadn't thought as much as I should about being a parent when I proposed to Renee, and now I could almost physically feel Julie slipping away from me. Maybe I should have read parenting books or talked to more people for advice or seen a counselor myself…

I had logged back onto the computer.

I wondered if this was near rock bottom for loneliness—searching for someone to talk to online without even realizing you logged on, like an alcoholic absentmindedly popping open a beer. But it was a weeknight and I often felt a tortuous, stretched-out sense after dusk, as if a slow-moving wheel was turning to start another long day.

Depressing.

I had started going to dating sites, but the idea of meeting someone face-to-face didn't appeal to me. But I had spent the last week corresponding with a woman who called herself Alison, and who placed an ad, asking for "something discreet." I had e-mailed her back, telling her I wanted the same, and we traded ideas. We even planned out a rendezvous, but it wasn't something I thought I'd go through with, since I assumed I'd be sitting in jail for murder by now.

Alison had sent me a message. *Are we still on 4 tomorrow?*

I glanced at Julie's sleeping body, curled in a corner of the couch.

See you then, I wrote back.

I took Julie to bed, tucked her in and closed her door. I headed back downstairs and tried to start preparing for my classes, but couldn't. Instead, I went to my bedroom, opened the window, lit a joint, and let it fill me. I didn't smoke weed as often as I used to, probably just once a week after Julie had gone to sleep. A couple of weeks ago, I splurged and spent a couple hundred on some California Mist down in Hampden. The high from it was sudden and overpowering. And it helped. I didn't like sleeping when I felt this lonely because I usually dreamed about Renee, but I let the sweet smell surround me and watched television until I finally fell asleep around three in the morning.

But I dreamt about Renee anyway.

CHAPTER 3

The Invisible Woman

I didn't have classes the next day so I took Julie to school then, for the second time that week, drove to Virginia and parked across from Chris Taylor's house. But this time, I didn't bring my gun.

Vengeance had rushed over me when I'd read about Chris's early release, the way that any hurried, powerful emotion does, like lust or rage. But like lust or rage, the action that sprang from my emotion wasn't thought out. When I imagined Chris Taylor standing above Renee and bringing that bat down over and over, being able to shoot him didn't seem like it would be a problem. I never expected I wouldn't be able to pull the trigger.

After about an hour, I saw Chris walk out the door wearing jeans and a white shirt under a brown jacket. He climbed into the Navigator and drove down the street.

I started my truck and followed him.

We drove out of residential neighborhoods and turned onto a wide street crowded with businesses. Chris pulled into a small strip mall, parked his car and left. I was following so closely that I almost took the space next to him, but drove around the lot until I saw the door he entered, then parked and hurried after him.

The room was so dim that I had to wait for my eyes to adjust, but after a few moments I realized I had walked into a small pool hall. Music blasted as I scanned the pool tables to my right and a bar to my left. A woman was standing at a counter in front of me, asking a question I couldn't hear.

"What?" I asked back.

"I need to see your ID."

"Oh, right." I took out my wallet and handed her my driver's license. I saw Chris Taylor at a table on the far side of the pool bar, shaking hands with a group of guys, all who looked about his age.

The woman handed my ID back to me. "Are you here for the bar or to play?"

"I'll sit at the bar." I truly sucked at pool and thought it would be a good idea to attract less attention by not sending balls sailing through the air. I found a stool at the long L-shaped bar around the corner from where Chris and his friends were setting up the table. I ordered a Guinness and watched him in the mirror.

The man who murdered Renee was twenty feet away from me.

He was there with four or five guys—it was difficult to tell because there were only a few pool tables and they weren't spaced that far apart. His friends seemed cheerful, smiling a lot, especially for men, and made loud conversation that I couldn't quite hear.

"You want another beer?" the bartender asked.

"Okay," I said, surprised I had already finished my first. I loved how dark beer filled my stomach, warming it like orange embers. "Guinness."

"I remember," the bartender said, sounding annoyed for some reason.

'*He's not the only one who's annoyed,*' Renee said, sitting on the bar stool next to me. '*You're not going to do anything but watch him, are you?*'

I took my beer and drank deeply from it, the wet foam covering my lips. "I think so, yeah."

"You say something?" the bartender asked.

I shook my head.

'*But you could do something. He's got to use the bathroom eventually. Follow him in there and slam his head over and over into the wall. Drown him in the toilet. Burn his eyes with the hand dryer.*'

The bartender walked to the other end of the bar.

"You don't sound much like Renee," I said, my voice low.

'*We've both changed since I was alive, Tom. You're not the same man you were. Did you think I'd stay the same?*'

"I didn't know what you'd do." I watched Chris in the bar mirror, watched as he shot and broke up the rack in the middle of the table. Balls rolled everywhere and Chris smiled as he walked to the other end of the table. He shot, missed, and winced in exaggeration. His carefree smile felt like a spear thrust into my stomach.

'*You don't care about me like you used to,*' Renee said plaintively.

I looked away from the game, from Chris, and stared below the mirror, at the colorful bottles lined around the bar. "Yeah, I do."

'*You don't!*'

"I do. Wait, are you talking about that chick I'm meeting later today?"

'*The chick you're—no. I'm talking about the man who killed me. You've changed. Look, if I was still alive, and you knew he was going to murder me tomorrow, would you stop him?*'

"Yes."

'*Do you think he should die for killing me?*'

"Yes."

'*Why?*'

"Because of...because of how much I miss you." My eyes were starting to cloud. I raised the glass and drank deeply.

'*Do you think you should do it?*'

The bartender returned, so I set the glass down and nodded.

'*So, why won't you? Can you? Can you do it?*'

The bartended glanced at me. "You need another beer?"

I shook my head.

I went into the bathroom and smashed my fist against the wall. Some guy washing his hands a few sinks away eyed me warily, dried his hands, and walked out.

I forced myself to breathe slowly, deeply, until the shaking in my arms and legs, the shaking that had taken hold of my entire body, calmed.

I still couldn't kill him. Here I was, helpless, standing in the bathroom of some pool hall in northern Virginia, seeing red like my face was being held down in a sink full of blood, still incapable of killing the only person I knew who truly deserved to die.

My back was tight, exhausted, like it had been trapped in the same position for days.

ᘓᕲᘒᕲ

"What are you doing?" Julie asked. It was almost six and I was dropping her off with Ruth and Dave in an hour. Then I was going to meet Alison.

"Looking for something on the computer."

"What're you looking for?"

"Just something." My laptop was spread over my lap, probably sterilizing me, and I was sitting in a corner of the couch so that Julie couldn't see as I Googled "hit men." There were a few articles about wives who tried to have their husbands killed and were subsequently arrested in undercover operations, or people who died in circumstances that led the police to believe that an assassination occurred, but no information about how I could hire someone.

I had thought I'd want to murder Chris myself, but the best option really was to pay someone else to do it for me. I should have realized that earlier, especially since I wouldn't get caught, and wouldn't have to give up Julie for prison, but I remembered my anger upon Chris's early release. I wanted his blood on my hands.

It took three months after Renee was killed for me to pick up my life and trudge forward—*trudge* being far too optimistic a word.

Three months after Renee was gone, in the empty cold of January, Dave and Ruth brought Julie back to my house. I can remember kneeling down to hug her at the door, her tears on my neck, and Dave and Ruth standing quietly on the porch as the chill wrapped around all of us. Julie's small body shook against mine, and I felt a closeness to her that I'd never felt before, even when I had officially adopted her a year earlier. She needed me, and no one else ever had. Not like that.

Everyone told me, from friends to family to the psychologist I saw, that I would recover in time, but their platitudes and good intentions only led me to a darker, terrifying realization—I wasn't going to recover. The abrupt sense of shock from Renee's death didn't dissipate. My pain was locked in some dark place psychology hadn't yet lit. I was able to return to work, but an enormous wound was carved into me and would not heal. The only thing that made me feel better was talking with Renee.

Ruth and Dave liked to watch Julie on Friday nights. They thought they were helping by forcing me to socialize, and I would oblige them by dropping Julie off at their home then pretend I was heading to a bar in Fells Point or a concert somewhere in the city. Instead, I would drive back home and sit in the bedroom and have imaginary conversations with Renee. I would tell her what I had done during the week, how Julie was doing, other things I thought she would like to know. I began to look forward to these conversations with urgency as the week drew to a close. I remember sitting in that dark bedroom after winter ended and summer had come, alone on warm summer nights talking to Renee's memory with the window open. I could hear cars passing on the street below, or neighbors murmuring, or the loud sudden excited shouts of children.

Grief, for a few moments, became beautiful.

The next day, I would drive to Ruth and Dave's house around noon to pick up Julie and invent some story about the prior evening, just enough for them to believe that I was doing whatever they thought was necessary to recover. All of my stories ended the same way. "...But, to be honest, we were all pretty drunk."

"Singlehood!" Dave would boom excitedly, while Ruth shot him a dark look.

I barely monitored myself, but I did watch Julie. She had never been an emotionally expressive or excited child, but there was a pall that hung over her after her mother's death that took a long time to lift. It eventually did, but I felt a disconnection to her that hadn't existed before Renee's death. Or maybe it did and I never noticed it because Renee was such a major figure in both our lives. But after Renee was gone, and after Julie's initial pain passed, there was an awkwardness to our relationship that I hadn't anticipated, almost as if we were reintroducing ourselves. Julie spent a lot of time with Ruth and Dave, and I spent a lot of time alone. I never made an attempt to fully be her father. Neither of us were willing to entirely commit to each other. And even after I realized that, even though I knew that was something Julie desperately needed, I was ashamed that I still couldn't do it. In almost every way, I gave her everything, and I cared for her and never hurt her, but I couldn't slip back into love with anyone.

"Can I use the computer?" Julie asked.

"What? No." I turned down the screen. "Are you bored? Do you need something to do?"

She smiled. "Yes."

"Did you finish your homework?"

"Yes."

"Are you sure?"

"Yes."

"Okay," I said. "Well, what do you want to do?" She was in a cheerful mood for once, and I wanted to encourage it.

"I want to look at puppies online."

"You're not getting a puppy," I told her.

Julie frowned. "I think it makes a lot of sense for me to get a dog."

"I don't think it does."

"Then let's make you a dating profile."

I wasn't sure whether to laugh or be amazed, so I did both, letting out a surprised bark of laughter. "What did you say?"

"I think we should make you a dating profile. It's time you met someone."

"How do you know what a dating profile even is?" I asked, bemused. Then alarmed, I said, "You don't have one, do you?"

Julie grinned. "No. But Suzanne, my friend? Her mom is getting divorced and she's been going out with all these guys she met online."

"I see," I said, briefly wondering if Suzanne's mom was named Alison. "I appreciate the effort, but I don't think I need to meet anyone through a dating site."

"Dad, it's been three years."

"Right."

"So maybe it's time."

I smiled because I always smiled when she imitated an adult. "Trust me, I'm fine. My life has everything it needs right now."

Julie looked more crestfallen than I expected. "Really?"

"Well..." I said, hesitantly then decided to make her happy. But I didn't want Julie to know I was already familiar with online dating, so I pretended to be naive. I had faint hopes that, if Julie thought I hadn't done something, she wouldn't do it either. "I'll see how it works. What do I need to say?"

Julie clapped her hands excitedly. "First, you need to go to a site."

"You have to be older to go to those sites."

"You're old enough."

"Thank you," I said. "But you're twelve, so you're not. I tell you what, let's figure out what I'm supposed to say, and I'll put it online later. Sound fair?"

She eyed me dubiously. "You promise?"

"I promise," I lied.

"Okay," Julie said, happily. "First, you have to describe yourself, then you have to describe the type of woman you're looking for."

"All right." I opened MSWord. "How would you describe me? Good sense of humor?"

"No."

"Really?"

"Write down your job," Julie said. "Women like men who are good with kids."

"But I don't teach kids, I teach adults."

Julie sighed. "Then lie!"

"Okay, okay."

Julie absent-mindedly scratched her calf. "Tell them where you live, but say Maryland. Baltimore might scare some people away."

I made a mental note to ask her about that statement later.

"Do you want someone who looks like Mom?" she asked.

"Let's not go for appearance," I said. "It might make me seem shallow."

Julie nodded.

"What hobbies should she have?"

"She has to be good with kids," Julie said firmly. "I don't want someone who doesn't like me. That sucks. And she can't be too tall, because then I'll feel really short. She can't be taller than you."

"Fair enough."

"And she has to take me ice skating during winter," Julie said. "And she has to like reading. That's probably important to you. Oh, and no glasses."

"What's wrong with glasses?" I asked.

Julie took off her glasses and fingered them. "They're ugly," she said.

"No, they're not. It all depends on the person. You, for example, look beautiful with or without glasses."

Julie made an unconvinced sound then said, "She also has to like going to the mall. Shopping."

"But I don't like shopping."

Julie looked at me. "Dad, this is for both of us."

"Oh."

She wanted a mother.

I hadn't realized how intensely Julie wanted a maternal figure in her life, or how poor a job I was doing at giving her what she needed.

Julie kept looking at me, her brown eyes wide and innocent behind her glasses. "What?" she asked, alarmed, as if she'd said something wrong. Then, her voice lowered, she asked again, "What?"

My heart broke. At that moment I couldn't do anything to risk losing her, like kill a man.

But then I thought about Renee and the moment passed.

ᏄᏄᏄ

It took more than an hour to fight through evening Beltway traffic after I dropped Julie off, but the Washington Harbor Court Hotel was easy to find. I left my car in a nearby parking garage, headed inside the long lobby and asked the front desk clerk if there was a keycard left for me under my initials.

The clerk spent so much time searching through his desk that I figured he was going to tell me no key had been left. I was so nervous that the thought relieved me.

"Room 606," the clerk said and handed me a keycard.

A woman slipped into my elevator. Her hair was long and blonde and she wore dark sunglasses that couldn't hide how attractive her face was. She flashed me a quick smile and I wondered if she was the woman I was supposed to meet, if she was Alison.

No such luck. I stepped out alone when the elevator opened to the sixth floor. Room 606 was three doors down.

I had been so excited when Alison and I planned this meeting that the worry I now felt surprised me. I almost hoped she decided not to show. And I couldn't stop thinking about Renee. My hand shook as I fumbled to put the keycard into the door. A dark room waited.

"Alison?"

"I'm here." Her voice was timid and high. "Tom?"

"Yeah." I stepped inside, so tense I could barely breathe. Renee's presence was so palpable I felt like she was with me, standing next to me.

I had never been inside a hotel room this dark. Alison and I had promised each other that this encounter would be completely anonymous, that the room's lights would be off and the curtains closed. I felt like I was peering into a cave just after the fire was extinguished.

"Want me to turn on the lights?" I asked, suddenly feeling the need to be completely aware of my surroundings.

"No, but can you close the door?"

I was even more blind when I did. I walked toward Alison's voice, my hand pressed against the wall, trying not to sound clumsy as my knee bumped something soft. I reached down and felt the edge of a mattress.

"I'm here," Alison said again, but she still sounded like she was coming from somewhere distant. "Lie down."

I patted the mattress as I stretched out. I smelled the sharp scent of perfume and sensed her body next to mine. My hand accidentally brushed coarse lace. *She's wearing lingerie?* I assumed she would be too cautious to be seductive. I remembered a time in college, when I was sleeping with a woman who had a boyfriend, and how I was constantly surprised that she liked being sexy. Guilt never pushed down her desire.

"I hung the comforter over the blinds to make it darker," Alison said. "I could still see a little bit from the lights outside. Like we said online, this needs to be totally dark and anonymous. So, this is dark enough, right?" She paused. "I'm sorry. I talk too much when I'm nervous."

"I break out into Tourette's. But don't worry, it'll help with the dirty talk."

She laughed. "All right," she said, and her body rose and settled over mine. "Let's give this a shot."

Her hips pushed down and Alison's body felt so much like Renee's that my hands were confused as they ran down the sides of her lace negligee. Her hair brushed over my face as she bent over me, and I smelled perfume on the side of her neck. Our noses touched, then our lips, and I remembered the night I proposed to Renee, when I realized I would never kiss another woman again. *Renee*, I thought and, ridiculously, tears came to my eyes.

Alison's hips bore down again and mine rose in response, almost as if a giant invisible hand was lifting me.

∽❀∽

Alison patted my chest and rolled off the bed. I could barely make out her shadow, but I heard her gathering her clothes.

"So," Alison said, the first word she had spoken since we finished, "tell me something about yourself."

"Well, I usually last longer than that."

"Uh huh. Something else. Where are you from?"

"I was born in Spain. My dad's white, but my mom's Spanish. We moved to Highlandtown, a blue collar Baltimore neighborhood, from Spain when I was a kid."

"So, you *hablo* Spanish?"

"What does *hablo* mean?"

"So you're not white or fully Spanish, is what you're saying?"

"Right. I'm not. I mean, yes—no."

"And are you really separated?"

"Yes," I lied.

"What happened?"

"She met someone else."

"Sounds rough."

"It was."

I heard the rush of Alison's zipper as it rose.

"Want to stick around?" I asked, hopefully. "Maybe have more sex?"

"I really have to go."

"Can I at least see you?"

"We said this was a one-time thing, remember?"

"I meant see you with the lights on."

A heavy sound, like a jacket being pulled on. "Afraid not. Sorry. It was fun, though."

"I know! I had a really nice…"

I heard the door open and shut, then I was alone.

I lay back on the hotel room's bed, still naked, feeling foolish. I tugged the cold condom off.

CHAPTER 4

Closure and Closer

Michael and Robin Rivers, Renee and Ruth's parents, sat on the cracked leather couch in their living room and stared at me. I was perched on the edge of an armchair in front of them, trying to figure out the best way to ask them to help me kill Chris Taylor.

"So…Chris Taylor was released from prison last week," I told them.

Neither responded for a few moments.

"I didn't know that," Robin said. She re-crossed her legs and held her top knee with both hands. She was tall, blonde, and her skin was the burnt golden complexion that comes from letting too much time pass in a tanning bed.

Michael shifted.

Renee sat next to him, perched on the arm of the sofa. '*Hey, Dad!*' she sang out, her voice light and childish.

"We haven't really made any attempts to keep up with the Taylor boy," Michael said, completely ignoring the figment of my imagination sitting next to him. He was tall with a thin, angular face, peppered gray hair, and blue eyes that had lost their shine. A beard wrapped around his chin and he wore glasses. The beard and glasses were new since I had last seen him months ago. And he seemed thinner than I remembered—hollowed cheeks showed, even with the beard.

I could see a little of Renee in her mother. Nothing in her father. Renee always said I reminded her of Michael, but I never saw the resemblance.

'*You really don't see it?*' Renee asked me. '*Because I totally do.*' She frowned. '*Is that weird? I hope I'm not weird.*'

"You hadn't heard about Taylor?" I asked. "Really?"

Robin was still holding her knee, the knee raised, like she was shielding her body behind it. She shook her head.

"Chris is free now," I said, trying to choose my words carefully, "and he doesn't deserve to be. Not after what he did."

Renee sighed and crossed her arms. '*They're never going to agree with you,*' she said.

"We never knew for sure," Michael also spoke carefully, "that he's the one who killed Renee."

'*See?*'

"We all know he did it. It doesn't matter what some jury said. Twelve other people might have decided something else."

"I want him to die." Robin's harsh words seemed out of place in the Bethesda home where they lived, with its quiet white-walled living room and extended bay window that faced dark woods. Out of place among their pale leather sofa and designer chairs situated around a glass coffee table that held a fan of home and garden and wine magazines.

'*Yay, Mom*!' Renee cheered.

"I want him to die," Robin said again, and she stood and walked out of the room.

A few moments of silence passed then Michael tiredly asked, "Tom, why'd you come here tonight?"

"I told you. It's not right that he's out of jail."

"What do you want to do?"

I knew better than to tell Michael what I wanted. "I'm not sure," I said.

"Trust me," Michael said, "we miss her as much as you do. A day doesn't pass when Renee's not in my thoughts. Not a day."

I was leaning forward, not realizing that my hands were squeezing so tightly my fingers ached.

"I appreciate how much Renee meant to you," Michael continued, unsteadily. "And I'm glad that you've stayed in touch with us all these years. I know it's not easy, raising Julie, even with Ruth's help."

I felt a sudden need to leave. I stood and said, "I'm going to check on Robin," and headed for the kitchen.

I stopped in the bathroom and called Chris Taylor, but this time there was no answer.

I found Robin in the kitchen, holding a glass of wine with one hand and leaning against the kitchen island with the other. A large blue bottle sat on the counter surrounded by small white piles of crumpled paper towels. The sink was full of unwashed dishes.

Renee stood next to her mother. '*I can't believe you didn't know Chris was released,*' she said to Robin.

"Isn't it strange that I didn't know?" Robin mused. She took a small sip. "I almost never think about the Taylor boy. That's probably why I said what I said in the other room. Remembering him reminds me too much of how I felt. All that—" Robin stopped.

'*Hate?*'

"Anger?" I supplied.

"Sadness," Robin finished, and took another sip. "And anger, too. Maybe even a little hate." Her blue eyes flashed at me. "You're still angry."

"Yeah."

"That's where Michael and I are different," Robin said, and she set the empty glass on the counter. "Michael was able to let his anger go. I'll always be angry." She paused, picked up the wine bottle, and poured the rest into her glass. "Chris Taylor could have died in prison and I'd hate his corpse."

Renee and I nodded.

"There's nothing that will make me happy again," Robin said, finishing her thoughts. Her gaze turned to me again but it was unfocused. I didn't even feel like she was talking to me. "I guess that's how I'm prepared to live the rest of my life. Some parents seem like they recover. Or maybe they're good at pretending they have. Not me." She almost seemed like she was about to smile, but didn't. "I'd probably go crazy."

'*Going crazy's not so bad.*'

"What if you had a way to get revenge, to do something about it?" I lowered my voice. "What if you could get to Chris Taylor?"

"You sound so obsessed," Robin observed. "Like you're going to sneak into his house and smell his brushes."

"Hair or toothbrushes?"

Robin smiled and took another drink. "Listen," she said, "I may be a little drunk, but I think I know what you're talking about."

"Do you?"

"I want to. God, Tom, you don't know how much I want to...but I can't." Robin was speaking louder than I liked. "I could never live with myself."

"You're not exactly living now."

'*No kidding.*'

Robin wasn't offended by my comment, she just smiled ruefully. "This is progress."

Now I didn't care if Michael heard me. "But you're just going to carry this pain forever? Without doing anything about it?"

Robin ran the back of her hand over her mouth. "Well, I imagine I'll be drunk most of the time." She held her glass out to me.

"I don't think getting drunk is the best way to deal with this," I said reproachfully, but I took her glass and finished it off.

'*Mmm,*' Renee said, licking her lips. '*Mom does have a point.*'

"That's actually not bad," I admitted.

"It's a Franciscan Cabernet."

"I don't know what that means." I didn't know a thing about wine and figured, someday, I probably should. Wine, classical music, and architecture, the three big cultural gaps in the education of Tom Starks. Coming in fourth—how to hire assassins.

"Do you want more wine?"

'*Say yes.*'

"Yes."

Robin opened another bottle, poured two glasses, and held one out to me. I took it. She pulled herself up onto the counter behind her and sat, her legs crossed, the top leg slowly swinging.

Renee climbed up next to her.

Robin looked at me as she drank, but I couldn't read her expression. She lowered the glass slowly and held it with both hands in her lap. Maybe it was the wine, but she seemed sort of attractive in this light.

'*Jesus Christ, Tom. Really?*'

"Tom, what do you have in mind?"

"What?" I asked, startled.

"Why are you here?"

"Oh. I want to hire someone to kill Chris."

She nodded. "And you think that's a good idea? With my granddaughter in your house?"

"She's not with me that much. She spends a lot of time with Ruth."

Robin smiled at her glass. "I imagine Ruth likes that quite a bit."

"She seems to."

"Look, I can't help you. Not with this."

'*Dammit,*' Renee said, softly.

"That's what you came here for, right?" Robin continued. "Help?"

I took another drink. "I don't know how to find someone."

"So you're asking me?"

"Honestly," I admitted, "I don't know what I'm doing."

"Did you try a seedy bar?"

'*Oh God, Mom.*'

I couldn't help laughing. "What are you, from the nineteen-forties?"

"Well, I'm not sure how someone does this," Robin protested then laughed herself.

We grew quiet.

I pushed myself away from the counter. "Do me a favor? Don't mention what we talked about to Michael."

She shook her head. "It's between us."

છજી

I sat in my truck outside of the Rivers' house, sent Alison a quick e-mail, then left Bethesda and headed back toward Baltimore. I turned up the heat and lowered the windows. Stars glided by and the woods on either side of the road merged into dense, dark shadows.

There was no other way.

I needed to kill Chris Taylor myself.

I drove into Baltimore and hated it. I hated night, when thoughts of Renee were like salt on slit wrists, when loneliness came like a shroud I couldn't shake off, when grief wrapped its hands around my neck. Julie was with Ruth and Dave for the night, so I was returning to an empty home.

I remembered a Saturday morning weeks ago. I had checked on Julie, making sure she was asleep, then left our row house, walked up the street to the top of Federal Hill, and sat on a park bench. It was early, a little after seven, cool but not too cold. A few people were out with their dogs, both the humans and animals in jackets. An overweight jogger wheezed past. From there, it was like I could see every row house and slum and chimney and painted door in the south side of the city. And there was Locust Point and the harbor and Highlandtown and Fells Point and Homeland—and there, in the distance, was where I proposed to Renee. And in front of me was the water, where her ashes were tossed.

Baltimore was such a small, suffocating city, no one was really separated.

Sometimes, I just wanted everything around me to stop, for the world to stop spinning, and to lose myself so deeply in memories that Renee would be next to me. Sometimes, I lay in our bed and thought about her so much that I could almost feel her body brush against mine…

I found an open spot on the street, pulled into it, and shut off my car.

I was home.

ભ્ય

I watched students file into my classroom the next morning. My classes at BCC were generally small and tended to be a mix of people and ages. There was always at least one person who was in their seventies, had never received an undergraduate degree, and, in a grim race against time, decided to pursue it now. And there were standard college students, kids in their late teens and very early twenties, some who didn't care and rarely showed up, and some who were so enthusiastic and determined that it broke your heart they had to attend a crappy community college. And there were one or two students in their thirties or forties, people taking a class because they had time on their hands and nothing else to do with it. Some of them wanted to be writers but, rather than writing, thought taking a class in literature would help their cause, and others just had an interest in whatever novel we were reading.

"All right," I told them, a few minutes after the ten o'clock start time had passed and most of my fourteen students had taken their seats, "I have a change in the syllabus. We were supposed to start reading *A Farewell to Arms*, Ernest Hemingway's story of doomed love and war, but we're going to read Alexander Dumas' *The Count of Monte Cristo* instead."

Hands rushed up.

"Yes, Marcia," I said, calling on the plump, and usually cheerful, forty-something brunette who always sat in the front row.

"But I've already bought *A Farewell to Arms* and started reading it. Now we have to buy a new book?"

"I know it throws a wrench in your plans," I told the class, "but I've spoken to the bookstore, and *Monte Cris-*

to will be available at a heavily reduced price. And, hey, it's not a bad thing to own a copy of *A Farewell to Arms*, right?"

Apparently, not many of my students agreed, because hands stayed up.

"All right, Sam," I said to the black, nineteen-year-old with tattoos everywhere, "what's up?"

"We seriously have to read a different book?"

"We seriously do. Well, you do. I've already read it."

A couple of hands lowered, but one remained.

"Sure, Tamara," I said, indicating the tall black woman in glasses, probably in her early twenties, sitting by herself in the corner.

"Can I just ask, why the switch?"

Because I don't really have any interest in teaching A Farewell to Arms *again,* I thought. Monte Cristo *is a better fit for my life.*

"Honestly," I lied, "I think you'd enjoy this book more. I understand if you have some concerns," I went on. "I don't care, but I understand. I printed out the first few chapters, and I want you to read five pages over the next few minutes and write down what you think is happening, both in the story and in the construct of the story."

I distributed the handouts then checked to see if Alison had e-mailed me. She hadn't, which made me sad, so I wrote her:

> *Hey, haven't heard from you and just wanted to see if you wanted to get together again? I'm free anytime, day or night. Just let*

*me know. Always up to see you. Ha, ha. Get
it? Up? Anyway, let me know. Tom.*

I decided the e-mail sounded too desperate and de-
leted it. I glanced up and saw that most of the students
had finished writing and were talking to whoever was
sitting next to them or checking their phones.

"All right," I asked, "who can tell me what's happening here?"

No one spoke, which was a little unusual for this
class. I felt like they were trying to punish me for changing books on them.

"I'll just have to call on someone." I scanned the
classroom and picked out the most confident looking student. "Sam, tell us what's happening here."

Sam stared at his handout, as if the answer to my
question would appear if he stared hard enough. But he
didn't speak, and I was about to prod him when another
hand rose.

"Yes, Song," I said, addressing the short, thin Asian
girl with streaks of red dye in her hair and a series of cir-
cles tattooed down her arms.

"A boat docks," Song said, "and this guy on land,
Monsieur Morrel, learns that the captain of the boat has
died."

"Right," I said. "So this book, which a lot of people
think is one of the greatest adventures ever written, opens
with a death. Why do you think Dumas did that?"

"Well," offered Sam, trying to redeem himself, "it
makes the book, like, really grim. From the start."

"Yeppers. And it does something else. What happens after the captain's death? How does this Danglars guy feel about Edmond Dantes?"

"He hates him," someone offered.

"He does, and he worries that Edmond's going to become the next captain. So things are changing, right?" I looked out and was encouraged by a few nods. "Death in books, just like in life, always changes the characters that are left behind. The captain's death leaves a void in a number of ways, but the most important, for us, is what it means for Edmond, the hero."

"That's not the only change," Song put in. "Edmond is going to get married, so his life was already going to be different."

"Right," I acknowledged. "And make a point to remember what happens in this chapter, and how everything is laid out. First, we hear of the captain's death, then we learn about Danglars' dislike of Edmond, and then that Edmond is going to get married. The order that these things are introduced is important. Dumas introduces Edmond's role in life ahead of his love, which is a pattern that gets repeated, and shows us what's important to Edmond. Does that make sense?"

If it didn't, no one said. A mixture of serene and blank faces regarded me.

We talked about the book until class ended, and I was about to follow the students out when Richard James, who ran the English department, walked into the room. He was an older man, bald and black and overweight, with kind eyes and a constant smile. I had known Richard for years, both as an undergraduate and a boss. I liked the way he looked at literature. He didn't analyze books to death, he just enjoyed their prose and poetry. I reached out to him after my medical discharge from the Army and, as it happened, he had just been hired to head the English department at Baltimore Community College. I assisted him in one of his classes, promptly decided to get my Masters, and BCC hired me full time.

And that was the point in my life, at twenty-five, just finished with graduate school and about to start the job that would become my career, when I met Renee.

"Tomás," Richard said, using his penchant for saying my birth name. "How's class been?"

"Just had a late switch in texts for the semester. *A Farewell to Arms* for *The Count of Monte Cristo.*"

"I heard about that," Richard said. "It's why I'm here."

I was dumbfounded. "One of the students already complained to you?"

He smiled. "They're not that fast. The bookstore is the culprit this time."

"If it's a matter of cost, then I can help pay for it."

Richard shook his head. "It's not the cost I'm concerned about, it's the change. Hemingway's novel is a classic."

"So is *The Count.*"

"Well, yes, but *Monte Cristo* lacks the literary qualities of Hemingway's novel."

"I know," I said. "I agree with you. But I just thought that the students would find Dumas's novel more interesting. It's a bit of a change in the syllabus, and that's not fair to them, but I'll make sure that it's not unfair to their grades."

"Just tell me next time, Tomás."

"Really?"

He nodded again. "I like to know."

"Okay."

"How else have you been?"

"You know, keeping busy."

"I meant, how have you been since Chris Taylor was released from prison?"

During the time just after Renee's death, when I sank into depression, Richard let me stay at his house while Julie stayed with her aunt. I was barely functional, and he helped me out a lot. I had told him last week that Chris Taylor was getting out early.

"I've been fine with it," I lied.

"Are you going to try and talk to him?"

"No," I said. "I don't plan to talk to him."

"You don't think that would help? Give you some closure?"

I felt the weight of the gun in my hand when I thought about closure, the rain hitting my face, the buzz in my pocket.

The buzz in my pocket?

I pulled out my phone and glanced at it. "I'm sorry, Richard," I said. "I have to take this. It's Julie's school."

"Understood."

I waited until he left the room then I looked at my phone again. A text message from a number I didn't recognize read, *heard u need hlp. meet us @ levees bar at 10 tonite. come alone. only chance u get.*

CHAPTER 5

This Isn't You

Levees was hard to find. Unlit letters ran down its front door in a dull red, and the two narrow windows facing the street were dark. Plus, it was in D.C., and I was barely familiar with the city. All I knew of D.C. were the monuments. I had never been to the neighborhoods I always heard about—Georgetown, Adams Morgan, Dupont Circle, Capitol Hill. To me, D.C. was nothing but a giant obelisk.

I wasn't sure what to do next. I could head into the bar, or sit and wait for other instructions—or start the truck, drive home, and forget I ever tried to arrange this meeting. That had been my impulse the entire drive from Baltimore, the thought that drummed through my mind. *I can still turn around. None of this has to happen.*

My phone buzzed. I pulled it out of my pocket and read the text message.

room 51

I glanced around and saw a motel called The Palms on the other side of the road, one of those long beaten motels that people use when they have nowhere else to go, either for the night or the rest of their lives. I slipped my phone into my pocket, opened the door, and crossed the quiet street. The Palms was only two stories, with doors facing the street and a couple of cars in the parking lot. Light shone from two or three windows, but the rest of the rooms were shuttered and dark, including number 51.

I was about to knock when my phone buzzed again.

its open

I stood rooted to the ground.

'*This isn't you,*' a voice said.

ᴇ∿ᴈᴇ∿ᴈ

People were screaming below us, seething back and forth in a wave of purple and black. Renee and I could see tiny explosions of white cold breath in front of their mouths.

"Okay, one benefit the hospital has over BCC," I told her. "There is no way BCC could afford a suite at this stadium."

She smiled. "It's amazing, right?"

We watched the Ravens run maniacally onto the field and the crowd erupted. For a second, even in the suite and behind glass, the noise overwhelmed us. The Colts came walking out stoically, and the cheering turned to boos, but didn't lose its intensity.

Renee and I watched the introductions, kick off, and most of the first quarter, making little conversation. The game, like most Ravens' games, was low-scoring and defensive, but the Ravens did score a couple of field goals.

"They'd better get a touchdown," I said. "They need to widen the lead."

"They need to do more than that."

"Like what?"

"They should stab them in the heart."

I thought about that. "Pretty sure that's a ten yard penalty. Maybe even fifteen."

"I'm just saying," Renee said. "That's what I'd do."

I nodded. The Ravens threw an interception and the Colts returned it to the six-yard line before being taken down.

"Shit!" I yelled out and stood.

"Do you see?" Renee countered. "Do you see why my idea would have worked? They'd better cut a throat. Slice off nipples. Drag a razor from their asses to their ribs."

"You don't, um, sound like yourself," I said.

Renee didn't reply.

"Hon?" I asked. "It's just a game." I stood and walked over to her, but she kept turning in her chair, keeping her face out of my sight.

"Renee?"

ल৯ल৯

The November chill slipped into my clothes.

My memories were getting weird.

I reached for the knob, twisted it, and pulled the motel room's door open.

The first thing I saw was the vague silhouette of a bed across from a stand with an old square television on it. There was a light deeper in the room, coming from the bathroom.

Someone was sitting on the bed. "You gonna stand there staring?" a woman asked. "Or come inside?"

I stepped into the room and the door slammed shut behind me. Someone shoved me toward the wall, hands roughly patting me down.

"Tom Starks?" a man asked.

"What?"

"You Tom Starks?" the man asked again, his mouth close to my ear.

I felt the point of a knife press into the side of my neck, pushing me harder against the wall. That knife controlled my entire body.

"Yes." My voice was a whisper.

"I'll cut you open if you fuck us over," the man said. "You understand?"

I nodded again, dizzy.

The blade bit deeper. "Say it," he urged me.

He moved and I winced. I could feel the teeth of the knife cutting through my skin.

"I understand."

He released me, but I stayed facing the wall, even as I heard him walk away. A thin line of blood trickled down to my shoulder.

The woman spoke. "That was my partner. You can call me Diane. And you can turn around now. Go ahead, turn around. There you go."

The room was dark, but my eyes adjusted to the lack of light. Diane was a big woman, maybe five-ten and a couple of hundred pounds, with wild blond hair, faded blue jeans, and a loose black sweater. She was sitting on the bed, a small table in front of her.

"What do you need?" Diane asked.

I gingerly touched the cut on my neck, and a sudden *thump* from the bathroom made me flinch. "What was that?"

Diane waved her hand dismissively. "Don't worry about it, Tom," she said, and then leaned back and called out, "Close the bathroom door."

I heard the door close. The room darkened further.

"What do you need?" Diane asked again.

"How do you know about me?"

"You've been asking for help. And not exactly discretely."

"How do I know you're not cops?"

"You gotta take my word for it."

"Do you have proof?"

She seemed amused. "What kind of proof would work for you?"

"I don't know."

Diane leaned forward. "This isn't a job interview. Tell me what you need."

Another *thump* from the bathroom made me jump. It sounded like an axe slamming into wood.

"There's this guy who got out of prison last week," I said. "His name is Chris Taylor. He was in there for killing my wife. Her name is Renee Starks."

"Was."

It took me a moment to realize what Diane meant. "Right. Was Renee Starks."

I paused to let Diane acknowledge the story. She didn't. After three years of Renee's death filling my thoughts, I automatically assumed everybody else thought about her, or at least knew what had happened.

Diane stayed silent.

"Chris said he didn't do it," I continued, "that he didn't know anything about it. But I never believed him."

"Sounds like you need a detective," Diane said, "not an undertaker."

"I need both."

Thump. Thump.

Diane was quiet for a long moment. "I tell you what," she finally said, "we'll look into it. Give us a couple of days."

"You don't need to know anything else?"

"I already knew what happened to your wife. Mack gave us the details."

It took me a moment. "Mack? From the gun store? It wasn't Robin?"

"Who called us? Nah, wasn't your mother-in-law."

A beat passed. "How do you—how do you know who Robin is?"

"We do our research." Diane leaned toward the bathroom and called out, "What do we know about Tom here?"

The bathroom door opened, and I heard the man's voice say, "In the Army for a time. A short time."

I felt like a hole suddenly opened underneath me. "How did you know—"

"You teach at Baltimore Community College," Diane said. "And you ran track in college. You drive a white truck. And you have a twelve-year old daughter named Julie."

Cold started to devour my body, from my feet to my waist to my throat. "How do you know about Julie?" I managed to ask.

"She goes to Whitegate," the man called out. "Up in Baltimore."

"Listen—" I started to say then stopped. A million thoughts were running through my mind, and all I wanted to do was leave this motel room and never see these people again. "I don't think I can work with you," I said and moved toward the door.

"Wait," Diane told me, and I stopped. "You don't have to worry about those people getting hurt…unless you screw us over."

Thump.

"We don't take chances, not with who hires us, not with the jobs we get. So we learn everything about you."

"How do I know Julie will be safe afterward? And everybody else?"

"You stay quiet about this, you don't have to worry. We'll look into the job and tell you how much it costs. You pay us half in advance, we do the job, show you the obit and then you pay the rest. Then it's over."

"That's it?"

I saw her smile, even in the dark. "Well, unless you piss me off."

e⁄⁾e⁄⁾

I left the motel room and barely noticed the door close behind me. I walked across the street on soft legs, opened the truck's door, and pulled myself into the driver's seat. I sat for a long moment, barely able to move, breathe, think—all I wanted to do was drive away.

'*Okay*,' Renee said, sitting in the passenger seat next to me. '*You need to calm down.*'

I started the truck and roared down the street. "I'm done taking advice from you," I told her, my voice wavering. "Did you hear what she said? About Julie?"

'*She's not going to do anything to Julie unless you go to the police. Come on, you expected her to threaten you, didn't you?*'

"Me, yes. Not my daughter. Our daughter."

'*These are the kind of people you're working with. What? You thought they'd be friendly assassins?*'

"I don't know what I was thinking." I pulled over to the side of the road, yanked on the emergency brake, and pressed my forehead against the wheel. "I don't even really know what I'm doing. None of this feels right."

'*Fair enough*,' Renee admitted. '*It's not right. What you're doing is wrong.*'

I shut down the truck, turned off the lights. "Really? You think so?"

She nodded. '*Of course, it's wrong. But you knew that, Tom. You've known that all along. Let me ask you something. If you don't hire these people, and Chris Taylor is free and happy, is that right? Do you remember how he was at the pool hall? Did he seem like he was upset?*'

"No."

'*And how have you been? How's your pain?*'

"Renee—I just can't do this."

'*What if Julie wasn't around?*'

"What do you mean?"

'*What if she had never been born? What if it was just you and me, and I didn't have a daughter who you thought could be in danger? Would you work with these people?*'

I didn't answer. I didn't want Renee to know she was changing my mind.

'*Listen,*' she said. '*You're just worried. Remember that time we were going to be late to the airport, and you were worried, and I calmed you down?*' Renee's voice had turned playful. '*Remember how I did that?*' She reached over to me and opened my pants.

A car pulled next to me, and I glanced over and saw Diane.

I shot down in my seat. I peeked over the wheel until the light turned green and then waited a few moments and clambered back up. Her car, a Dodge sedan, was crossing the intersection.

'*Tom?*' Renee asked. '*What are you doing?*'

I started the engine and pulled into the street. "Following her."

'*Why?*'

"She seems to know everything about me," I said, grimly. "It's time I learned something about her."

'*Okay, remember how I said hiring them was a good idea? Messing with them? Definitely not.*'

"I'm going to stay a block behind her. She won't even know I'm here."

'But she'll see you! The streets are empty! And she knows what kind of car you drive. And you don't know this city. What do you expect to find out?'

"I'm not sure," I admitted. "Something for leverage."

'You already know she's a hit man! What else do you need?'

"More than that. Look." I pointed left. "She's turning into…oh."

'She's going to KFC, Tom.'

"Stop nagging."

I followed Diane into the parking lot and around the restaurant. Her car stopped in the drive-through and I waited around the corner. I leaned forward, peeking through the windshield.

'Do you see anything?'

"Nothing yet." I frowned and grabbed the door handle. "I'm going to get out."

The door flew open and I fell outside. I struggled to my feet and someone grabbed me then shoved me against the truck, knocking the air out of me. My knees buckled and I gasped.

I heard Diane's voice next to my ear. "Hi Tom."

I tried to talk normally, but the air was slow to return. "You like chicken, too?" I croaked.

"Restaurant's closed," Diane said. She stayed behind me, and her hands felt like iron manacles around my arms. Her body pressed against mine, crushing me against the truck. "You better have a good reason for being here."

"Coupon?" I gasped.

"Better than that. Jesus, why are your pants open?"

I turned to the side, anything to escape suffocation. "I wanted to see where you were going."

"Why?"

"I don't know what I was doing."

Diane was quiet for a moment. "Want to hear a secret?" she asked.

"Um…maybe?"

"Look at your shoulder."

I looked to my left. "I don't see anything."

She sighed. "Other one."

"Oh." I craned my neck and looked in the other direction. "I still don't see—" I stopped talking.

A red dot was crawling up my shoulder.

I forced my head to the other side, struggling to get away, and turned to the window. I could see the dot crawling up my neck and face in the reflection, almost feel it, like a small poisonous insect, waiting to bite.

"The secret is," Diane whispered, "we're watching you. You were following me, and my partner was following you. If you had pulled into a police station, you'd be dead by now. Do you understand that? We don't take chances."

In the reflection, I watched the dot hover next to my eye. Diane was nothing but a giant shadow behind me.

"I understand."

"If this is too much for you, say something now. We'll leave, and you never met with us. This night never happened. Your choice."

I stared into the truck, looking past the reflection, into the empty passenger seat.

"Let me know what you find out," I said.

Diane released me, but I didn't turn around. I stared into the window until she left, until I heard her car start and the dot vanished. Still, I stayed.

CHAPTER 6

Hours After Midnight

Nervousness ate at me like maggots after Diane left. I barely slept when I got home, and Ruth dropped off Julie first thing the next morning. Alison had e-mailed me back and asked to see me that night, and the idea of being with Alison made me feel a little better. I needed distractions.

"Do you want to do something this afternoon?" I asked Julie. "Go to the mall, watch a movie? It is Saturday, after all."

Julie looked at me seriously. "I want to paint my nails."

"You heard that I said the mall, right?"

"Yeah, but the polish is chipped. I need to touch it up before tonight." She was going to a sleepover at a girlfriend's house, and I liked this girl. Tracy was a nerdy twelve-year old who always had a book with her and, according to her parents, had yet to receive a grade less than a B+. They lived in a beautiful row house in Canton, near

Julie's school, and I always heard Tracy playing classical music on the piano whenever I dropped Julie off. I hoped some of their sense of class would rub off on Julie, since I usually let her watch terrible reality dating shows or whatever was on MTV. And we couldn't afford a piano.

"Can I hang out with you while you do it?" I asked.

"Just don't distract me."

Five minutes later we were sitting at the kitchen table. Julie had three bottles of nail polish in front of her and was using a clear liquid to remove pink paint from her fingernails. The awful smell of nail polish remover floated to me.

"Who taught you how to do that?" I asked. "A friend or Aunt Ruth?"

Julie didn't look up. Her brown hair fell around her face, framing it, and she kept tucking it behind her ears and pushing it away from her glasses. Julie's glasses always made me smile, because they were a little too big on her and made her young face look comically old. "Aunt Ruth."

"Did you ask her, or did she offer?"

Julie's expression remained concentrated. "I asked."

"You're pretty good."

"Thanks."

I pressed on. "Do your girlfriends at school wear makeup yet?"

"A couple of them. All the older girls do."

I tried to remember when girls started wearing makeup when I was in school. I had no idea. It seemed to just happen, like breasts. Julie and I didn't have many personal conversations, but I knew she was at an age where she would start going through changes...even if I didn't exactly know what "changes" meant.

"Do you need any new clothes?" I asked.

"I bought some with Aunt Ruth a couple of weeks ago."

"Right. But I mean, like, shirts. Are you..." I didn't know how to finish my sentence. "...getting bigger?"

Julie set the cotton ball on the table and looked up at me. "Like fat?"

"No. I just meant that you, well, you're getting older. I thought you might like clothes that were more grown up."

Julie looked annoyed. "What's wrong with my clothes?"

"Nothing. I like the way you dress. Here, all I'm saying is that if you ever want new clothes, let me know. I'll take you shopping."

Julie frowned at me for a couple of seconds then turned back to her nails. She briefly examined them and pushed the three bottles of nail polish toward me. "Shopping's always good. Which color do you like?"

I looked over the three bottles, different shades of red that I could barely tell apart.

"I'm wearing my tan sweater tonight," she added, as if that would help me out.

I pointed at the second. "I like this one."

Julie picked a different, brighter color and opened the top. "This is the one I want to use."

"Then why'd you ask?"

"I thought you wanted to help."

Renee used to do the same thing, but remembering Renee reminded me of Diane, which reminded me of how nervous I was.

"I think it looks good on you," I said. I left Julie to her nails and took a shower. The hot water vanished just before I finished and I stepped out of the shower shivering. I dried, worried about how much a plumber would cost, then checked my e-mail and read a message from Alison.

Just wanted to let you know that im SO looking forward to seeing you tonight!

I finished dressing and went back to Julie's bedroom. She was lying on her bed, reading a large book. I sat on the edge of the bed and poked the top of her head.

Julie sighed crossly and looked up. "What?" she asked.

"What what?"

She pushed up her glasses. "You've been acting…weird. All day."

"I'm sorry. I just got some…news."

"About what?"

"Work."

"You didn't say anything earlier," she said suspiciously.

"Well, I found out about the news just now."

"On a Saturday?"

"Hey," I said to change the subject, "how are Aunt Ruth and Uncle Dave getting along?"

"Better. I didn't used to like it, back when they fought when I was there, but now it's okay."

"They don't fight in front of you anymore?"

"I hear them when I go to bed."

"What are they fighting about now?"

"*Everything*. But don't worry. Uncle Dave doesn't know what happened."

"Doesn't know about what?"

"About you and Aunt Ruth, in the backyard that night. Uncle Dave doesn't know about it."

I glanced up fast. "*You* know about it?"

Julie looked intimidated. "Well…I heard you."

I stood. "You did?"

She nodded.

"You really heard us?"

"Just that one time."

"It only happened one time." I took a slow breath and sat back on the bed. "Listen, Julie, come here."

She didn't move. "You're not going to freak, are you?"

"Not anymore." I indicated the spot on the bed next to me. "Come on, sit down."

Julie did, a little farther away than I had indicated.

"Back then," I told her, "well, that was a really tough time for all of us. And your Aunt Ruth and I kind of turned to each other. It was a mistake, and it shouldn't have happened, and it never happened again."

"Okay."

"You haven't told anyone about it, right?"

Julie shook her head.

"You promise? Because it just happened once, when we were very, very sad, and it would hurt a lot of people if Dave—if Uncle Dave found out." I paused and thought about his boxing trophies. "Especially me."

"I won't tell him," Julie said. "But can I ask you something?"

"Sure."

"What about before?"

"Before what?"

"Before Mom died." Julie's hands were clasped, and her fingers were rubbing each other. She spoke like she didn't want to know the answer.

"Never," I said. "Not once."

She looked away from me. "You promise?"

"I promise."

When Julie turned back toward me, her face was empty of expression. She was already learning how to hide her emotions. "I didn't think so, but I wanted to make sure."

"You know how much I loved your mother, Julie. She meant everything to me."

Julie touched her hair, softly pulled at the tips. "Me, too."

ּ◌ֺ

I downed another beer at the lobby bar of the Harbor Court Hotel. The idea that my well-being now resided with a temperamental twelve-year-old, who was constantly mad at me, wasn't exactly reassuring. The only positive note was that I was more worried about Julie than I was about Diane.

But what really bothered me was that I couldn't stop imagining what Julie heard. It made me feel terrible to think she'd listened to me and Ruth, in the backyard beneath her bedroom window, and realized what we were doing—her step-father and her mother's sister. Her dead mother's sister.

And so I decided to get drunk. With twenty minutes until I was supposed to meet Alison.

I fumbled with my cell phone and almost knocked my beer over.

"You all right?" the bartender asked.

"Yuh," I said, and I tried to focus on the blurry numbers. A jazz singer standing under a sign that read *The Sara Jones Quartet* was in a lounge across the lobby. I heard her voice floating through the room, with nothing but a lonely bass beating its heart in time with her words:

"Embrace me,
"My sweet embraceable you.
"Embrace me,
"My irreplaceable you.
"Just to look at you,
"My heart grows tipsy in me…

I watched the singer, a beautiful wisp of a woman, and I wanted her cheerful voice to carry me into a world where pain turned into music. I felt like I started to go there, but grief rose and pulled me back.

Art can do a lot, but it can't save you from real pain.

My phone. I mashed the keypad and a list of names popped up. I selected the one I wanted, my hand shaking.

"Tom?" Ruth asked when she answered. "What's going on?"

"Hey," I said, and glanced at the bartender. He was standing at the other end of the bar, watching me warily. "How are you? You doing okay?"

"Are you drunk?" Ruth asked instead.

"Perhaps," I said craftily.

"Where are you?"

"Well, I'm in this…I just don't…I'm sorry I called."

"Is everything okay? Do you need help?"

"Ruth…Julie knows."

Ruth was silent for a moment. "She knows what?"

"About what happened. With us."

Her voice was tight. "Why did you tell her?"

"I didn't! She told me. She overheard us."

"Oh God."

"She said she's not going to tell anybody."

"Are you sure?"

"I feel very confident," I said, nodding knowingly. "I'm nodding knowingly."

Ruth's line disconnected.

I sat at the bar, trying to fight off the sudden drunken rush, and tapped my cell phone against my chin. I didn't feel like going upstairs, but I slid off the barstool, made my way toward the elevator, and rode up alone.

I wandered down the sixth floor until I reached the room Alison had reserved, opened the door, and, like last time, I was surprised at how dark the room was. A slit of yellow light lay on the floor to my left, coming from underneath the bathroom door. I tried to see into the dark and guessed at the vague outlines of a chair and table to my left and a bed to my right. I stepped forward and stumbled.

"Tom?" Alison's voice. "Is that you?"

I looked up from the floor. "I'm not sure. It's pretty dark."

An abrupt laugh. "I'm in the bathroom, so go ahead and turn on the room light. I'll turn the light back off when I come out."

I clumsily rolled to my knees, reached out with my left hand, and my fingers bumped the wall. I pressed my palm against it, used it to stand, then ran my hands blindly up and down until I found the light switch. I fumbled with it and finally flipped it on.

The hotel room was so nice that I wondered if it was a good idea for us to keep our rendezvous in pitch-blackness—we were wasting a terrific room. Two thick beige armchairs formed a small sitting area to the side of a fancy wooden stand from which a large plasma TV hung. A small circular glass table with an intricately-designed brass base was positioned between them. Like last time, the comforter had been removed from the bed and hung over the drapes.

The bathroom door to my right was closed, and the wall curved in front of me to reveal the base of the bed. I followed the curve to a king-sized mattress protruding like a flat white tongue from a wide cushioned leather headboard. Two shining brass lamps hung on either side of the headboard, all underneath a large black and white photograph of gazelles wandering an African plain.

I stared at the photograph and walked toward it until I bumped into the bed and pitched forward onto the mattress. I lay still, wondering if I should try and sober up or just admit to Alison that tonight was a bust. I should have eaten before I came, that would have helped. I rolled to my back, looked up at the ceiling, and heard the bathroom door open. Everything disappeared into darkness as the room's lights went out.

Movement in front of me. I pulled myself up to a sitting position, reached out, and felt something cool and smooth.

"Leather boots?" I asked.

"Sexy, right?" Alison sounded proud.

"I don't know if you'll find my sneakers as much of a turn on."

"That's not helping the mood."

"I'm sorry. I'm so sorry, Alison, but I'm kind of drunk."

More movement, and I realized she was sitting on the bed next to me.

"Is everything okay?" she asked, her voice close in the dark.

"I lied to you earlier."

"About what?"

"I'm not separated."

There was a moment's hesitation before she spoke. "You're married?"

"I'm a widower."

"You are?"

"Yeah."

Her voice still held that hesitation. "When did your wife die?"

"Three years ago."

"Am I—am I the first person you've been with since her?"

"Just you, yeah."

I felt Alison lie down, felt her body next to mine.

"Tell me about her."

"Really?" Her request made me warm. "Like what?"

"How did you meet?"

೧ഉ೧ഉ

I contacted her through an online dating site and, after trading a few e-mails back and forth, we decided to meet for coffee in Hampden. This happened near the holidays, deep in December, and I was a little depressed. The holidays always brought me down, like they did a lot of people. I was still sore from my last relationship and terrible at online dating. It seemed like women could sense that I was wounded, something about the way their eyes darkened whenever I talked about my ex.

I walked into the Common Ground coffee shop and recognized Renee's short black hair and wide brown eyes from her profile picture. We made an awkward introduction and she let out a slow smile that, somewhere inside me, started to burn.

We found a table.

"Do you come here a lot?" Renee asked then suddenly laughed. "I can't believe how that sounds, like I'm totally trying to pick you up."

"It's not your fault," I assured her. "I'm wearing a new shirt, and it probably has you more attracted to me than you thought you'd be."

"Right, right," Renee said, still laughing. "Good thing you told me. What I meant was, do you come to Hampden a lot?"

"Probably not as much as I should."

"What do you mean?"

"I don't know...I just feel that someone who lives in the city should make a pilgrimage here, like, once a year. What about you?"

"I'm a pretty good pilgrim," Renee replied. "Especially with my daughter. I bring her here during Christmas to see the lights." She raised a hand. "I told you about my daughter, right, or should I just ask for the check?"

"You told me. Totally cool. I like kids," I lied.

"Do you have any? I don't remember."

"No kids." I thought for a moment. "You don't remember?"

Renee grinned. "No, I do. I'm just making sure your story's straight. You wouldn't believe how many of the guys I've met online lie. Actually, you wouldn't believe how many of them are married."

"Really?"

"Lots."

"What about you? Have you ever been married?"

Renee shook her head. "No. You?"

"Me neither."

"Have you been close?"

"Sort of. My ex wanted to get married."

"So why didn't you?"

"Well, I should correct that. She wanted to get married to someone else."

Renee laughed then abruptly stopped. "Oh, I'm sorry. You're serious."

"Yeah, it's—" I was going to start talking about my last relationship, but decided against it. "It's no big deal. What about you? Ever been close to marriage?"

"There was one guy," Renee said. "This one lawyer I was dating, but it didn't work out. We're still friends, though."

"Is that hard? Being friends with someone you were close to?"

She shrugged. "Not really. You don't keep in touch with any of your exes?"

"I had a few I stayed in touch with, but it usually ended when one of us started dating somebody else."

"That does kill it," Renee agreed. "You know that part at the end of a relationship, when you feel like you can stay friends and hang out?"

I nodded. "And you're thinking singlehood isn't that bad, but that's because you're not really single yet?"

"Exactly!" Renee beamed. "And you're comfortable with the person, but you're not fighting because there's no pressure anymore? That's a nice point in a relationship. When things are over, but you haven't let them end."

"I do like that," I agreed. "I also like the third date.

"Really? Why the third?"

"The first date is all introduction, and as the guy, you sort of feel that the woman has made up her mind about you within the first few minutes."

"Oh, it happens faster than that," Renee assured me.

"And the second date is usually fun, but there's still pressure. If you do really well on the first date, then you have to make sure you keep your momentum going and keep her interested."

"Good point."

"So if you survive that, then you're on the third. And things are usually pretty easy at that point. Plus, you've usually had the first kiss out of the way, so there's no worry about that."

"Cripes," Renee said. "I'd hope the first kiss is out of the way by then." And she looked at me and laughed.

We kept talking as our untouched coffees cooled—about her childhood in Delaware, her love of Anne Tyler's novels, her adolescent dreams of being an astronaut. And she told me about Julie, and life as a single mom.

"Dating is hard," Renee said. "I'm lucky that my sister and her husband love watching her, but I hate leaving her. I went to the store and bought a gift for her before I met you tonight so I wouldn't feel too guilty."

"Is she getting spoiled for Christmas?"

"Oh, definitely. What about you? Are you going to visit your family?"

I frowned meditatively. "I'm not sure I can call the people at Blockbuster family."

Renee laughed. "Aww."

"Can I tell you something that's totally going to sound like a line, and I'll probably regret saying it, and you won't want to go out with me again because of the complete and total cheesiness, but I want to say it anyway?"

"I guess so."

"You have the most beautiful eyes, really, that I've ever seen. I'm being honest. And I know how corny that sounds. I'm sorry."

Renee smiled. "Well, you're right that I'd think that was cheesy. Because I do. But you're wrong about the other thing."

"About your eyes?"

"No, my eyes are awesome."

"So what was I wrong about?"

"I do want to go out with you again…"

ɔɔɛɔ

"How did you meet?" Alison asked again.

I blinked, clearing my thoughts. "In Hampden, this one neighborhood in Baltimore."

"That's it? That's the whole story?"

I shrugged. "That's it."

"So, was she the perfect woman or something? How come you haven't been with anyone else?"

"I don't know if Renee was perfect. We just didn't have time for things to grow old."

"How long did you date before you got married?"

"Not that long. She was moving because of work and we had to make a choice…"

ɔɔɛɔ

"I don't want to leave," Renee said, one summer evening, nine months after we'd first met. "But it's my job. They want me in L.A." She played with the black wooden beads of her string necklace.

We were sitting on a high green hill in Patterson Park, at the base of a huge colorful Japanese pagoda, watching Julie roll around in the grass. Patterson Park was a series of hilly fields that had been dangerous a decade before, but now it was filled with picnickers and children playing sports. We liked coming here on the weekends to people-watch and let Julie run around. From the base of the Pagoda there was a split through the trees and buildings where you could see

Highlandtown and, beyond that, sun sparkling on the blue water.

"Honestly," Renee went on, "I wish I could quit my job and stay with you here in Baltimore. I don't want to go, and I don't want to move Julie. Everyone in L.A. seems like they have perfect bodies and too much money. They're all beautiful out there."

"And you'd rather be here with me?"

She laughed. "I meant that I wouldn't fit in."

"You'll fit in fine."

"But I'll be sad without you. I mean, even those trips I took to Boston..." Renee's eyes darkened. "I just didn't like being without you."

We were silent.

"I'll do what I have to," I told her. "If that means the long distance thing, I'll do it. Los Angeles isn't far away. A few hours by plane. And we can have weekends together."

"I'll probably have to work a lot of weekends. New hospital, and new on staff? I'm not going to get the best schedule."

"I just can't believe there aren't any hospitals here that need nurses."

"I'm sure there are, but I can't stay unemployed much longer. If Claire can really get me a job at UCLA, then I don't have a choice. Maybe something will open up here and I'll come back, but for now..." She let the sentence float away then sighed and said, "I kind of wish I wasn't in love with you."

"A lot of the women who date me say that."

"I guess we could try long distance. I mean, we have to try, right?"

"We could. But let's just get married instead."

Renee smiled. "How would that help?"

"Well, you could stay here until you found another job, and I could support you and Julie."

"Tom, that's really sweet, but—"

"Look," I said, starting to take myself seriously. "Why not? I love you, you love me, Julie seems to find me almost bearable—"

"She likes you."

"Renee, why not?" I turned toward her. "Let's get married. Stay here and live with me, and I'll take care of you and Julie forever. I mean, until I get fired or something and then you have to support me. We'll trade off."

"Tom—"

"Listen, I've never loved anyone like…I feel like I've never loved anyone until now. I don't have a ring with me, but I do want this. I do."

"Are you serious?" Renee asked, smiling.

The dying sun lit her brown eyes beautifully.

❧❧

I woke suddenly and looked over at the alarm clock. Hours after midnight.

I could feel Alison lying next to me on the bed. I was sober now and melancholy. The warm sour taste of sleep was in my mouth.

"Are you awake?" Alison asked.

"Yeah."

"You fell asleep while you were talking."

"Wow. So I'm that boring."

"Can I ask you something? And will you be honest?"

"Maybe."

Her voice was small. "How did Renee die?"

"Car accident," I lied.

"I'm sorry."

Silence.

"What did she look like?"

Just over five feet, with short brown hair and dark eyes. She wasn't stocky but she wasn't thin either, she was somewhere in-between. She had a small mole to the side of her left eye, nothing more than a black dot and she always wanted to have the mole removed. But I liked it. She wore mildly-unusual jewelry, maybe a high second earring in one ear, or rings on her toes, or string necklaces with large flat turquoise stones. She loved wearing sundresses.

"What did she look like?" Alison asked again.

A friend took a picture of us walking down this narrow street in Fells Point, and I look miserable, for some reason, but Renee has one arm slung over my waist and she's standing on her tiptoes and I'm leaning down so she can kiss my cheek. That's how I remember Renee.

"What did she look like?"

I threw up everything I ate and didn't sleep. I could barely move. My parents flew from Florida to stay with me, two elderly ghosts flitting through the house. Julie stayed with Ruth and Dave while we tried to recover from her mother's murder.

In a daze, I went to the top of Federal Hill and looked at the frozen grass coated with ice and the quiet empty waterfront. I had a bottle of sleeping pills clutched in my coat pocket.

There was no miraculously-timed intervention that saved my life, no interference from the heavens. I sat there for hours, squeezing the bottle in my hand, but, in the end, I just didn't have the courage.

"What did she look like?"

"Short. Brunette. Fun at parties."

"Whoa," Alison said. "I didn't ask for her life story."

I smiled, even if having a conversation in complete darkness was odd. Listening to our voices felt like watching a play blindfolded, nothing but lines of dialogue, the spectators invisible but present.

And I smiled because I was starting to like Alison. Even if she was still a stranger.

And maybe that was why I sought out someone in the first place. I needed that connection, the touch of someone both distant and close. Just a shadow of someone.

"What about you?" I asked. "Feel like sharing something about yourself? You can lie if you want. I think I'm still a little drunk, so I won't be able to tell."

"I won't lie. Ask me anything and I'll give you an honest answer."

"Why'd you agree to meet some guy you met online in a hotel room?"

"Hmmm. Ask something else."

"Really?"

"Yeah." I felt Alison turn over, felt her elbow push into my chest.

"Got kids?" I asked.

"Nope. You?"

"One daughter."

"What's her name?"

"Julie."

"How old is Julie?"

"Twelve. She's not mine, though. I mean, she is, but she was my wife's biological daughter. I adopted her when we got married."

"And you're raising her on your own now?"

"Yep."

"Good man," Alison said approvingly. "How's life as a single parent?"

"Awkward. Confusing. But sometimes, it's painful."

She laughed. "Wait until she's a teenager. I was a mess my teenage years. How tough was it for her after her mom died?"

"Honestly, I was pretty depressed, so I don't even know how Julie was. It was hard on both of us. I probably should have been there for her more than I was."

"Probably."

I was a little stung. "Well, it wasn't easy for me."

"No, but there's some people in your life that you owe everything to. Family, some friends. That's how I've always looked at things."

I didn't like the tone in Alison's voice. I felt judged. I stayed quiet until she spoke again.

"You still miss her. Renee, right?"

"Yeah. I do."

"So…when you're with me, and it's dark like this, are you pretending that you're with her?"

I thought for a moment. "No."

"Really?" Alison moved, and the elbow pressed into me lifted. I felt her head and her soft hair on my chest. "I figured from the start that you were pretending I'm someone you loved, or someone you wanted but couldn't have, like a woman at work or something."

"I guess it would make sense to imagine that you're Renee, but that's not what I'm doing." I swallowed. "Renee's kind of always in my thoughts, except when I'm with you. This is like an escape from her."

"Sounds like this is an escape from everything," Alison said.

"Maybe it is."

We were both silent. I closed my eyes, not that it mattered much in the dark. I felt her fingernails trace my stomach and ribs.

"So, what about you?" I asked. "Why are you here?"

"Just for the sex."

I nodded.

Alison laughed. "It's probably not just for the sex. Okay, I don't know why I'm here. I need something, but I'm not sure what it is. But I think that I'm getting it with you. As long as you don't turn into a freak show or stalker or something."

"No promises."

"I guess that'll have to work."

"So," I said, "I know you don't want to tell me too much about yourself, or why you're here, and that's fine. But..." I wasn't sure how to say what I wanted. "Is this an escape for you, too?"

Her head lifted as Alison considered my question. "Maybe," she said. "But I don't really look at it as an escape."

"No?"

Her hair rustled against my body as she shook her head. "It's never really an escape, is it? Escaping, going back…all that seems like just another way, sometimes, to say that you're going in a different direction. Still moving forward, though. Forward's wherever you're headed."

ぐぁぐぁ

Almost dawn. Alison had gone.

I rolled out of bed, stood, stretched, walked over to the door, and flipped on the lights. My jeans and sweater were on the floor, in a jumbled pile with my boxers and socks. Alison and I had sex once, quickly, before she left. It almost felt like an afterthought, something we had to do, but once we started, some deep feeling in me rose. Our kisses and undressing had turned impatient.

"You brought a condom, right?" Alison asked.

"Yeppers."

"Put it on. And don't say *yeppers*."

I fumbled around the sheets until I found my pants, took the condom out of the pocket, and tore open the packet.

"I'm not really good at these," I told Alison, but it slipped on easier than I thought it would.

I turned around and she pulled me on top of her. I held her hand and, together, we guided me inside of her. This was different than the first time we had been together. Then it had been quick and easy and surprising, surprising because I kept expecting one of us to stop. Now, there was something different, something beyond two strangers. Now, as her hips slowly and then furiously rushed up into mine, there was something we both wanted. And there was an intimacy I hadn't expected, but it seemed Alison felt it, too. We kissed as we fucked. I held the back of her head and she grabbed and squeezed my shoulders, her legs circling me, pulling me deeper and refusing to let me go.

And then her body seemed to turn into warm water beneath mine and, in that moment of sudden surprising tenderness, it was as if I found whatever was missing, whatever had been lost, here in this dark room, in her.

I held Alison close to me and the intimacy of my arms seemed to surprise her. She said a faint "oh" and relaxed.

"I think I…I can't believe I just came," she said, her voice amazed.

"Yeah?"

"I *never* come with guys. Never." She paused. "And it even happened after you said *yeppers*."

I brought her head to my chest and kissed her forehead. "Shh," I said.

"Why are you saying 'shh'?" she asked.

"Because I'm…comforting you?"

"Why do I need comforting?"

"I don't know?"

"Uh-huh." She moved away from me. "I need to go."

I heard Alison start dressing.

"You don't want to talk more?" I asked.

"Nothing else to talk about." The sounds of clothes being pulled on stopped. "I'm sorry. I don't know why I'm being this way."

But my thoughts were already somewhere else. *Nothing else to talk about*, Alison had said. It triggered something in my mind. "It's okay," I said, distantly. "No problem."

Nothing else to talk about.

"Tom?" Alison said, and I heard her walk to the bed. Her hands found my arm, and I felt her lips kiss my forehead. "We'll talk later, right?"

"Yeah, definitely."

"Okay. It's just…tough to explain, afterward." She left me and, moments later, the room door flashed open then closed and I sat up in bed.

I knew what her words had triggered.

I had to talk to Chris Taylor.

CHAPTER 7

The First Cut

I adjusted my wig, tamped down my fake mustache and looked at myself in the rearview mirror. It wasn't the best disguise, but it was the only disguise available at Target a month after Halloween and, besides, I wasn't too worried about Chris recognizing me. At this point, it didn't really matter if he did. I just wanted to talk to him, and I wanted to do it before Diane and her partner got back to me. I wanted another chance to learn the truth myself.

I left my truck and headed through the chilly night toward his house, a long brick rambler with a blue front door and blue accents around the windows. Dearborn Drive was barely lit this late, and no cars passed on the road behind me. I walked up to the front door and rang the doorbell.

I heard someone talking, a distant voice that grew louder as it approached, then the door opened and Chris stood in front of me, a phone in his hand.

He wore long black sweatpants and a white T-shirt that made his shaved head seem like it was shining. Everything about him seemed to shine, as if he had just emerged from a bathtub. Maybe he had, or maybe he was starting to recover from prison.

"Hi," I said. "Are you Christopher Taylor?"

"Yeah."

"My name is Alan Smith, and I'm a recruiter with—" I immediately forgot the name of the company I'd invented on my drive here. "—Alan Smith Recruiting. We work with..." And now the story was gone, too. "—we place people who got out of prison with...people who hire people who got out of prison."

A little sloppy.

"Oh—okay," Chris said. He stared at me for a long moment then blinked. He didn't recognize me. I mentally celebrated my fake mustache.

"Who told you—" he started to ask, then he glanced around and lowered his voice. "Who told you I was in prison?"

"We get notices from the courts," I told him. "They did tell you about employment assistance, right?"

Chris's expression relaxed. "Right. Yeah, they mentioned that. I just didn't expect you to show up at my house on a Sunday night. What did you say your name was?"

I had no idea. "Alex Smith."

"Right." He smiled. "Do you want to come in? Have a drink?"

"Sure," I said, and I followed Chris Taylor inside his house.

છઝઝ

We sat in his kitchen, a room with dark windows looking out behind the house, two open bottles of Dominion Ale between us.

"So, what kind of work are you hiring for?" Chris asked.

I felt a bit more relaxed now that I had his trust. "I work in referrals. So I meet with you, find out what you're interested in, and see if I know any employers that make a good match."

Chris nodded. "Well, I'd really be interested in anything. I mean, I can't be too picky. Something in construction would be fine. But, honestly, anything."

His voice was so innocent, so open and honest, that I was momentarily disarmed. "Can I ask you something?"

He nodded. "Sure."

"What were you in for?"

Chris leaned back in his chair. "They didn't tell you?"

I shook my head.

Pain flashed in his eyes as he looked away. "It's not something I want to talk about. I'm sorry if that sounds rude. I was arrested on false charges. My conviction was overturned."

"So you were innocent."

"Found innocent. Eventually. Yeah."

I watched him as he tipped his bottle to me and drank. The house smelled like cherry, like red fragrant candles.

Chris pushed back his chair suddenly and stood. "I'm going to have some bread. You want some?"

"Sure."

Chris turned his back to me as he walked over to the kitchen counter and, when he turned back around, he had a long serrated knife in his hand. A thick piece of bread was in the other. He set the bread down, opened a cupboard, took out two plates, and slid one to me.

"You can have the first cut," Chris said as he sat back down. He turned the knife around and held the handle out to me.

The knife was heavy in my hand.

"I'm sorry that's all I have to offer," Chris said, apologetically, but I barely heard him. All I could do was look at the knife. "We barely have anything to eat. It was either bread or cereal."

"This is fine."

"'Welcome your stranger into your home…kindness …something, something.' I think there's a Bible passage that goes along those lines."

I cut away the crust. The long jagged blade slid easily through the hard bread. "You're religious?"

"My mom's the religious one," he said. "She's at Bible Study now. I'm trying to get better about going."

"What led to that?" I asked. The question sounded too personal. "I mean, if you don't mind me asking." I held out the heavy knife and he took it.

"Not at all. Like I said, I'm not too religious, but I should be."

"You've done a lot that needs to be forgiven?"

Chris looked at me sharply and I had a sudden sensation. I felt like he and I just simultaneously realized that, throughout this entire conversation, neither of us was telling the truth. I wanted to look at the knife in his hand, but instead I looked into his faded, beaten blue eyes, and they seemed angry, as if a tiny point of light inside of them had exploded. I couldn't look away.

Chris did. He glanced down at the knife and slowly brought it to his other hand.

He sliced his bread in half.

"Not that much," he said. "Can I ask you something?"

"Sure."

"When did you lose it?"

Silence for a moment. "What do you mean?"

He touched the side of his head. "Your hair. It's pretty obvious that you're wearing a wig."

"It is?"

He grinned and nodded. "Sorry."

"I started to lose it about three years ago."

The phone rang, startling me so much that I almost knocked over my beer.

Chris leaned back and took the cordless phone off the wall behind him.

"Yeah?" he asked, then he looked at me. "Can you give me a second?"

"Sure."

He stood and left the kitchen.

I quietly pushed back my chair. I walked to the doorway and saw Chris at the other end of the hall, his back to me, the phone pressed against his ear. I couldn't hear what he was saying.

There was another hallway to my right, a long dark hall with rows of doors on either side. I slowly stepped out of the kitchen and into the hallway, watching Chris's back as he talked.

It was so dark that I could barely see the doors on either side of me. I pushed open the first door to my right and peered into a large bedroom filled with a big bed covered in decorative pillows and lit with a reddish glow from the pink shade of a table lamp. This probably wasn't Chris's room, so I closed the door and kept walking. The next doorway was only a few steps away, and it was open. I stepped inside and turned on the light.

This bedroom held a small bed and a dresser. A long duffel bag sat on the floor with clothes sprawling out. I pulled out a pair of jeans and examined them. They looked like they would fit Chris.

I walked over to the dresser and pulled open the top drawer. A man's white underwear and T-shirts. I looked underneath them and found nothing, slid the drawer shut and pulled out the next one.

I didn't know what I expected to find. A clue, maybe, something that would confirm that Chris had killed Renee, anything incriminating. But this second drawer just held more t-shirts.

I closed it and listened intently, trying to hear if Chris was still on the phone. Not a sound.

I walked to the doorway and peered down the hall.

Nothing.

I went back into the bedroom and opened the dresser's third drawer. Empty. The fourth drawer was the same. I knelt down to pull open the fifth and final drawer and found jumbled socks.

I felt desperate, as if I couldn't leave without learning something. I turned toward the duffel bag and emptied its contents on the floor.

And that's when I saw it, in the corner of the room leaning against the wall. The shine of a metal baseball bat.

The world skidded to a stop.

I didn't move. I just stood still and stared. It wasn't the same baseball bat, obviously, because that bat was locked up someplace with other crime evidence. But seeing the same instrument used to kill Renee stunned me. Angered me. Snakes rushed through my blood.

"Hello?"

Chris's voice startled me so much that my sudden anger vanished. I turned to the door, but he wasn't standing in it.

"Hello?" Chris called again, his voice coming from down the hall. I walked to the bedroom doorway and peeked outside. I saw a flash of his body walking past the entrance to the hallway, back toward the front door. He must have thought I left.

I turned off the room lights and hurried out. There was an open door across the hall, and I saw the outline of a sink. I ducked inside and closed the door behind me, waited a few minutes and opened it again.

Chris was standing at the end of the hallway. "Mr. Smith?"

"Hi," I said. "I just needed to use the bathroom."

He watched me.

"All that beer."

ଓଓ୬

I walked back to my truck with a copy of Chris's resume. I wished I had something else, like certainty that he had killed Renee. But I was far from certain. Now I wondered if my earlier hesitation to murder him came from a doubt I hadn't realized.

I climbed inside my truck, crumpled Chris's resume, took off my wig, and threw both in the seat next to me. I started the engine and checked my phone. A text message:

what r u doin?

An unrecognized number had sent the text, but I knew it was from Diane. I looked around and saw her dark sedan parked down the street. I slowly drove toward it, stopped next to her window, and peered inside. I couldn't see anything. But I heard my truck's passenger door open and when I turned, Diane was clambering inside. The truck sagged a little under her weight. She pulled the door shut behind her and pointed down the street.

"Drive."

I did, surprised I wasn't scared. Then again, I wasn't sure there was any reason for Diane to be mad at me.

"So, I'm here checking out our suspect. Why are you here?" she asked, then gestured toward the side of the road. "Pull over."

I pulled over. I could see her more clearly now than in the darkened motel room the other night. She had short curled blonde hair and a long face with small eyes, a squashed nose and thin lips.

"I wanted to talk to Chris myself. I wanted to see if there was anything I could find out."

"That's what you're paying us for."

"The thing is," I admitted, "I felt like, no matter what you learned, I'd have doubts. And now that I've talked to him, I'm really not sure. I saw a baseball bat in his room. Do you think that means anything?"

"Yes," Diane said flatly. "It means he plays baseball. But I didn't know you were a mind reader. You could tell he's innocent?"

"Well, no, but—"

Diane raised a hand, stopping me. "Listen, Starks. Let us figure out who's innocent." She glanced down, picked up the crumpled resume, and smoothed it out. "He played trombone in the marching band in college?"

"I don't like how the trombone sounds," I told her.

Diane nodded. "May be enough of a reason right there to kill him. By the way, you grow hair quick."

It took me a moment to figure out what she was referring to. "Oh." I touched my mustache and peeled it off. "That was fake."

"Really."

"It's from Target."

"Listen, Starks. I'm glad I found you. I need to ask you something."

"I don't know if they have more mustaches."

Diane grinned. "Not that. Here's the thing. You're a nervous guy, and we're not used to working with someone so jumpy."

"You don't want to work with me?"

"Not if we don't trust you. And with our business, well, we have to have trust."

"Okay."

"Starks, did you tell anyone about us?"

"No."

"You sure?"

"Positive."

"What about before? You asked Mack for help. Anyone else?"

"I mentioned it to Robin," I said, and a thunderclap smashed inside of my head. "I mean, I never said anything about you two, specifically…"

It was too late. Diane was staring at me intently. "What did you say?"

"Nothing, I told you. Nothing. I asked her if she knew how to…how to find someone…"

Diane kept watching me as she settled back in her seat. "So she'll know."

"Know what?" I asked, mentally kicking myself for my mistake, trying to play dumb.

"When Taylor's killed, Robin will know you hired someone to do it. She'll know you were responsible."

"No, she won't."

"And when she learns he's dead, guilt might start up with her," Diane went on, ignoring me. "If she starts asking you questions, no offense, Starks, but you're not exactly a vault."

"She's not going to ask…"

"So, the thing to do," Diane said, as if she was thinking out loud, "is make sure she stays quiet."

A thick moment hung in the air. "What does that mean?"

"I'm not going to let this get out of hand," Diane told me. "I don't want a mess of bodies to bury. I'll talk to her. I'll tell her she needs to stay quiet."

"Wait, what?" I felt like the situation was already getting out of hand. "You don't have to worry about Robin. I promise. She'll be happy that the man who killed her daughter is dead. Trust me." *May have killed*, my mind added.

"She might, but my experience tells me to expect the unpredictable. And I don't like the unpredictable."

"Listen," I said, seized by a nervousness I had felt before, the kind of overwhelming fear that feels like it was devouring you. "Let me talk to her. Please. Doesn't that make more sense?"

"I can deliver the message better."

"Please," I said, begging. "Let me. I'll call her right now."

Diane pursed her lips. "All right," she said. "Call her right now. Tell her to meet you at a bar near her house. And tell her not to bring Michael."

"Okay." I hated that Diane knew the names of everyone I cared about.

"And then you and I are heading to that bar. Pick someplace quiet."

೮ꝰ೮ꝰ

"You know," Diane said, about an hour later. "This isn't exactly what I had in mind."

"I don't know any other bars in Bethesda," I told her, defensively. We were standing outside the door to a brightly-lit Chili's.

"She inside?" Diane asked.

"I don't know," I said and pushed open the door.

I spotted Robin almost immediately, sitting at a table near the bar by herself, a glass of wine that looked hopelessly out of place at a Chili's in front of her. "She's over there," I said to Diane. There was no response. I glanced back and Diane had already sidled to a bar stool. She was fast, I had to admit, for a bigger person. I turned and Robin looked up at me and smiled faintly as I approached, but the smile left as I sat down across from her.

"So, Tom," she said, "why'd you bring me out here? What's so important?"

"Well, here's the thing," I said uncertainly, fighting an urge to glance over my shoulder. "Hi."

"Hi, Tom. Why am I here?"

"You look well." She did actually look nice. Robin was wearing a tan turtleneck sweater with jeans and her hair was brushed back, giving her a slightly disheveled look that she made attractive.

"Thank you," Robin said. "But why…" She looked up and past me, just as I felt a hand on my shoulder. I turned and saw Diane.

"Jesus Christ, this is taking too long," Diane said, and she slid into the booth next to me, shoving me into the wall. "Robin Rivers?"

Robin seemed startled, but she adjusted well. "Yes?"

Diane's voice lowered. "Tom here told you about his plan the other day, right? To hire a hit man to take out Chris Taylor?"

Robin quickly looked at me. "Yes."

"I'm one of the people he hired."

"Oh," Robin said, faintly.

"Can I get you two anything?" a cheerful voice asked, and I saw a beaming waitress standing next to our booth.

"Nothing," Diane said, without looking up.

The waitress didn't stick around.

"If we do this job," Diane continued, "then I need to make sure you stay quiet. In fact, you need to forget you ever talked to Tom, starting now."

"I understand," Robin said, her voice still distant.

Diane leaned forward. "You understand now," she said. "I need to make sure you understand later." She reached across the table and took Robin's purse, pulled it over and opened it up.

Robin reached for her purse but Diane, without looking up, caught her by the wrist with one hand and brought Robin's arm down to the table. Her other hand kept searching inside the purse. I saw pain flash across Robin's face.

"What are you looking for?" I asked Diane.

"Something she needs..." Diane muttered, then her eyes brightened and she pulled out a small green notebook. "Ha!" she exclaimed. "Perfect! Can't believe you still carry around an address book." She let go of Robin's arm.

"Why do you want that?" Robin asked.

She looked at me, but I couldn't meet her eyes. I saw red marks on her wrist and looked away from that, too.

"Insurance," Diane said. "You mention what we've talked about to anyone, and I'll make sure bad things happen to the people in here." She stuffed the address book into her pocket.

I could feel Robin's stare, but I didn't lift my eyes from the table.

"Listen—" Robin started, her voice hard.

"Your instinct is to keep your family and your friends safe," Diane cut her off, her voice harder. "So you want to make a stand. You're a cornered dog, and you want to bark. But you've got to fight that instinct, Robin Rivers. You want to make a move to help your people, and I'm telling you that the move is to do nothing at all. I've got no reason to come after you. This will be over, and everyone in this book will be safe. The only person who can put them in danger is you. You hear me?"

Now I looked up at Robin. Her face hadn't lost any of its anger, but she nodded, slowly. Then she turned toward me, and fire flashed behind her eyes.

"You're responsible for all of this," she told me.

But it was like that fire was spreading. I felt it rush over me. Anger, spurred by tension.

"Do you know what happened to me?" I asked, but my voice was so low even I could barely hear it.

"Sorry?" Robin asked.

"I don't give a damn about anyone in your address book," I said and leaned forward. "Do you know what my life has been like since Renee was killed?"

"Yes," Robin said. "I actually do."

"No, you don't," I told her. I was having problems keeping my voice steady. "I'm alone in the world. Do you understand that? I know how much it hurts to lose her. But I can't make peace with it, like Michael did, or distract myself with a bullshit marriage, like Ruth, and I can't get drunk and let that take everything away. I have to deal with this pain, every day, every moment, and if I let myself look into it, just for a second, it runs over me. I can't live like this anymore. Do you understand?"

"Tom," Robin said, "I—"

"If you get in our way," I told her, and the thickness of my tone surprised me, almost as much as what I said next, "then I don't know what I'll do to you."

Robin stared at me, then blinked and looked back and forth between me and Diane. I wanted to say something else, to retract my threat, but I couldn't. My throat felt hot.

"You're going to go home," Diane told Robin. "And you're going to tell Michael that Tom has been missing Renee a lot recently and wanted to talk to you about it. Understand?"

Robin nodded.

"You're going to forget about this conversation, and your earlier one with Tom. Understand?"

Robin nodded.

"You do those things, and you'll save the lives of your friends and family. Understand?"

Robin nodded.

"Go."

Diane waited until Robin left the restaurant to speak again. "Well, Starks," she said, "I didn't know you had it in you. Look, I have goose bumps."

I looked at her arm but she was already out of the booth. "I'll be in touch," she said, then she was gone.

CHAPTER 8

Cemetery Gates

Thoughts of the confrontation with Robin distracted me throughout class the next day.

"All right," I told the students after they filed in, "Everyone enjoying *The Count?*"

A mix of nods. Middle-aged Marcia said, "I don't really like the main guy, Edmond. I understand what he's doing, but I think vengeance is wrong."

I nodded. "Edmond Dantes is an anti-hero. You're supposed to like him, or at least understand him, even if he does or says things you morally disagree with. Someone like, say, one of Quentin Tarantino's characters. Did anyone here see *Kill Bill?*"

Every head nodded.

"Uma Thurman's character is a late descendant of Edmond Dantes."

A questioning hand rose.

"Not literally," I said.

The hand lowered.

"Everything he does is for revenge. And so you have to ask yourself if his revenge, and the measures he takes, are warranted."

What if Robin panicked and called the cops? What if they arrested me in class? I'd lose my job, my family, everything.

"Professor?" someone asked. "Are you all right?"

I cleared my head. "Edmond is tough to relate to," I went on, "a lot like Thurman's character. You can enjoy the fun Tarrantino has with the movie, but at the heart, it's nothing but murder."

"Yeah," Song said, "I guess what I like about it is that you don't know who's going to live and die. I hate reading books from the writer's point of view, what's that, like first-person? Because you know they can't die."

"A first-person narrator can die," I said. "It can happen, especially in modern literature. A lot of times you don't even really know who's telling the story."

Robin knows everything.

And she's angry.

You're getting in over your head.

"Someone read the first line on page twenty."

A woman named Carla volunteered. "'May God forgive me,'" she read, "'that I should rejoice in good fortune brought about by another's death.'"

"Okay, so here Edmond is asking for God's forgiveness because another person's death helps him. But, later on, Edmond will seek the death of others, and he will consider that he is doing God's work. So…"

I forgot my point.

"So what does that mean to you?" I asked, lamely.

"I think it means," Song offered, "that Edmond feels bad because the captain was just an innocent man, but the people he wants vengeance against aren't innocent."

"So murder can be justified?"

"Well," Song said, "maybe back then. I mean, they had duels, right?"

"And they had the death penalty," someone else put in.

"Murder was almost acceptable when it came to revenge," I said.

"I have a question," a student named Bryon asked. He was a chubby black kid who rarely spoke. "It's about this line on the top of page thirty-four. 'Joy has that peculiar effect that at times it oppresses us just as much as grief.'"

"Okay, what's your question?"

"I got no idea what it means!" Bryon said helplessly.

Some kids, including Bryon, laughed.

"Any volunteers?" I asked.

Song spoke again. "I think he's saying that any emotions can be, you know, blinding. Especially when they're really passionate. Like love."

I nodded. "Anyone else?"

No other volunteers, so I spoke. "I agree with Song, but it's interesting that Edmond speaks the line. Because there will be a point in the novel where Edmond isn't going to feel grief or joy again. But he is going to be blinded by an emotion. It just hasn't been introduced yet." I looked around the room. "Any other questions?"

I had two more composition classes that day then I rushed to Whitegate for an appointment with Julie's school counselor. By the time I opened the door to Rose Carpenter's office, I was almost thirty minutes late, out-of-breath, and worried about getting scolded.

In other words, back in school.

"I'm sorry," I said. "I got caught up at work and—"

"It's no problem." Rose waved my concerns away. "I'm just glad you called me for this meeting. Julie has been a concern of mine for a while."

I studied the two chairs facing her desk and sat in the one to my left. "Why's that?"

Rose seemed surprised. "I'm concerned any time someone in a child's immediate family has died. No matter when it happened."

"Right." I suddenly wondered if Rose and I had met before, maybe during the distracted months following Renee's death. But she didn't look familiar. Rose was a short and slight black woman probably in her late thirties with shiny, straight black hair that dropped past her shoulders and a narrow, pointed face. A small bookcase was behind her, filled with various books on adolescent development and counseling. Her desk was devoid of any family photographs, and only two certificates hung on the wall, a Bachelors of Science in Psychology and Masters in Education, both from the University of Maryland.

I saw a psychiatrist, briefly, after Renee's death and was surprised by the similar lack of personal effects in her office. I assumed it was because the therapist wanted to protect herself from the weirdoes she counseled.

I wondered if Julie and I were weirdoes.

'*Kind of,*' Renee said, sitting in the seat next to mine. '*And how could you threaten my mom?*'

"Should I have come before now?" I asked.

"I'm the one who should have done more," Rose said. "I did leave you a couple of messages, but that was it."

"You did?"

Rose seemed as surprised as I did. "You didn't receive them?"

Renee tapped me insistently on the shoulder. '*She's lying. I can tell. By the way, Tom, about my mom, what the hell?*'

I brushed my shoulder. "I may have," I told Rose, "but after my wife died, I really wasn't talking to anyone. Everything was a blur."

'*I know. I wish I could have been there for you. How could you—*'

"I should have been more persistent," Rose was saying, "but I was already meeting with Julie. I'm sure she told you about that."

She hadn't, but I nodded anyway. Julie and I didn't talk much then. Even after she moved back into the house, we acted like roommates instead of family. And then, when I realized she needed more than that, that Julie needed a family, I felt overwhelmed.

'*When Julie was a baby,*' Renee said, '*I just wanted to hold her, to squeeze her chubby arms, to blow on her stomach, to kiss her face forever. I couldn't stop looking at her. I didn't expect to feel what I felt when Julie was born. I started falling in love with her.*'

"I've never felt that way with her," I said.

"I'm sorry?" Rose asked.

"Oh, I'm sorry. I meant that I remember those meetings. She did tell me about them."

Rose looked at me strangely. When she continued speaking, the strange look stayed. "I really like Julie," she said, "and I think she feels the same toward me. Or felt the same. It's been a while since she and I talked. I honestly thought she was doing better until I looked at her grades. I hadn't realized they had dropped so much."

'*Her grades are dropping*?' Renee asked, dismayed. '*Jesus Christ, Tom.*'

"I don't know why they have either," I said, a little defensively. "She's doing all of her homework. I'm also a teacher, by the way."

"But for a community college…" Rose's voice trailed away. "She's turning in her assignments, but she's not testing well. There's a disconnect between the grades she receives on her homework and the grades she receives on exams. I take it that you're not being made aware of her test grades."

'*No, he's not!*'

"I guess not."

Rose didn't react to what I said. She was probably used to poor examples of parenting walking into her office. "It also appears," she continued, "that Julie's test scores have lowered across the board. So it's something affecting all of her grades."

"Could it be something at school?" I asked. "Maybe she feels alienated."

"I haven't been told of anything that's affected Julie. She has been distant, but that's not abnormal at her age. I think—and this is a safe assumption—that this downturn has to do with her mother's death."

'*Well*,' Renee said, '*no kidding, doc.*'

"Have you considered a therapist?" Rose asked.

I almost glanced to the chair next to me, but restrained myself. "You think I need one?"

"I meant for Julie."

"Oh! She saw one. But she hated it so much that I promised her she wouldn't have to go back."

"Any reason why?"

"I didn't press Julie on why. I think he made her...actually, I don't know."

"You're not her natural father, right?"

I hated the term *natural*. "No."

"Who is?"

"I don't know. He left right after Julie was born, and my wife barely knew him. I don't think Julie ever met him."

'*Admittedly, not one of my better moments*,' Renee said.

"Was the adoption easy? Did she accept it?"

"Oh yeah. Julie asked me to adopt her."

"She did?" Rose's face broke out of its seriousness with a smile. "I'm sorry, but that's really cute."

"Thanks," I said distantly, the memory of that day, that afternoon, stealing over my body like sunlight...

❧❧

The sun on that hot Fourth of July, the sweat starting to dampen my shirt as I sat with Renee and Julie on a crowded Federal Hill. Julie lay on her back, a wet washrag covering her face.

"So," I asked, "when do the fireworks start?"

"We still have a few hours," Renee said grimly.

"If I melt, can you just face my puddle toward the show?"

Julie laughed.

"Sweetheart," Renee told her, "don't encourage him."

"You're not going to win this one," Julie told me, turning to me with her face still under the washrag. "Mom loves this holiday."

"You don't?" Renee asked me.

This was the first Fourth of July we celebrated together. I usually spent the holiday with friends, indoors, maybe briefly venturing outside for some barbeque, but Renee wanted to come to Federal Hill. The entire area was covered with blankets and food and groups of people talking and laughing and eating and sweating together. "I'm not really into crowds or heat. Or fireworks. But everything else is cool."

Renee frowned at me as Julie laughed.

"This is the only time it feels like the whole city comes together," Renee said. "And you can see the fireworks really well from here."

Julie lifted the rag off her head, sat up, and pointed to a row house just off the hill with a rooftop deck. "Those people have the right idea," she said. "We need one of those decks." She lay back down and covered her face again.

"I'll head back and build one," I offered. "I think we have enough time."

"Both of you shut up," Renee said serenely, "and enjoy the day. Besides, Tom, Julie has a question for you."

"She wants to know the signs of dehydration?" I asked.

"Tom..." Renee said, and I saw something serious in her expression.

I had no idea what Julie was about to ask.

She lifted a corner of the towel and peeked out at me. "So...I was wondering...do you want to be my dad?" She lay the towel back down and faced the other direction.

I studied Julie, not moving under the towel, and pride beat like a drum in my chest. I had told Julie, just before Renee and I got married, that I wanted to adopt her, but I wanted it to be something she wanted as well. I had known so many people who complained about difficult relationships with their step-parents or step-children. I never wanted Julie to feel like I forced my way into her life.

"More than anything in the world," I said.

"Okay, cool," Julie replied. I lifted the washrag for a moment, saw that she was smiling, and set it back down.

ഛഈഝ

"Thank you," I told Rose, "and thanks for helping me out. I really appreciate it."

"I'm always happy to help Julie," Rose said, "but I think she needs someone outside of the school, preferably a specialist in adolescent grief. And someone unfamiliar with her may actually be a benefit. In cases like this, a child often feels that he or she has either distance or power over the remaining authority figure in their life. Especially if the connection isn't natural."

It took me a moment to understand what she was saying. "But I've been her father for years."

"But that may not resonate with Julie as much as it does with you. Do the two of you discuss her mother?"

"Not often, no."

"Why not?"

"We're trying to move past that."

"Are you sure Julie's ready to?"

"I think so. She's been trying to get me to date other women. I guess she and I both need to move on."

"She's been trying to set you up?" Rose asked and laughed a little. "Well, that's a good sign. Still, though, Julie needs to talk to someone, and the sooner the better. I'll start meeting with her. She and I had a good relationship last year, and I might be able to build on that." Her eyes flicked up to me. "If that's okay with you, of course."

"Oh, yeah," I said. "I want her to talk to someone." The unspoken sentiment, that it wouldn't be me, hurt.

"Great. We'll set up regular meetings."

I barely registered what she was saying. Something else was on my mind. "Do you," I asked Rose, uncertainly, "think I'm making a mistake?"

Rose seemed surprised. "How?"

"By how I'm raising Julie."

"Oh." That neutral expression returned. "I really have no idea how you're raising her."

I felt like fidgeting, or telling her about Diane, but wisely restrained myself on both counts. "I'm trying, you know, but it's just...there's a lot to figure out. And a lot going on."

"If it helps, there's no one way to deal with what happened. It's different for everyone. But it seems like her mother left a good kid for you."

☙☙☙

After my meeting with Rose, I decided to pick Julie up from Dave and Ruth and have her spend the night with me.

But Julie scowled when we arrived home and I told her about Rose.

"Why'd you do that?"

These were the kind of tense comments Renee had been wonderful at calming. She was so attuned to her daughter's emotions that, when I was frustrated, Renee could empathize with her, even if she disagreed. But Julie's emotions always came from somewhere I could never understand.

"Because your grades are slipping, and your teachers thought it would be a good idea."

"You should have asked me first."

"I'm sorry that I didn't," I said gravely, keeping my amusement to myself.

Julie turned from me, stormed down the hallway, and slammed the door to her bedroom. "I'm not meeting with her!" she shouted.

I headed downstairs. I had papers to grade for tomorrow's classes. I idly flipped through them but didn't have the energy to even start. Instead, after about twenty minutes, I went back to Julie's room.

She was sitting on the bed in her pajamas, a notebook open in front of her. The room was quietly lit by the lamp next to her bed. The light green that her room was painted always reminded me of dawn, of dew on grass. Her furniture was still small, the dresser and nightstand made for children younger than her. She and Renee planned on buying a new bedroom set but never had, and Julie never brought it up to me.

"I'm sorry," I told her. "I should have told you that I was going to talk to Ms. Carpenter. You don't have to meet with her if you don't want to."

Julie studied me, and I wondered if apologizing was the right thing to do. I couldn't remember Renee ever apologizing to Julie, or my parents apologizing to me. "It's okay, Dad," she said. "But can I ask you something?"

The word *Dad* felt good. "Anything."

"Do you feel like something's missing?"

"What do you mean?"

"I mean with us."

Her question's seriousness and sadness surprised me. "Why? Do you feel like something's missing?"

"I guess."

I didn't know how to respond.

"Can I ask you something else?" Julie went on.

"Okay."

"What's an institution?"

"What do you mean?" I wondered where these questions came from.

"I mean a Baltimore institution."

"Julie," I asked, "has someone been...talking to you about your life?"

"I have to write about a Baltimore institution for school."

"Oh!" I was relieved. "There are two types of institutions. One is a place where people go to get better, or to study. The other is something that's part of a history or tradition. Like the Orioles. That's the one you probably have to write about."

"So I should write about the Orioles?"

I leaned against the doorframe. "No, you should write about something more cheerful."

"Like what?"

"Baltimore has lots of things that it's famous for. You could write about the Domino Sugars sign, or row houses, or Edgar Allan Poe, or—"

"Who's that?"

"Edgar Allan Poe? He was a writer, and he lived here around the eighteen hundreds."

Julie sat up in bed. "What did he write?"

"He wrote a lot of things, but he's mainly known for writing scary stories."

"And he lived here?"

"Lived and died here. He was found on a street corner, and no one knows how he died. I don't think they ever found out."

"Wow."

I didn't know why this was impressing Julie so much, but I didn't want the conversation to end—even if talking about death made me uneasy. "In fact," I contin-

ued, "every year, on the anniversary of his death, someone used to visit his grave and leave a rose and a bottle of
alcohol. But I think that person died."

"Really? His grave is here?"

I nodded.

"I think I want to write about that," Julie said. "Can
we go see his grave?"

"Sure," I said, and I had an idea. "Want to go right
now?"

"Are you serious?"

"I am," I told her.

Ten minutes later I was locking the front door and
Julie was standing next to me, wearing jeans and a sweater with a thick jacket and a hood pulled over the top of
her head.

I drove through Federal Hill, following the curve of
the harbor, and headed toward the stadiums up Light
Street. Downtown Baltimore was quiet this cold night.
Only a few men and women were out, shuffling along the
sidewalk in their thick coats, their heads lowered, hands
shoved in pockets. I tried to tell Julie everything I knew
about Poe on the way there, all of which I had learned on
Wikipedia while she was getting dressed. I wasn't proud.

"He ended up marrying his cousin," I told her.

"Eww."

"Well, yes. And she was a lot younger than he was,
but the marriage didn't last long. She died of a disease
called consumption." I hoped Julie wouldn't ask what
consumption was, because I had no idea.

"What's consumption?"

"It's a disease people got in the old days. It made
them really sick," I decided to make up the rest, "from

eating bad food. But that was years ago, before they could fix it."

"Did people die from consumption when you were a boy?"

"How old do you think I am?"

Julie ignored the question. "Did he ever get married again?"

"I don't think so, no."

"Can you tell me about sex?"

I almost slammed on the brakes. "What?"

"Can—can you tell me about sex?" Julie asked hesitantly.

"Why are you asking?"

"I just wanted to know about it." Now her voice was hushed, and her eyes looked away from me.

"No." I took a breath. "You're twelve. You're too young to think about this."

Julie was silent.

"Do you have a boyfriend?" I asked. "Is someone talking to you about..." I didn't know how to finish the sentence.

"No. My friends at school talk about it. I don't have a boyfriend."

That last sentence was spoken a few moments after the other, and there was something sad in the pause.

I pulled over to the side of the street and yanked out the emergency brake. "What do you want to know?" I asked.

"I don't know...how old were you when you did it? For the first time?"

I wasn't sure if I should lie to her or be honest, so I lied. "I was twenty-one," I told her.

"Were you in love?"

"Yes." Another lie.

"What was it like?"

"Well, I didn't know what to expect." I spoke slowly, chose my words carefully, but the truth in what I said surprised me. "I really didn't know what I was doing."

Julie laughed. "Really? Were you ready?"

ભ૭ભ૭

It was my best friend's—sadly, I can't remember his name anymore—sister, Sherry. I was sixteen, spending the day at his house one summer because he had a pool and it was one of those murky Maryland summers when the humidity dampens your clothes the moment you step outside. He was already swimming when I arrived. I went into his bathroom to change and walked in on Sherry, seventeen and about to head off to college. She was changing into a bikini, her hands behind her back as she tied the top. Her elbows were pointed up on either side of her head like the tips of angel wings.

I was going to step outside but she told me to stay and asked me to close the door. I did, nervous because I had never been this close to a girl, much less one wearing so little. I managed to answer whatever questions she asked, although I had problems concentrating the closer she moved toward me. Suddenly, we were kissing on the bathroom floor, and she loudly said, "OW."

"Are you all right?" I asked.

"Yeah," she said. "My elbow. Here, let me get on top."

"Okay."

"And put this on." She handed me a condom.

"I'm not really good at these," I told her.

I unwrapped the condom and tried to apply it, but it was the first time I had ever tried to use one. I was nervous and the lubricant made it slip out of my hand and fall to the floor.

Sherry picked it up, stretched it out, and slipped it over me. "Okay," she said, "are you ready?"

✁✁

"No," I said to Julie, trying to clear my mind of the memory, "I wasn't ready."

"Who was it with? Just tell me her name."

"None of your business and no. Why are you asking me all this?"

"I just always hear my friends talk about it, and I don't know if they're being honest."

I thought for a moment. "You know you can ask me anything you want."

"I know that."

I took off the emergency brake, but didn't pull out into the street. "Will you promise me something?"

"Okay."

"Before you do anything like that for the first time, let me know?"

"Okay."

I shook my head. "You're saying that now, but you're going to feel differently when it happens. It's really important that you tell me. There are things you need to know to keep yourself safe, and I'll help you with that. If you don't feel like you can talk to me, then tell Aunt Ruth. Just tell one of us."

"Okay. I promise."

I drove down the street. We hadn't been that far from Westminster Church. The black iron gate leading to the cemetery was to our left.

I parked. A fence protected the church and cemetery but, after nervously glancing up and down the street, I was able to boost Julie over the top and climb over afterward. We found ourselves on a red-bricked path next to the massive, almost overbearing church. Gravestones and monuments were on either side of us, and the path was lit by sunken lights. We walked around the church, stopping to examine the names inscribed into stone until we finally reached Poe's, marked by a raven carved on the top of a large headstone with a single rose and bottle of cognac below.

Tombs were all around us, and we had to stand with our backs to the path. The bare arms of a sprawling tree stretched toward us. Julie looked around nervously and held my hand. "It's scary here."

I didn't disagree with her, even though I was more scared that, at twelve, she was asking me about sex. I wondered if there was a boy out there pressuring her. I wanted to ask her about it, but I knew that if I pressed she might retreat.

A thought floated through my mind. If Diane and her partner killed Chris Taylor, I might not have to leave Julie. Ever since the thought of revenge first occurred to me, I hadn't anticipated keeping her.

Until now. After all, the police hadn't come yet. Maybe Robin heeded Diane's advice.

And my advice.

"So," I asked, "what are you going to say in your paper?"

"I guess what you told me about him?"

"You need to add a little more. Something from you, something that you learned from being here."

"Like, his grave is in a creepy place?"

I laughed. "How about this? Why do you think Edgar Allan Poe is so important to Baltimore?"

Julie shivered. The cemetery *was* creepy and cold, and despite what I was telling her, I wasn't exactly sure what she could learn here either.

"You said that people didn't like him when he was alive, and he died here, and then they only liked him after he had gone?" Julie asked.

"Pretty much."

"Well, no one likes Baltimore. The kids at school who moved from other cities, like New York and D.C., always talk about how much better their cities are."

"They do?"

"Yeah, but I know this one girl named Jennifer who left Baltimore because her parents were worried about crime and they went back to New York and then she wrote my friend Meg and told Meg that she liked Baltimore more than she had thought."

I was mystified. "And that makes you think of Edgar Allan Poe?"

"Because he wrote scary stories, but everyone liked them."

"So," I said, wondering exactly how she had made this connection, "you think that Baltimore can be a scary place, but also beautiful? Like the way people feel about what Edgar Allan Poe wrote?"

"Yeah. Or like when I think about Mom."

"What do you mean?"

"I mean, I get sad when I think about her, but it also makes me happy to remember her."

I was silent for a moment. "Come on." We started back to the entrance. "You found your starting point."

"You think so?" Julie said, doubtfully.

"Definitely."

We walked in silence for a few steps then she spoke. "Thanks for driving me here to help with my paper."

Something about her sentence made me smile. It reminded me of Renee, of an immediate possessiveness that I had always found funny. "*Thank you for my flowers*," Renee used to say, when she would come home and find a bundle of grocery-store flowers I had left on the counter.

This whole evening reminded me of Renee, and I suddenly realized that she would have loved to have come here, probably with her camera, and would have asked me to hold a flashlight over Poe's tombstone as she took a picture of it.

Renee and her camera. The innocent artist. She never took a class or studied photography, and doubtless she would have been better if she had, but there was something alert and alive in her photographs, a life and excitement that came before a student's rules and restraints.

Her themes were simple, even clichéd—a close-up of a flower, a person's lengthening shadow, Julie's wide joy. But, still, there was life.

I had come to this cemetery once before, a year into teaching and in the midst of my Masters, flush with the idea that Poe's grave would give me momentum, inspiration for whatever short story I was writing that I hadn't yet learned would never be published. I had come here, ambitious and stupid, and sat in front of Poe's grave for an hour, waiting to be touched by the master's spirit. It was the kind of act that only the young at heart, or in art, undertake. I sat, eyes closed, my manuscript rolled in my hand, waiting. But the earth stayed silent. My candle wasn't blown to life.

"Dad," Julie said. "I do love you."

"I love you, too."

"But I want to stay with Aunt Ruth from now on," Julie said. "Instead of going back and forth."

Her words ricocheted through me. I stopped just before the cemetery gates. "What?"

"I just think things would be better that way," Julie said, seriously, standing in front of me. "Remember how I said that, sometimes, it feels like something is missing? It doesn't feel like anything is missing when I'm with her, with her and Uncle Dave, you know?"

Julie kept staring at me, her eyes wide but focused, peering at me intently through the dark.

"I just think it would be better for me," she said. "You'll see."

CHAPTER 9

Bananas

I fixed breakfast the next morning. Julie walked silently downstairs, sat at the kitchen table, and started to eat. She kept looking in my direction. I avoided her glances.

"I really think I'm going to do well on my report about Eddie Albert Poe," she said.

"Edgar Allan Poe," I corrected her.

"Edgar," she repeated, dutifully. "Will you help me on it?"

I wanted to say no, but couldn't. "Sure."

"Cool."

I stared down at my waffles, unsure how I should act. I didn't think it would be right for Julie to see me hurt or sad.

I drove her to school after breakfast and headed to BCC. I was grateful to teach that day. I wanted to lose myself in the lesson.

ᘓᔓᘓᔓ

"How many of you feel the novel shifting?" I asked the class. "Can someone summarize what happened?"

"Edmond is sent to prison," Marcia said, "and he stays there for…four years, I think? And he finally meets another prisoner."

"What stuck out to you?" I was asking the class for their input more than I usually did, but I needed the distraction. I didn't want to think about what Julie told me.

"Well," Marcia said, "you mentioned philosophical lines last time, and I noticed a line on page ninety-three, when the other prisoner tells Edmond, 'If you wish to discover the author of a crime, endeavor to find out in the first place who would derive advantage from the crime committed.' That kind of reminded me of that old saying about Watergate. 'Follow the money.'"

"Good point," I said. "And for Edmond, finding out who truly sent him to prison leads him to escape that prison. And vengeance saves him from suicide. And, later, when Faria tells Edmond about his fortune hidden in Monte Cristo, vengeance leads him to money. It also leads him to family, given that the other prisoner adopts Edmond. What about his escape?"

Silence from the class, and I started to remember Julie. I said abruptly, my voice harsher than I expected, "Come on!"

"What about it?" someone asked, timidly.

"How does Edmond escape?"

Sam spoke. "After the prisoner dies, Edmond hides in his burial wrappings, and then he's carried out to sea and thrown overboard. So he swims to an island, finds a passing boat, and pretends that he's a shipwrecked sailor."

"Good," I said. "But what *really* happened?"

Nothing.

"Could you make an argument," I went on, "that Edmond uses death to gain life? Could you say that the prisoner's death gives him life? Think about this— Edmond has to die in order to live, and when he lives again, he's reborn into the Count of Monte Cristo. His escape from prison is like a birth. After all, he is in a small, dark wrapping that he has to emerge from. Not only that, but he's been tossed into the sea. Baptized. He's been cleansed of his old life. But the remnants of that old life, especially his vengeance, stay with him. So the Count of Monte Cristo becomes more than a man in a lot of ways. He's almost a spirit, a wraith." I stopped speaking and blinked. "I'm sorry," I said. "I should have let some of you contribute to that."

The class laughed.

"Can someone tell me where something similar occurs?" I asked.

Song raised her hand and started speaking, her other hand holding the pages of her book open. "When he finds the treasure, in the chapter *The Treasure Cave*."

"Okay. What happens?"

Song studied the book as she spoke. "Well, he has to walk through a couple of caves, which is kind of like the same thing, right? Like, it's kind of gross, but on page one hundred and forty-one, it says, '…in the cave, the

atmosphere of which was warm rather than damp...'"
Song paused for a quick laugh, "'fragrant rather than fet-
id'...it's kind of, like, vaginal."

The class laughed with her.

"Okay," I said. "And Dante has to go through the
caves and dig through the hard stones and then, finally,
inside a chest, he finds his treasure. So what happened?"

"Well," said Sam, "it's kind of like he died earlier
and then was born again."

I nodded. "Exactly. And this isn't the only time that
happens to Dante, but it's the most important. This chapter is what allows him to become the man that we follow
for the rest of the story."

caca

After class ended and the students left, I grabbed my
laptop, stuffed it into my satchel, and hurried into the
hall. I had another class, but it wasn't until the afternoon.
I walked out into the cold, gray day and headed toward
the parking lot. I climbed into my car and remembered
what Julie said.

I rubbed my eyes.

It took me a few minutes to compose myself, but I
eventually started my car and drove out of the lot. I had
an idea.

caca

I knew my plan didn't make sense when I thought of it that afternoon, but I was still excited as I walked Julie upstairs that evening.

"What is it?" Julie kept asking. "What do you want to show me?"

"You have to wait," I told her, listening to my voice as I spoke. Definitely calmer than the day before. After all, despite the ominous feeling that Robin was going to turn me in, I didn't have to hire Diane and her partner if I didn't want to. Nothing was in motion yet. And even if I did hire them, Julie wasn't in danger. I had played out as many different scenarios as I could imagine, and they all ended in one of two ways, and neither involved Julie getting hurt. One, Diane and her partner found and killed Chris Taylor, I paid them, and the job was over, or two, Diane and her partner got arrested, I got implicated in the crime, and Julie lived with Ruth and Dave.

But I still felt guilty about Julie being even remotely involved, and so I did something for her, something that might convince her to stay with me. We reached the second floor, walked to her bedroom. I opened the door and turned on the light.

Julie looked up at me questioningly then stepped inside. Silence, then she asked, "What's that?"

"What do you mean?" I stepped in after her and looked down at the small, red plastic cage holding a fat, lop-eared light-brown rabbit. The rabbit sat on its haunches, sneezed, rubbed its nose on yellowed paws then looked up at us through crusty eyes. His hair was matted and stuck together in places.

"Why'd you buy me a rabbit?"

"You said you wanted a pet."

"But, like, a dog." She was looking down at the rabbit as she spoke.

"A dog is a lot of work. And this is kind of like a dog, but he stays in a cage and doesn't need to be walked. Besides, I don't have a lot of time to train a dog."

"Huh," Julie said.

Julie had always wanted a pet. Now she had one and was hesitant. I wondered if she suspected I was using this rabbit as a way to keep her.

"Did you ever have a dog?" she asked.

"Growing up I did."

Winky had been a mix between a basset and a lab, with a big head, but short squat legs and a happy eagerness that never failed him, even when arthritis eventually took over his body.

His condition deteriorated to the point where he could barely move without whimpering, and I remembered the last time that my parents took the dog to the vet, in winter, carrying him wrapped in a blue blanket as he breathed hoarsely.

I left for college later that year and my parents never brought another dog into their life. Their house always seemed quiet and dark—lifeless, bloodless—afterward.

I worried that our house might seem that same way to Julie.

The rabbit sneezed.

"Where did you get it?" she asked.

"At a pet store in Cantonsville. It was a pretty dumpy store, to be honest. I kind of felt like I was saving his life by getting him out of there."

"Well, that's nice," Julie said. She finally knelt and peered closely at the rabbit. "He is sort of cute." She turned, looked up at me, and smiled. "Thank you."

"Sure."

"His cage seems small," she said. "Can we get him a bigger one?"

"I had the same thought," I told her. "I actually have a bigger one, but it's in the car. It's a little big for your room, so we can keep it in the den."

"I can't keep it in my room?" she asked.

"Well—"

"But I want him to be here when I go to sleep at night."

And that was it—the assumption that she would be spending her nights with me, and not with Ruth and Dave. "Sure," I told her. "Let me get it and I'll set it up."

I walked downstairs, beaming, lifted the cage out of the car, and carried it upstairs. I could hear Julie's soft voice cooing to the rabbit already, "...and I'll brush you and feed you," she was saying, "and I'll give you lots of carrots or whatever you want, and I'll take pictures of you and put them online..."

The cage was actually a dog pen. Julie lifted the rabbit out of its small pen—he stayed limp as he was carried, and I was a little worried by the rabbit's lack of struggle. He lay stiffly on the bed, paws tucked underneath his body. Julie sat next to him, petting him with one hand and holding a book I bought about rabbits with the other.

"It says that they like fruits and vegetables," she said as I assembled the pen. "And they like to keep themselves very clean."

I glanced at the rabbit as I tried to snap the locks in place. "They must not have been writing about your rabbit."

Julie laughed, a hyper, little, delighted laugh. "Should we give him a bath?"

"What does the book say?" I was struggling with the cage. The door for the pen had to be attached, and the locks were stubborn.

"It says…" I heard Julie flipping pages. "It says that you should only bathe rabbits when they're really, really dirty. I don't think he's that dirty. Do you, Dad?"

"Hell yes. But we're taking him to the vet soon. The vet can give him a bath."

"Okay."

"What are you going to name him?" I asked, still trying to fit the cage together.

"Renee."

The entire cage almost came apart in my hands. "What?"

"Renee."

My voice sounded smaller than I had expected. "You can't name him that."

"I want to name my bunny after Mom."

"But…they told me that he's a boy rabbit. He needs a boy's name."

Julie was quiet for a moment. "I thought you'd like it if I named him after Mom."

"I do like it," I said. "I just think it would be better if he had a different name. But I do like your idea," I added hastily. "I think it's really nice of you."

"Now I have to think of another name for you," Julie cooed to the rabbit.

I turned back to the cage, surprised at how fast I was breathing.

"Albert," Julie said. "Frankie, Steve, Bugs…"

The door finally snapped into place. I tested it, swinging it open and closed, making sure it latched. "Come over here," I said.

Julie obediently hopped off the bed and stood next to me.

"This is how you open the door," I told her. "See? But don't let him out tonight. He's had a long day, and we should let him get used to his new home."

"Okay."

"Do you have the box?" I asked.

"It's here," Julie said.

She lifted the cardboard box I had been given at the store. I took it and stuck it in a corner of the pen, with the opening on the side. I had already placed a bin filled with hay in one corner, with a bowl with water next to it and a litter box in the other. Although I was still skeptical that rabbits could be litter trained.

"All right," I said and stepped back to study the cage. "It's good to go."

"Come see your new home," Julie sang out to the rabbit, but the rabbit stayed in its stiff position on the bed. Julie sighed, reached over, and picked him up. His eyes widened as he was lifted. She placed it on the floor next to the cage's open door and, after a few moments, the rabbit hopped inside, took a mouthful of hay, and bounced into its box, dragging hay across the carpet after him.

What a stupid animal.

But at least my daughter was happy. I glanced at the clock. Almost eleven.

"Time for bed, hon. You have school tomorrow."

"All right," Julie said happily, and she closed the cage door. She walked over to me and reached up to give me a huge hug, wrapping her small arms around my neck. "Say goodnight to Bananas," she told me.

"What?"

"Bananas," Julie said. "That's my bunny's name."

I let go of Julie and reached down to tap the top of the box. "Goodnight, Bananas."

"I'm sorry for what I said the other night," Julie told me. "About going away."

"Oh," I said and tried to hide my surprise, my happiness. "That's okay. We all say things we don't mean sometimes."

"I don't really want to live with Aunt Ruth and Uncle Dave forever. Aunt Ruth just made it sound like a good idea. I want to stay with you."

✞✞✞

Ruth answered after the third ring.

"Hello?" Her voice was sleepy.

"Ruth."

"Tom…what's going on? Is something wrong? Are you drunk again?"

"Julie told me what you told her."

Her voice lowered to a whisper. "What did I tell her?"

"About her moving in with you and Dave."

"Wait a minute." I heard shuffling sounds then the sound of a door closing. "Tom?" Her voice was clearer.

"Why are you trying to convince Julie to live with you?"

"Why am I...oh." Ruth paused for a moment then she sighed. "I'm sorry. It wasn't like that."

"What was it like?" I asked. I was sitting in my bedroom, the room dark.

"Look—we were talking, and Julie said that she wished your house was more like ours. Okay? And I asked her why she said that, and she said that our house felt more like a family."

"Well, if you had a daughter, and she said that, I still would have told her that it was important to be with her own family."

"Tom, Julie *is* my family."

"You know better than that."

Ruth's voice was defensive. "Well, maybe Julie has a point. Maybe you should listen to her."

"I do listen to her. If you—"

"No," Ruth interrupted me, heatedly. "I don't think you do. You're not a bad father, Tom, but you're not everything she needs. Have you noticed that she's changing? Did you know that her grades were dropping, or did her teachers have to tell you? Do you even know that she's unhappy? Do you think she even feels a *real* connection to you?"

I was quiet.

"You're losing her," Ruth continued. "These are important years for Julie, and I'm worried about her. And if I said more than I should have, then it's because I was thinking about Renee, and what she would have wanted."

"Renee wanted Julie to be with me."

"Renee wanted Julie to be happy. And she wanted her to achieve everything she could." She paused. "I just think it will be harder for you than it will for us."

"You're right," I said. "It will be hard. But I don't know anyone who said being a parent is easy." I felt my anger grow, a hot rush. "And I don't need you second-guessing me in front of my daughter."

"That wasn't what I wanted to do."

"Bullshit."

"Watch your goddamn mouth," Ruth said, her voice snapping. "Don't talk to me like that, or you can find someone else to watch Julie."

"I'm happy to."

There was a pause.

"Go to hell, Tom," Ruth said, and she hung up.

৩৩৩

Hours later, I was sitting on the living room couch, watching TV downstairs so I wouldn't wake Julie.

My living room was always uncomfortably cold. It was the most unused room in the row house, long and narrow and difficult to illuminate. Even now, only a faint glow, cast from a lamp on an end table at the far side of the couch, provided dim light. The fireplace, which was so dirty that its charm had been forgotten, was shadowed and quiet. The room was large, the chair I was sitting in was large, the entire house was too large for just me.

An aching nervousness was beginning in my stomach and spreading. And not just because I kept threatening members of Renee's family.

I couldn't do this alone.

I couldn't raise Julie without help. I wouldn't be able to get through a single day without Ruth. I'd have to leave work early to pick Julie up from school, instead of Julie taking the bus straight to Ruth's house, and there were some days when I just couldn't leave early, especially now, near the end of the semester when students needed me for conferences. And she could only have so many sleepovers at Tracy's. I could try and find a nanny…but money was an issue. Christmas was a month away and my mother wanted us to visit her in Florida. I needed to start saving.

I pushed open the living room curtains and peered outside. The street in front of our row house was lined with cars and trees, and all of the other houses were dark. I stared out and wondered, like I always did, how other families managed. How did other parents pay their bills, find enough time to spend with their children, and deal with their own issues? I had felt overwhelmed *before* Renee died. Now I was on my own, alone, and I had no clue.

I turned off the TV, made my way upstairs as quietly as I could to Julie's room, pushed open the door, and peeked inside.

A steady crunching sound. Bananas was furiously gnawing at something through the bars, his neck stretched forward and his long lopped ears back. I bent down to peer into the pen. Bananas stiffened and then raced into the box, almost knocking it over, and from inside came a solid thumping sound.

I reached down and felt the baseboards. They were rough, half-eaten, and I remembered Julie flipping through the book and telling me that rabbits liked chewing wood.

I considered putting something over the baseboards to protect them, but couldn't think of anything that wouldn't wake Julie. She was sleeping on her stomach, her cheek pressed against the pillow and her small arm wrapped around it. I watched her while Bananas hopped out and started gnawing again at the wood. Then I went back to my bedroom and lay down, but couldn't sleep. I picked up my phone to send Alison a text, asking if I could see her soon.

But I already had a message.

From Diane.

be ready to pay.

CHAPTER 10

However

A note taped to the bathroom door in the hotel room instructed me to turn out the lights, get naked, and join Alison in the tub.

I was a little desperate to be with Alison. I'd spent the day teaching composition classes and texted Alison right after confirming that Julie could spend tonight with Tracy. I needed something removed from Diane and her partner, Robin, and Julie, and…everything. I didn't want to spend this night alone.

"Hey," I called out.

"Hey you," Alison called back, from behind the closed bathroom door. "Coming in?"

"Hold on," I told her. I quickly shed my clothes, turned off the light, and opened the door to the dark bathroom. I stepped onto cold tiles and awkwardly reached down until Alison said, "Okay, that's my nose."

I felt her body move forward and I settled behind her, slowly sinking in the warm water. She leaned back into me.

"I probably should have said this before now," I said, "but I think I need to pee."

"Right now?" Alison asked, disbelief in her voice.

"Maybe."

"Then you should."

"In here?"

"No! The toilet."

"But I'd have to turn on the light. My aim's not that good."

"Well…"

"It's okay. I can hold it."

"Are you sure?" Alison asked. "This is something I want you to be sure about."

"I can do this."

"Really?"

"I'm good. Talk about something. Distract me."

"Okay. I actually want to ask you to do something."

"Is it anal?"

I felt her body turn toward me. "What?"

"What, what?"

"Did you just ask if I want to have anal sex?"

"I wouldn't ask you that. But, do you?"

"No!"

"That's okay. We keep it so dark that it'd be like throwing a spear at a bee."

She paused. "This conversation is kind of making me re-think our little relationship."

"I get that."

"Anyway, shut up. I want you to listen to this," Alison said.

I felt her reach over the side of the tub, fiddle with something, and low music started. Drums, guitar, a woman's soft, almost cautious voice over a low bluesy beat.

"You, um, don't have a band in here with us, do you?"

A sharp bark of laughter from Alison. "No, that's an old CD player. You're stupid."

"With sticks flying all around you,
"Breaking every little thing that you do.
"I'm gonna fly…
"All night.
"I might drive…
"All night."

"So what's bothering you?" Alison asked, and it took me a moment to realize she was referring to my text from earlier: *Things not good. Can we get together?*

"Oh. It's just…nothing. I just kind of needed to be with someone else."

"I feel the same way."

She leaned back and we kissed, our tongues briefly playing, like flashlight beams dancing around each other.

"They see your heavy heart and its wound,
"A bat flying around your room."

"I'm just not that good a father. I don't think Julie wants to live with me anymore. Even though I bribed her with a pet rabbit."

"Did you really want to be her father?"

"What do you mean?"

"Hearts are gonna break down,
"Baby's gonna take down and lie.
Draw me a line,
"Shake it and make it unwind."

"I mean that you fell in love with Renee, and you married her, but what about Julie? Were you as excited about her as you were about Renee?"

I didn't respond.

"Some people never get a chance
to lie awake and wonder,
"lie awake and wonder, unleash their brain.
"Some people never get a chance
to walk around and wander,
"walk around and wander,
"Don't you think that's a shame?"

"People always hate their stepparents," Alison went on.

"Julie doesn't hate me."

"Yeah, but she knows you didn't love her right away. Not the way you loved her mother."

"What's your point, Alison?"

"Is this upsetting you?"

                         "A crime?
                     "And a shame…"

"A little."

"Is that why you just peed on my back?"

"That was unrelated."

"Look, I was just trying to see where Julie's coming from. She's *your* daughter. You adopted her, you raised her. Don't let anyone tell you differently, not even her. No matter what, you two share one thing in common. Her mother."

                   "Draw me a line,
             "Shake it and make it unwind…"

"Can we talk about something else?"

"Okay." Alison was quiet for a moment. "Do you like this song?"

"Yeah."

"A woman named Abby Mott sings it. She's from Baltimore." Alison paused again then asked hopefully, "Do you really like it?"

"I do."

                   "Draw me a line…
               "Make it unwind…"

                         ৵৶৵৶

"So, are you religious?" Alison asked, lying in bed next to me in the dark.

Our bodies were dry although her hair was still wet, draped over my arm, the side of her face on my chest. I felt warm and relaxed. The meeting with Diane felt like it happened years ago.

"You're just hitting all the fun topics tonight."

She laughed. "Sorry, I'm curious about you."

"I'm kind of Catholic."

"What does *kind of* mean?"

"It means I was raised Catholic, but I like having anonymous sex with you so it's not working out too well. And I stopped turning to God after Renee was...after she died. Religion just seemed like a luxury."

"What do you mean?"

"It makes sense to believe in God when everything is going good. But when your wife dies, or your dad has some incurable disease, or a plane crashes into a pair of towers...believing doesn't feel right. So I just couldn't practice anymore, not after I lost Renee. What about you?"

"I'm not religious, but the reason's not as deep as yours. Basically, I like doing my shopping on Sunday." She paused. "I'm sorry for bothering you about your daughter earlier. I know it's tough."

"You don't have kids, right?"

"No." Her voice was soft then she cleared her throat. "All my sentences ended in periods."

I laughed. "Do you want kids?"

I liked feeling her jaw move against my chest when she spoke. "I did, I mean, I do. But it's not going to happen for me."

"Why not?"

"My ex and I were trying to have a kid, and it wasn't working. So I went to the doctor a few months ago. He told me I couldn't conceive."

"Oof. Sorry."

"It hit us both pretty hard," Alison said, quietly. "I mean, I always liked children, and I just thought I'd end up with a couple. I never thought it wouldn't happen."

"What happened with the ex?"

"We were both so sad afterward that everything ended up falling apart. I guess it's good we didn't have kids, after all. I've thought about that a lot."

"You still keep in touch with him?"

"No."

I realized that she was crying. I slowly rubbed her back.

"So you've never been married?" I asked.

"No."

"Why not? Are you...ugly?"

She laughed, a sudden loud laugh. "*No!* Jerk. I think I just dated the wrong guys. Kind of like now."

"Can I ask you something?"

There was a moment's pause. "What?"

"Can I see you?" I asked. "Can I turn on the lights?"

I felt her head shake. "No."

"Then will you tell me what you look like?"

"I feel like you already know. I'm short, Vietnamese, dark hair..."

"You're Vietnamese?"

"Yeah, why?"

"I had no idea."

"Does it matter?"

"No. I just didn't know. Alison doesn't seem like the name for a Vietnamese woman. I thought it'd be something like...Toy, or something."

She laughed. "Well, I was born here. I've never been there. And, hey! Tom's not exactly Spanish-sounding."

"Technically, it's Tomás. But nobody calls me that."

"What do they call you?"

"Everyone's always called me by my last name, Starks."

"Starks." I felt Alison nod. "I could see that."

"So," I said, wondering if it was okay to ask this, since she didn't seem to be crying anymore, "this ex of yours. Were you pretty serious?"

"We dated for about a year. So, kind of."

"Who was the first person you were in love with?"

Alison laughed. "You sound like a teenage girl."

"Come on. Just tell me."

"You first," she said. "Tell me more about Renee."

"Why?"

"I like listening to you talk about love."

My voice was hoarse. "But it makes me sad."

"But it sounds beautiful."

გელე

"I told a friend about our meetings," Alison said, an hour or so later.

"What did your friend say?"

"She said that I was an idiot and this was really unsafe."

I nodded. "I could see that."

"So I gave her the hotel name and told her the room number. And if I don't call her in two hours, then she's going to break down the door and shoot you."

"Fair enough."

"I told her that you seem okay. Plus, it's almost like we're sort of dating now, isn't it?"

Something about her question turned my body cold.

Alison must have sensed my change, because she added, abruptly, "I mean, dating as much as you can without actually seeing the person."

I didn't respond, and she went on. "So, new subject."

"Okay."

But she didn't want to entirely give up. "I mean," Alison pressed, "I know it's not *really* dating, but it's some sort of a relationship. We're learning a lot about each other, and it feels sort of more honest this way, doesn't it?"

"I guess." I felt like I needed to say more, so I added, "But there's a lot that seeing someone can tell you."

"Well," Alison said, "like you'd know about my tattoo."

"You have a tattoo?"

"Isn't that so weird?" Alison marveled. "We've been naked together, like, three times now, and you have no idea about my tattoo."

"What is it?"

"It's really dumb. Wings on my back."

"Really?"

"Really. They're not huge or anything. I don't know what I was thinking. What about you? Got any tattoos that you regret?"

"Nope. No tattoos."

"And no regrets?" Alison asked.

I thought about Diane and her partner. "I don't think I've done my biggest one yet. It'll probably happen soon, though."

"What does that mean?"

Raw anxiety sharply rose. I tried to force it back down. "I don't know."

"Should I be worried?"

I realized Alison's body was stiff. "Oh! No. It's nothing. I'm just...I'm just worried about my daughter. I always think I'm making mistakes by how I'm raising her."

I felt Alison relax. "The fact that you're worried means you're doing a better job than you probably think you are. Most of my friends with kids never seem to care. They treat children like a burden." She laughed. "As long as you're not putting her life in danger, you're probably fine."

After a few moments, Alison asked, "Tom?"

"Sorry. Just thinking about something you said."

"Can I ask you something?" Without waiting for me to answer, she continued. "Does this bother you?"

"What's that?"

"Not being able to see me. It's just so weird to me, now that I think about it, how little you and I know about each other. We met for sex, which is really superficial, but then we kept meeting and talking, without knowing a thing about what we look like, so now it feels…deeper. To me, anyway. But does not seeing me bother you?"

"A little," I admitted. "Not too much."

"I kind of like it that we can be anything to each other." She paused. "Do you want to pretend I'm Renee?"

The wind was knocked out of me. "No," I said, unsteadily. "I like being with you."

"Are you okay?" Alison asked.

"Yeah," I said. Rolling our bodies over so that she was underneath me, I sank between her legs. "I'm okay."

'*Are you sure you're okay?*' Renee asked.

I backed up until I reached the end of the bed, then lowered myself to the floor. I tugged Alison's thighs toward me until they rested over my shoulders. "Yeah," Alison said, as her hips rose, "you're definitely okay."

I kissed the insides of her thighs. Her hands found my shoulders and I felt her nails tracing, then digging.

'*She's wrong,*' Renee said. '*You're definitely not okay. Although I am impressed with your powers of concentration.*'

Alison's hips lifted again. I slid my hands under her butt and her cheeks filled my palms.

'*I miss you, Tom,*' Renee told me. '*I miss you so much. Too much.*' And I felt her touch, her hand and then her mouth closing over me. I could feel her lips.

I let my tongue slip inside Alison. Her thighs briefly closed over my ears and then separated, spreading even farther, almost lying flat on the bed.

I took one hand out from under Alison and reached down, my fingers rolling over Renee's strained nipple.

"Get inside me," Alison implored.

I climbed up and over her. My hips rose and I felt hands on my lower back, pushing them down, guiding them into her. '*It's me, Tom,*' Renee said. '*You're in me now. Do you feel it?*'

"Do it slowly," Alison asked, and her body lifted under mine.

Renee's hands pushed me down, her soft hands on my lower back. Alison's arms and legs wrapped around me, Renee's breasts pressing into me.

'*I miss you when you're not here,*' she told me.

I miss you, too.

ღღღ

Saturday morning. I sat on the floor in Julie's bedroom, waiting for her to come home, watching Bananas eat hay. My phone buzzed. Another message from Diane.

2nite. Levees. 8 pm.

Maybe I was that tired, but her message didn't raise any emotions in me. Not fear or excitement, nothing. I wrote back. *Do I bring money?*

Moments later.

no cash. just bank acct #s

A beat passed.

u can give robin the book back

You're going to bring it tonight?

nah left it in your place last night. check bedroom closet

I jumped up, rushed to my bedroom, and threw open the closet door. Robin's green address book was on the

top shelf. I looked for my phone, couldn't find it, and realized I had left it in Julie's room.

I hurried back to her room. My sudden movements
must have startled Bananas because he had hopped inside
his box and was thumping the ground angrily.

I picked up my phone.

How did you get in here last night?

Diane didn't write back.

CHAPTER 11

Beneath the Surface

Diane didn't respond to any of my texts but, aside from the address book, nothing was disturbed in the house. I was still worried and didn't think it was a good idea to stay there with Julie. My meeting with Diane and her partner was tonight, and their unpredictability unnerved me.

So when Julie was dropped off just before noon, I promptly asked if there was anything she wanted to do.

"I don't care," she said. "We could just hang out and watch TV."

"Something out of the house."

Julie offered a light careless shrug. "I don't know."

The shrug was new, a gesture that, somehow, she had taken from her mother. Every day, she looked more and more like Renee. I had been an only child and unable to observe someone else grow up, so it was fascinating for me to watch Julie mature. Her cheeks were getting rounder now that she was twelve, and her stomach and breasts had begun to fill out. Renee had been short and a little overweight and Julie was inheriting her body. She had Renee's light skin and long black hair and—behind the large round glasses she always wore—wide, sad, brown eyes. I could see a faint trace, like an outline, of the woman she would become.

"I tell you what," I said. "Why don't we go ice skating?"

"Down by the harbor?"

"How about Highlandtown instead?"

"Where's that?"

"Where's Highland…You've been there. It's where I grew up."

That shrug again.

Julie added a sweater to her outfit, I threw on a coat, and we headed out. The drive was only twenty minutes, and I found parking near the outdoor skating rink. We left the car and walked through the cold air.

"Looks like a dump," she pronounced.

"A little bit. Want to see the house I lived in?"

"Don't you want to go ice skating first?"

"Nah, let's do this."

We walked up a few streets to a light blue house on the corner of Highland Street, on a hilltop intersection of four streets, and stopped in front of it.

"You grew up here?" Julie asked, in disbelief.

"I did."

"Isn't it abandoned?"

"Maybe. It doesn't have the charm it used to." I'd come here hoping that Julie would like it, or that she would take something from the experience, but she could care less. Her arms wrapped around herself. She was probably pretending to be cold so we would leave soon.

I turned back toward my old house. It *was* a little dumpy. Some owners after us had added a wooden balcony, but now the wood was worn and on the edge of collapse. The blue paint on the house needed a re-coating, and it didn't help that the house next door actually *was* abandoned. But I remembered growing up here, especially my early teenage years. I would spend summers lazily watching television, a little lonely because I lacked siblings, and I always imagined one day buying this house back and filling it with family. I loved Highlandtown. I hadn't shared those dreams with Renee, but that was because it wasn't actually a dream I was really aware of. It just felt like something that would someday happen.

"All right," I told Julie, "want to head to the rink?"

Ice skating consisted of me watching Julie skate. She wasn't bad, but she took the curves clumsily and had a tendency to flail out her arms, despite whoever was around her and how close they were. But that made her fun to watch, and she did have an unnatural ability to stay on her feet. I wondered if there was a sport she would be good at, maybe gymnastics. Renee never wanted Julie to do sports because she thought they would be a distraction from school, despite my counter argument that running was the only thing that kept me in college.

Julie stomped off the ice when she finished and headed over to return her skates and retrieve her shoes.

"Ready to go home?" I asked, while we waited at the counter. Then I remembered Diane's break-in.

"Home," Julie repeated offhandedly. "Sure."

We walked back to the bench so that Julie could put her boots back on.

"Hon," I began hesitantly, "listen. I'm going to need you to move in with Ruth for a little bit. I'm sorry."

Julie looked up at me. "What do you mean?"

"You have to stay with Aunt Ruth and Uncle Dave a little longer."

"Why?"

"Because—I'm really busy these next couple of weeks, and it would make things easier if you stayed with them."

Julie scowled. "So when things are busy for you, or hard, you don't want me around?"

"Only when they're this hard, I promise." I hoped that would be enough, and that Julie would understand. But her scowl deepened, and she angrily thrust her feet into her boots.

"You can't do that. The other night you asked me to stay and now you want me to leave? You can't pick and choose when you want to be my dad. Nobody does that."

Her voice was loud, and a fat woman next to us, kneeling to tie ice skates onto a row of three waiting children, glanced over in alarm. I gave her an apologetic look and a small smile. The woman didn't smile back, and she didn't turn away.

"Listen, Julie," I said. "You know that's not what I'm doing. I just have some things to do now that I need time for. And Aunt Ruth and Uncle Dave love you. They love having you there."

"They probably love having me there more than you do," Julie said defiantly.

One of the three kids started to say something, but the fat woman shushed him.

"That's not true."

"They've never once asked me to stay somewhere else. Not once. They *want* me there."

I was growing angry, not just at Julie, but everything—Diane, Renee, the nosy woman next to us. "It's different for them," I said.

"Why?"

I thought about the meeting tonight again, about Diane and her partner and what I wanted to do. There was no way I could keep Julie. "Because they don't have to raise you like I do. They do it when they want."

"Sorry I'm so hard to deal with for you," Julie said hotly. She kicked her heels against the ground.

Something in me snapped.

"I didn't ask for this," I said quietly.

"What?" Julie asked.

"I didn't ask to be your father."

Someone gasped, either the fat woman or Julie or someone else, but I didn't care. I was facing Julie but my mind was somewhere else. I didn't even see her. All I saw was Renee's body on a table in the morgue, the side of her head caved in.

But then Julie sniffed, and Renee faded.

I hated seeing Julie cry. I always had. Her lips thickened, her eyes swelled behind her glasses, and her cheeks pushed together.

"I didn't mean that," I said. "I'm sorry."

Julie kept concentrating on one of her boots. She had a knot in the shoelace, and I tried to help her with it. My fingers felt too clumsy to untangle the small knot. I was just making it worse.

"Aunt Ruth's going to try to keep me," Julie said. "You know she is."

"I won't let her." But my words sounded lame when I spoke them. I couldn't stop thinking about Renee, and Diane, and my meeting tonight.

"I don't want things to change again," Julie said. "They're always changing."

"I didn't want things to change either," I said slowly. "But sometimes things happen that you can't control."

"Change always happens to me," Julie said plaintively. "Why does it keep happening to me?"

"It's not just you," I said, and now my voice was quiet.

"I lost my mom, and now I'm losing you."

"I lost her, too!" I said. Suddenly I was on my feet, yelling. Julie was still sitting on the bench. "I lost her, too. She died and left me alone with you."

Julie's head was down.

"Do you understand that?" I asked. I looked over at the fat woman, but she wasn't watching me anymore. She was busying herself with her kids, but she was the only one. Everybody in the ice rink had turned toward me. I glanced back at Julie.

She stared down, holding onto the knot in her boot.

⋘⋙

I stayed on the living room couch, until Ruth and Julie had finished packing, and rose when Julie came downstairs, but she didn't stop to say goodbye. She just brushed past me and hurried outside. Ruth did the same. She hadn't said much during my apologetic phone call, nothing beyond asking when she should pick Julie up.

I went upstairs to Julie's bedroom after they left.

I wondered how she was doing at school. I hadn't asked her about her homework since the parent-teacher conference. I was so plagued with thoughts of Renee and my meeting with Diane that I hadn't made time for Julie. I remembered last year when I offered to help Julie with her math homework—complex fractions. She was confused and so was I, and she suggested that we use the computer to find the answers, but I gamely worked out the equations with her by hand. We had been up till almost midnight, writing out long division, but it was a nice night.

We ate potato chips, drank soda, and puzzled over the math problems, turning goofy as the night grew later. Then Julie told me the next day that her teacher gave her a D because most of her answers were wrong. After that, I still helped her with her homework, but I sheepishly went online to check what I didn't understand.

Bananas was still here. Ruth had allergies which meant that, for now, the rabbit stayed with me. He was sitting at the front of his pen, facing me, leaning back on his haunches. His nose rapidly lifted up and down.

"Hey buddy," I whispered and lifted the rabbit's ear. Bananas stood still, stiff. I rubbed his ear, feeling the velvety skin between my index finger and thumb. It was like touching the inside of a jewelry box.

Nine hours until the meeting with Diane, unless they broke in again and kidnapped me. I wanted a distraction. I picked up Bananas, carried him downstairs. We sat on the couch and flipped through channels, looking for something on television to watch. I couldn't find a thing except some reality show about people trying to buy a house, so I kept it on and watched Bananas instead. He didn't do much except sit on the couch in a small huddled ball for a few minutes, then he stretched and tentatively hopped to the corner. I went to the kitchen, grabbed a large piece of lettuce, brought it back, and laid it before him. He started eating it, watching me the entire time.

I actually started to get into the reality show. An older couple was looking for a winter home in Bermuda and couldn't decide between two properties, one that looked out over heartbreakingly perfect blue water or a larger, pink palatial home farther inland. The couple's conversation turned into an argument, and I was so engrossed in their debate that I didn't realize I was absent-mindedly petting Bananas, rubbing his ears together.

He seemed to enjoy it. His eyes were closed and his body had flattened on the couch. He looked so comfortable that I didn't want to disturb him. I even ignored the black pellets that rolled out of his butt and toward the back of the cushion. Petting him was different than petting a dog or a cat, because Bananas showed no inclination of moving, and we ended up sitting on the couch for the next hour and a half, watching people on TV trying to decide where they wanted to spend the next phase of their lives.

Eventually, one of the couples had a daughter who looked like Julie, and that made me sad, so I switched around to find something else to watch but didn't have much luck. Bananas stood, stretched and yawned then hopped to the floor, as if he could sense a change. I decided to send Alison a text:

Got a couple of free hours?

I received a reply a minute or two later.

Hey u, visiting friends in philly for the day. cya when i get back?

Well, damn.

I stood up from the couch and tried to figure out what I could do. The silence of the house didn't help the nervousness bubbling just beneath my surface, so I thought it would be best to head outside. I carried Bananas back upstairs, deposited him into his pen then grabbed a jacket and my car keys and headed out. As I stood on the front porch, a memory floated toward me…

രൃരൃ

"Mom's late," Julie sighed. "So now you have to make me dinner."

I looked over at her, sitting in the passenger seat. "Corndogs and cokes, if you can keep it a secret from your mother."

Julie nodded solemnly. "You know, dinners like that are the reason I'm happy you married Mom."

"Well," I told her, pushing my car door open as she did the same, "I'll just go ahead and accept that as a compliment."

We headed up the sidewalk to the front door and Julie asked me to carry her.

"Really?" I asked, but lifted her and carried her up our porch steps. "Oh, my God. You're so heavy."

"Dad, stop," Julie said, hitting me lightly. "Now I'm going to get one of those eating disorders when I become a teenager, and it'll be all your fault."

Inside, there was a message on the answering machine from the police about Renee, and another from the hospital.

Renee.

ↄ०ↄ०

The memory resolved something inside me. I headed to my car and drove to the movie theater to see if something was playing, but the only movie with a start time I could make starred Adam Sandler, and I didn't want to spend my last day on earth watching an Adam Sandler movie.

It was then I realized I was treating today as if it *was* my last day on earth.

But nothing was going to happen tonight. I was just going to decide if I wanted to hire Diane and her partner. Even so, I couldn't help this premonitory feeling, this sense that everything would change after my meeting. And maybe it would. If my life story was a book, then tonight would be the point where a major change occurred, where I took an action that served as a dividing chapter, a page turned from the person I had been to the person I would be.

That idea had a very strange effect.

I was exhilarated.

I went to McDonalds, ordered a Big Mac with fries and a large Coke, then drove to Patterson Park, walked to the spot where I proposed to Renee, and treated myself to a makeshift picnic. The hamburger and fries tasted strangely good, almost as if I had been deprived from taste for years. It was a bit chilly outside, but I welcomed the weather, enjoyed feeling the wind whisper around my collar and under my jacket, against my skin. It was the kind of evening wind that carries memories of childhood. A group of people were playing flag football on one of the fields below the hill I was sitting on, and I watched them, sipping my drink. I hadn't been able to come here ever since Renee died, but I felt fine now.

'*You're happy because you're going to move on,*' Renee told me.

"You think that's it?"

She nodded and sat down next to me. '*Can I have a fry?*'

"'Course."

We ate and watched the football game for a bit. One of the men, wearing a Ray Lewis jersey, caught a short pass for a touchdown and ran around like this was the single greatest moment in his life.

"What am I moving on from?" I asked.

'*From me.*'

"I don't think that's it. I don't think I'm going to move on."

'*So what are you so happy about?*'

"That I'm finally doing something. I'm finally doing something about this. That's why I'm happy. And because, even though I'm a little freaked out, it's probably going to be easier than I suspect. Diane and her partner seem like they know what they're doing."

'How come you didn't feel this way the other day then? When you went to Chris's house with your gun?'

"I'm not sure."

'Because you knew you weren't going to do anything.'

I was about to take another bite out of my hamburger, but paused. "Yeah, maybe."

'You were afraid.'

I took the bite. "Yeah, maybe," I said again, my mouth full. "So what?"

'Nothing. Just making a point. Maybe your commitment to this isn't what you think it is. Maybe you're excited now because this is coming closer to happening, but you know you can still put the brakes on it whenever you want. Maybe you're teasing yourself.'

I swallowed. "I'm not."

'I don't know if I believe you.'

"That's fine. But if Diane tells me that she has information and is ready to do this job, then I'm paying her. And that thought makes me really happy. Anyway, why are you acting this way? You're the one who wanted me to do this."

'Right. And I want to make sure it gets done.'

"It will. Not because of you, or because of me…but because of us."

Renee's head leaned against my shoulder, and I felt wisps of her hair when the wind blew them against my face. *'Okay.'*

"You know," I said, still watching the game. "I probably would have been a pretty mediocre football player."

'We're getting closer to being together,' Renee told me.

CHAPTER 12

When the Waves Came

I sat outside the Palms Motel and thought about Julie. Strange that, even while waiting to meet a pair of hit men, my thoughts were focused on a twelve-year-old girl and her resentment. I tried to think about Renee, Alison, anyone else, but I couldn't. Julie's sad face, staring down at her boots at the ice rink, kept pushing through.

Someone rapped on my window.

Diane.

She motioned for me to follow her and headed toward a white van parked down the street. I left my truck and locked the door. It was cold. I zipped up my jacket and hurried after her lumbering figure, then realized I had left my phone sitting in the cup holder.

"Hey," I said when I had reached the van. "My phone is back there—"

"You won't need it," Diane said and pulled open the back door, shoving a black curtain aside. She climbed in and I followed her.

"Sit down," she ordered.

Two long benches ran down either side of the van. I sat on one and she sat next to me. She wore black jeans and a humungous sweater. Both articles of clothing strained to cover her. There was something impassive about her face, and I realized that she rarely made any unnecessary movements, even in her expressions.

"What are you looking at?" Diane asked.

"I'm wondering how you got into my house."

She shrugged. "I knocked. No answer. Figured I'd put the address book next to your weed."

"You should have told me."

"Well," Diane said and smiled. "I wanted you to know we could get to you. Anyway, I got some information for you. Carr and Bailey. Ever heard of them?"

I was still angry, but I let her lead the conversation. "What are they, a '70s rock band?"

Diane grinned. "Nah. They're the ones who helped Chris Taylor treat Renee's head like a softball."

Her words struck me like arrows.

"You okay?" Diane asked.

"How'd you find that out?" I asked, after a moment. "The police never said anything about this."

"They had Carr and Bailey listed as suspects, but never drew anything on them. One of our contacts linked them to it. And that's why you're here. We want to know if you can identify James Carr. See if you remember him from anything your wife said."

"We're going to talk to him?"

"Not you. He's not going to see you. But we want you to listen to what he says. He won't even know you're there."

"Okay."

"But we get paid first," Diane said. "Twenty-five hundred for each man."

"Six thousand dollars?"

"Seventy-five hundred, English teacher. Carr, Bailey, and Taylor." She pulled out a Blackberry. "Your choice. Pay now, or never."

This was a chance for me to stop what I started, but it was also my only chance to find out the truth. I had learned more in five minutes with Diane than I had in three years.

"I'll pay," I told her.

Diane turned the Blackberry on. Light illuminated her face as she squinted and typed on the keyboard.

"Where's your partner?" I asked, as she typed. "Up front?"

She shook her head. "He's already with James Carr. They're waiting for us."

⊱⊰

I stayed in back while Diane drove. An hour passed and I had no idea where we were. I asked Diane once and she wouldn't tell me.

"I like vans," I offered, approvingly. "What is this, a V8?"

"Yup."

And that was the only conversation we made.

The van finally slowed and Diane pulled into an empty parking lot at some rest stop. She held up a finger, climbed out, walked around the van, and opened my door. I stepped outside and another van pulled up next to us. Diane motioned for me to climb in. I pulled myself into the passenger seat as a curtain separating the front seats from the back slid shut. Diane sat in the driver's seat. The entire switch took no more than twenty seconds.

Diane held a finger to her lips as she drove and, eventually, the road we were traveling on turned rough. She pulled to a stop after about twenty minutes and the curtain was quickly pulled aside. A man stepped through.

He had a long lean body and blond hair that dropped in a nonchalant way, as if he had just emerged from a shower, and a long pockmarked face with blue, bedroom eyes.

He looked like he was in his late thirties. He pulled out a pair of gloves from behind his seat and slipped them over his hands. I noticed the butt of a gun protruding from his jeans. He motioned for me to step outside and followed me when I did.

He guided me a few steps away from the van, stopped, and spoke in a low harsh voice I recognized from the room at the Palms Motel.

"I'm letting you see me," he said, "because Diane thinks we don't have a choice tonight. Carr's been gagged and blindfolded in back, so don't say a word. But if you need to talk to us for anything, you call her Diane and you call me Bardos."

"Bardos," I repeated. "Why Bardos?"

He turned and walked back to the van.

There were moments in my life when I felt a fear so strong that it actually enveloped me, like fear was a tangible, wrathful being with hands and eyes and teeth. I felt it once, as a child, playing late into the evening and ending up lost in the woods, and again the day Renee died, and now. Fear, like hands touching my shoulder, cold teeth pressing into my spine.

Still, I followed Bardos.

ೲ

I sat in the front passenger seat, the windows around me covered in black plastic and a long piece of cardboard blocking the windshield. My body was turned so that I could see through a hole in the curtain that Diane had shown me, but neither Diane nor the prisoner were in my line of vision.

"I'm going to take out my gun," I heard Diane say. "And if you make a sound, I'll shoot you in the face. You understand? Nod if you do." There was a moment's silence before she continued. "Good. Ready?"

More silence, and I heard the man take a sudden, loud breath. I couldn't see anything through the hole in the curtain, so I turned toward Bardos. He was expressionless, staring into the cardboard-covered windshield.

"Is your name Carr?" Diane asked.

"Yes," the man said, his voice calmer than I expected. I peered through the curtain hole again. I couldn't see anything but the bench.

"First or last name?"

"Last."

"What's the first?"

"James."

"James Carr, good." Diane sounded like she was going through a checklist. "You ever heard of a woman named Renee Starks?"

"No."

"Really? What about Chris Taylor? Heard of him?"

"No."

"What about a man named Robert Bailey?"

"No." He actually seemed to be getting angry. "Who are you?"

"Three years ago," Diane said, instead of answering, "you and Bailey beat Renee Starks to death."

A slight pause before he spoke. "I don't know what you're talking about."

"Yeah, you know exactly what I'm talking about," Diane said, and Bardos rose from the driver's seat. He reached into his coat pocket and pulled out something shiny. He didn't look at me as he pushed the curtain aside and headed to the back.

"What are you going to do with that lighter?" Carr asked. I heard a *snip* and then Carr screamed.

The scream abruptly stopped.

I was breathing hard. I had never heard a grown man cry out in pain like that.

"Stick the rag in his mouth," Bardos said.

Snip.

I jumped as the screaming started again, muffled and incoherent, like a wild animal.

"You tell me the truth," Diane said, calmly, "or you keep getting burned."

I was staring through the curtain hole so intently that my eye hurt. I hadn't expected torture. I heard my own breathing and wondered if it was this loud the entire time, if the man named James Carr heard me, if he knew I was here. Part of me wanted to stop everything, like this was a movie I could leave and the scene would abruptly end.

But only part of me.

I saw Bardos' back as he knelt over Carr. I smelled a raw grotesque smell. Flesh being burnt.

"Did you murder Renee Starks?" Diane asked.

Carr was breathing wildly. "I don't know who that is," he said, his voice hoarse.

"Hold out his ear," Bardos said. Carr's body was in front of me now, the back of his head pressed against the hole in the curtain.

Moments later, those muffled screams. The curtain shook, the van shook.

"Did you murder Renee Starks?" Diane asked again.

Carr said something indecipherable.

"Other ear," Diane said.

"No, no," Carr said, his voice slurred. "We didn't know her name. We just got the job. We never got her name."

"What do you mean, the job?" Diane asked, her voice sharp. "You're pros?"

"Yeah." The word came out thick, full of liquid.

I was barely breathing. The smell of charred flesh was overpowering me.

"Carr and Bailey," Diane said. "I've never heard of you."

"You wouldn't have," Carr said.

"Chris Taylor. Did he hire you?"

"I don't know who that is. All I know is that it was for some guy in Boston."

Boston?

"All right," Diane said. "We got someone that needs to see you."

Then Diane exclaimed loudly and I heard smacking sounds, something repeatedly being hit, and then there was a loud thunderclap. Bardos cried out. I was reaching toward the door handle when the curtain was shoved aside and James Carr rushed through.

He was a big man, bald with a round scar, like a clover, under his right eye. He wore a yellow tank top and black shorts. Half of his face was drenched in blood, and his right ear seemed like it was hanging loose. He was holding a tiny gun, pointing it at me.

"Get out of my way," he growled.

I opened my door and James Carr rushed through the opening, inadvertently knocking me out of the van with him. We fell to the ground and he rolled to his feet then limped off into the woods.

I was confused, disoriented—but, more than anything, terrified by the violence I had just witnessed. I couldn't go back into the van.

I ran into the woods.

Blind in the night.

I heard Carr ahead of me, crashing through the underbrush. I rushed forward through branches until my leg acted up and I tripped and fell to the ground.

"Who the hell?" Carr exclaimed. He turned and ran past me, back into the clearing. I was trying to stand when I heard a sudden, single *clap*. I crouched down and looked back to the van.

The headlights illuminated Carr, walking slowly toward the van with his gun pointed ahead of him. The side door slid open and a thick figure lumbered out. Carr fired and sparks exploded against the side of the van. A flash of light came from the other person. Carr cried out, dropped his gun, and stumbled backward. The figure calmly walked toward him.

Diane crossed the headlights.

☙ぬ☙ぬ

Do you remember? You were there, the night we stayed in that cheap motel in the middle of a long overnight trip, three months into our marriage, alone because Julie was with your sister. You liked it. I was apprehensive because of the torn wallpaper and dirty tub. I swore I saw something scurry out of sight when I turned on the lights, but you just grinned and said, "Hey, it's an experience."

I was reluctant, but it had been a long drive and we were tired. And something about the mischief in your eyes compelled me. I don't know what happened to me after we made love, after I had stood on the floor and held you as you faced me, your feet on the bed. I don't know why I broke down, why the silent, squalid room stirred desperation in me, but I couldn't help myself. A fear touched, plucked firmly like the string of some sad instrument, its mournful tone resounding through me. "I'm afraid that I won't be able to provide for you and Julie someday," I told you, my face buried into the mattress. "And we'll end up in a place like this."

"No," you told me. "We'll provide for each other."

c∕∂c∕∂

Carr rose to his feet and pulled out something from behind his back. A tiny knife. He held it behind his other arm, using his forearm as a sort of shield, and circled Diane. She watched him, the gun lowered at her side.

c∕∂c∕∂

And you were with me when we went to my grandfather's funeral in Nevada, where he and my grandmother had moved for their retirement. I was surprised to see how much my father was affected. I had been distant from my grandfather and, stupidly, selfishly, assumed everyone else was, too. But my father suddenly fainted, his body buckling and sinking to the floor amidst concerned cries and grabbing hands. He recovered right away, blamed the alcohol and the heat of the Nevada day, and said he was fine. And I, alone among everyone there, believed him.

But you were the one who insisted we stay an extra day, and you were the one who decided we should help my grandmother adjust. And you were the one who, at night, when we went walking around the retirement neighborhood where they lived, took my hand and led me to the pool. We went swimming in the heat and the dark, and I remember leaning against the side of the pool, your weightless, naked body floating next to me, over me, your wet hair over my arm as we kissed.

ɔɛɔ

Carr lunged forward and Diane moved quickly, her gun smashing against Carr's face. He cried out in pain and dropped to one knee. Diane stood before him, motionless, saying something to him I couldn't hear.

ɔɛɔ

You flailed next to me in the water during a week-long trip to the beaches of North Carolina in the summer. We went swimming while Julie played on the sand, and we were the only people on the beach that late in the day. We swam out, too far, and when the waves came, we didn't have enough strength to swim back. The water was high and we must have drifted. I plunged down to see how deep the water was, and my foot barely touched sand before I had to push back up. The exertion exhausted me. I looked at you.

Your head slipped under the surface, and your struggling arms found me. I held you and we sank into the ocean. Then I gathered my strength and pushed off again, your arms over my neck when we broke the surface. I swam as best as I could before the waves pushed me back. I tried to cry out for Julie to get help, but you said no, you didn't want her to come in. We sank again. I touched sand and pushed up, swallowing too much water on the way.

I held you and, with everything I could, swam for the shore. We were on the sand and Julie was laughing. I looked over and you were lying next to me. I crawled over to you. You were breathing, not choking, hands over your stomach, face cramped in pain.

⌒⌒⌒

Carr dove forward again but Diane swung her leg away and brought the gun down on the back of his head. He lay sprawled, limbs jerking, and then rose to his knees and crawled toward her, blood running down his face. Diane walked backward, still speaking too quietly for me to hear. He reached for her with the knife, but she caught his arm and pulled it behind his back.

He cried out as she took the knife from him, and then she cut his throat.

Diane stared at Carr until his body stopped shaking. Then she walked back toward the van and climbed inside. She returned moments later, holding an axe. She completely undressed Carr's corpse and then brought the axe down on him, over and over.

Every blow sounded like someone landing after falling from a great height. Once his head, arms, and legs were separated from his torso, Diane went back to the van, brought out plastic bags, and placed Carr's body parts inside them. She took the bags into the van, came back, and set the ground on fire where he had bled and died. She let the ground burn as she stared into the woods, sometimes looking directly at me in the dark.

⌒⌒⌒

And it was you I watched in the night, asleep, your body curled away from mine. You were impossible to wake, despite my prodding when something happened on TV or when I wanted to make love. I used to tease you for the way you would squeeze your eyes shut when you wanted to go to sleep, as if that would help. Maybe it did.

I stayed awake, hopelessly awake as the time passed midnight or two in the morning, and it was *then*, early in the morning, when I would sometimes feel this desperate love for you, this sense of astonishment that you were lying next to me. I felt lucky, but it ended up a waiting game.

✂✄✂

It seemed like lifetimes passed as the fire burned and Diane stared in my direction. "Tom, you out there?" Diane called. "Come on Tom, get back here." She paced back and forth, letting the axe swing by her knees. "Bardos is going to be okay. Bullet just nicked him. Can't say the same for you, unless you come back here."

I didn't move, barely breathed.

"You saw too much. Saw a man get chopped up. But if you don't get out here, I'm going to think you're getting scared. Getting cold feet. And if you're scared, then I don't think I can trust you. You might end up telling someone. This is why Bardos was right, and I messed up by bringing you here. You didn't need to see it happen. You just needed to know it did. But now you've looked, and I figure you can't look away. And I can't trust you're going to forget."

Diane stopped pacing and held the axe with both hands.

"Come out here, Tom, and let me finish this. This way you get to pick how it happens. Trust me, every person I've ever dealt with—at the end, they wish they could have controlled it. That's all they wish at the end."

I stayed still on the dark, hard, cold dirt.

"Be seeing you soon," Diane said, and she stomped out the fire. She took a long walk around the clearing, climbed back into the van, and drove off.

I tried to think about Renee again but I couldn't even remember what her face looked like.

All I heard were my breaths, my wild animal breaths.

CHAPTER 13

Love, and So Many Other Things

I walked past the burnt ground where James Carr was killed and headed into the woods next to the van's path, following it but staying hidden in case Diane was waiting for me.

I stumbled through reluctant branches. The night chill rushed into my clothes and over my skin, and it seemed like hours passed until I heard traffic. I stayed in the woods and approached the sound, my hands in front of me as thorns clutched my jeans. I finally saw lights ahead and emerged onto the side of a highway. A small ditch ran along the road and I dropped into it.

Headlights flashed past. I stayed low in the ditch and followed the road, hoping to come upon a sign that would tell me where I was. I didn't think anyone could see me, but I heard a car swerve and stop and, when I turned around, a door opened.

I ran, tripped and fell flat on my face. I tasted mud.

"Hey," a man shouted. "Do you need help?"

I picked myself up and started limping away.

"Hey! Excuse me!" he shouted again.

And I slowed. He might be the only chance I had.

The man was tall, thin and black, with glasses, and he stood about twenty feet away, looking down at me in the ditch. "Are you okay?" he asked.

"No."

My answer made him hesitate. "Are you in trouble?"

I didn't know what to say. "I need a ride."

He looked around. "Yeah?"

"Just to a gas station."

"Okay," he said reluctantly. "Come on. But don't try anything. I got mace." He paused. "And a gun."

I climbed out of the ditch and limped to his car, some type of silver sedan. I pulled open the passenger door and ducked inside. He walked quickly around the car and got in, adjusted his mirror and gave me a doubtful look. Then he said something under his breath that sounded like a brief prayer, started the engine, and pulled out onto the highway.

"Thanks," I told him. "I really appreciate this."

"It's okay," he said, staring straight ahead as he drove. "Christian thing to do."

"My name's Tom."

"Kevin."

I saw a sign for Interstate 95. "Are you going to Baltimore?"

"Yeah. Why? You live in the city?"

I nodded.

"Me, too. I'll take you to your home, if you want. Just don't tell me the trouble you're in. I don't want to be involved."

"No problem." I briefly imagined telling him about my night, and memories of Diane and her axe rushed at my face like frightened birds.

"What?" Kevin asked. "You okay?"

"Yeah, sorry. Just…just had a bad moment."

"You on drugs?"

"No. Just a tough night. Sorry."

Kevin nodded, still staring straight ahead as he drove. "Looks like it."

"Yeah." I settled back into the passenger seat and tried to let myself calm down. An alarming amount of sweat was on my forehead and over my chest, and my heart was beating too hard. "So," I asked, trying to divert my thoughts from Diane, "Kevin, what do you do?"

"I'm a therapist."

"Like physical therapy?"

"No." Kevin tapped his forehead. "Up here. Psychology. But don't take that as an invitation."

"To what?"

"To tell me anything." He paused. "I'm sorry. I don't want to get involved."

"It's okay. I don't want to get anyone involved with this."

Silence took over as we drove. I looked out the window, at the dark silhouettes of trees and bushes on the side of the interstate, and tried my hardest not to think about Diane cutting Carr's body apart. I could still hear the sounds of the axe driving through him and into the ground, like footfalls, growing louder as they approached.

"So," I asked, noticing a rosary wrapped around his windshield mirror, "you're a psychologist and a Christian?"

Kevin nodded. "I always say I hedged my bets. If one way doesn't work, I've always got the other."

"What led you to psychology?"

He shrugged. "Just picked it when I started college because it sounded neat. I figured I'd change majors when I found something else I wanted to do more, but I never did."

Kevin and I didn't talk much more as he drove me into Federal Hill. I asked him to stop a few streets away from my house. I didn't want to take the chance that Diane was waiting for me. "It's here," I said, pointing to some row house where the lights were still lit.

I opened the passenger door, stepped outside, walked up the sidewalk to the porch, climbed the steps, and pretended to knock on the front door. Kevin drove off.

I headed back to the sidewalk. The street was lined with a mix of cars. I worried that Diane had switched automobiles and was waiting for me. So I stayed in the shadows, trying to see into each car before I passed it, but all of the cars looked empty.

I knelt and threw up into the gutter.

I spit, wiped my mouth on my sleeve, stood, and hurried up the sidewalk. When I neared my house, I hid in shadows and watched for a few minutes, worried I'd see Diane. All I needed was to get to my bedroom closet, where I had a stash of emergency cash hidden in a shoebox. I thought about getting my gun, but just thinking about my gun nearly nauseated me again.

I finally hurried across the street, fumbled my keys out of my pocket, and opened the door. The row house was dark and quiet, but I was too scared to do anything other than rush upstairs and dig through my closet. I found the shoebox, took the cash and a spare credit card, and left.

But I stopped at the front door, cursed myself, and went back to the kitchen, got something out of the fridge, and then ran to Julie's room.

Bananas hopped to the front of his cage.

"Here," I said. I dropped an entire head of lettuce and a handful of baby carrots into his cage. "Make it last." I filled up his water bowl and hay bin, and then I left the house.

I headed to Light Street, waved down a cab, and climbed inside.

"Where do you want to go?"

I gave him the address for Ruth and Dave's house in Homeland and asked him to hurry. The ride took fifteen minutes, but my legs couldn't stop shaking the entire time.

"You need me to wait for you?" the cab driver asked as he pulled to a stop in front of their house in Homeland.

"Yeah," I told the driver. "Wait for me, but don't wait out here. Come back in ten."

My impulse was to pick up Julie and take her on the run with me, but I knew that wasn't a good idea. Diane was going to catch me eventually.

Dave opened the front door after I pounded on it.

"Starks?" he frowned. "What's going on?"

"Is Julie here?"

"Sure. Do you need to see her?"

"Right away." I stepped inside their giant house, looked around, and let out a small cry when I saw the living room. Everything in it was overturned. Couch cushions were all over the floor, clothes were everywhere, and the floor was strewn with different toys, magazines, and books.

"What happened here?" I asked, my voice panicked. "Did Diane do this?"

Dave gave me a baffled look. "Julie and I were just playing. Who's Diane?"

I saw a pair of glasses and brown hair peer out from behind the couch.

"Julie?" I asked. I walked over to the couch. She stood slowly, perplexed, and then that look gave way to anger. "What are you guys doing?" I asked.

"We were having game night," she said.

"Game night? What game?"

"I made it up. It's sort of a combination of chess and charades," she explained. "We're setting up the battlefield."

I shook my head. "I didn't even know you still... played. I thought you were too old."

"Game night's cool."

"Listen, hon," I said, trying to keep the urgency out of my voice. "I need to talk to Uncle Dave alone for a few minutes. Can you wait in the other room?"

She was about to speak, but something in my expression must have convinced her, because she promptly spun around and walked out.

"Are you okay?" Dave asked, after she had left. "You don't seem like yourself."

I watched Julie leave and, when she was out of earshot, I turned toward him. "I'm in a lot of trouble," I said. "So much trouble that...listen. I need you to take Julie and Ruth and get out of town, right now. Where is Ruth, anyway?"

Dave watched me. "Upstairs with a migraine. What did you do?"

I thought about Julie in the other room and a huge lump started to overtake my throat. "It's bad. I messed up. And I'm worried about your family, and Julie."

"Do you owe someone money?"

"I owe them more than that."

Dave's face was stoic. "So you want us to leave town for a few days, while you get this straightened out?"

I nodded. "Go anywhere. I know you have that beach place in St. Michaels. Take Julie there."

"I'm not doing anything," Dave said, "unless you tell me what's going on. Jesus Christ, Tom, it's eleven at night."

The taxi horn blared. I went to the door, opened it, and held up my hand, asking the driver for five minutes. When I came back, Julie was standing next to Dave.

"What's up?" she asked.

And it was at that moment that everything froze.

I saw myself, wild-eyed, unkempt, terrified. And there was Julie, comfortable in this giant home, happily playing some weird game. This wasn't a life I could give her. Even if things had been safe, Julie would be better off here than she would with me. I loved her—but she had love here, too. Love, and so many other things.

I walked over to Julie and knelt. "Hey," I told her. "I have to get going, but I just wanted to see you. I'm sorry for what I said the other day."

"Okay."

"Uncle Dave and Aunt Ruth are going to take good care of you. But I want you to know that I love you, and I care about you."

"Okay."

It didn't seem like I was going to get anything out of her other than "Okay," so I touched Julie's cheek and stood. "Let me talk to your uncle again."

I watched her head into the other room.

"Tom," Dave said, quietly. "You need to tell me what's happening."

"I can't do that," I said. "What I can tell you is that, if a woman named Diane calls looking for me, then tell her you never saw me. If she shows up at your door, call the police."

"What did you do?"

"I can't—"

"You can't tell me. Fine. All right, we're going away. We'll leave. But I'm not telling you where." Dave put a giant finger to my chest. "You fix this, you hear me? You fix this, for us and for Julie. And when this is over, then we're going to talk about Julie, and where she's going to live."

"But you are going away for a few days?" I asked. "You promise?"

Dave nodded. "Fix this."

"I will." I opened their front door and headed toward the cab. I wanted to say goodbye to Julie again. I wanted to tell her something that would express everything I felt toward her, but instead I left.

I climbed into the back seat and a terrible thought struck me.

"Can you do me a favor?" I asked the driver. "Can you take me around the corner?"

He turned to look back at me. "Listen, bud, this is getting—"

"Just around the corner, and then I'll pay you double what all this is worth and you never have to see me again."

"Sounds good to me."

We coasted down the street, pulled to a stop after the first turn and I gave the driver my credit card. "If anyone asks," I told him as he charged it, "you never saw me, right?"

"Sure, whatever."

I stepped outside, watched him drive off, and trotted back toward Ruth and Dave's house.

I couldn't leave, not only because I had no idea where to go, but also because I couldn't simply hide and hope Julie made it away without any problem. Diane may have followed me, or she might be watching their home. I walked down their street, spotted a large gap between the houses across the street, and hid, crouched behind a tall fat bush.

I didn't wear a watch and my phone was probably still sitting in my truck outside the Palms Motel, or, more likely, Diane had it. So I didn't know how much time passed, but I grew desperately cold. I wanted to hurry across, pound on the door, and ask what the hell was taking Ruth and Dave so long.

I tried to imagine what happened after I left. Dave probably took a moment to consider what a massive screw-up I was and then woke Ruth and told her everything I told him. Ruth would have been indignant about leaving, and irritated about her migraine, and would have argued with Dave and that likely led to a fight. Dave probably stormed out of their bedroom and Ruth grumpily climbed out of bed and started packing. Dave, fuming downstairs, heard her, told Julie to collect her things, and started packing as well.

What a happy household.

I wrapped my arms around my chest as I slowly walked away, bouncing up and down in the cold. Finally, I heard their front door open and scurried back behind the bush. I peeked out and saw Dave pop open the trunk to his car and drop a suitcase in, and then he walked back to the house and grabbed another. Ruth emerged behind him. And in the doorway, I saw Julie.

Something broke inside me, and I heard her voice from the other day, asking why everything in her life always changed. She was standing with her small suitcase, going to yet another house, watching two silent and angry adults—at least, in my mind, they were angry. Years had passed since Julie had been in a real home—especially since I barely provided her with one—and she was being uprooted again.

Dave and Ruth walked into the house and closed the door. Julie stood outside, alone, holding her suitcase at her side like a little businesswoman. The image made my eyes cloud. I rubbed my face with my sleeve.

A sudden thought. I could rush across the street, promise Julie that everything would be okay, and hurry back before Dave or Ruth saw me. I could tell Julie that this was all some sort of game and everything would be straightened out when she came back. I would give her the life she wanted.

I started to stand, but the door opened and Ruth and Dave emerged. They locked the house behind them and Julie climbed into the backseat of their car. I still wanted one last goodbye and I didn't care anymore if they saw me, so I stood and walked toward the street as the BMW backed down the driveway. But the car sped down the street before I could reach them.

And then Diane's van drove past.

❡❧❡

I thought I imagined it.

It was the kind of moment you anticipate so much that, when it actually happens, it seems unreal, like a first kiss or first punch. But I watched the van, stunned, and didn't even realize I had stepped into the street to stare at it until the brakes lit.

Diane's head suddenly poked out the window then disappeared and the van rushed backward.

"Shit!" I exclaimed to no one in particular. I turned and ran in the opposite direction. I wasn't sure where I was going, and the old injury in my leg was acting up, so it was more of a hurried hobble than a run. I looked over my shoulder and saw the van turn into a driveway, back out, and drive toward me, and a distant part of me realized this was a good thing. Better for Diane to follow me than Julie.

That said, it wasn't much better for me.

I turned and limped between two houses as the van rushed past. I headed past backyards and into the next street and saw the van waiting at the edge. I hurried across that street and into another and the van rushed toward me. It was so close that I could see Diane's face in the driver seat.

I turned back around, slipped into the gap, and heard the van squeal to a stop. I went to my right, thankful that Homeland didn't have tons of streetlights. I needed shadows. I passed a door and thought about banging on it and pleading for the owners of the house to let me inside, but knew that wouldn't work. Chances were they wouldn't let me in—or, worse yet, they would, and Diane would kill us all. I hobbled past a high porch, stopped, and hid beside it.

I tried to keep my breathing quiet as I listened. I was out of breath and my body wanted to suck in as much air as possible, but I forced myself to stay silent. A large shadow flew past and I could tell it was Diane. She was much faster than I thought. I waited until she passed two other houses then I hurried in the other direction.

Headlights hit me.

I turned and raised a hand to cover my eyes. The van. I looked back toward Diane and saw that she was coming back.

I dipped between two more houses and limped back the way I had come from. I headed toward a children's park across the street behind a cluster of trees. I didn't have anywhere else to go and my lungs were burning. My injured leg was so stiff that I felt it might completely give out at any moment. I hobbled into the park as headlights shone behind me.

The small park had a slide, a merry-go-round, monkey bars, a sandbox, and a few goofy plastic caterpillars that children could ride. Nothing that would help. I hid behind the trees and looked around desperately, hoping a car was driving by that I could flag down for help. I was so desperate that I was willing to risk someone else's life. But there were no cars, and no one in sight. I thought about shouting, having neighbors open their doors and windows to witness what was happening, because Diane couldn't kill me in front of witnesses. I even opened my mouth but stayed silent. The trees hid me from easy view, and I didn't know how close Diane was.

I limped into the park, and a rough idea started to form.

It wasn't very good.

I stepped through the sandbox and kicked off one of my shoes. Then I looked for a place to hide. I saw Diane's shadow on the other side of the trees and climbed onto the slide, lying on my back on the cold metal.

And, for the most terrible, terrifying moments of my life, I waited.

I couldn't hear a thing. Diane moved with a lot of stealth for her size. I remembered watching her nimbly move around Carr as he flailed at her, but the memory affected me so much my body started to shake, so I tried not to think about anything. I looked into the dark starless sky above me, waiting for her voice.

I heard something, a small sound. Breathing. Someone controlling their breathing.

I listened to Diane walk past my head, by the top of the slide, and I realized how lucky I was that she had chosen that side. If she walked by the other end, near my feet, she would have seen me.

I waited.

Finally, I lifted my head. I saw Diane walking away from the sandbox, my shoe in her hand. She kept walking in that direction until she left the park and I couldn't see her any longer. Even so, I stayed on the slide for a few more minutes, scared she would come back.

I slid to the ground and hurried toward the trees. I waited, staring intensely into the street, and then rushed across. I hid between houses and watched the street again, waiting to see if I was being followed, but the van didn't emerge.

I headed into the next street, trying to remember how to get back to the main road where I could find a bus or a taxi and suddenly I was bathed in the van's headlights.

I turned and ran, even as I heard the van's door open. I felt a hand on the back of my shirt and spun around to see Bardos. I saw a red splotch of blood on his shoulder, pushed it, and he winced in pain, his knees buckling. He stumbled. I yanked my shirt free and hurried across the street. As I glanced back, I heard the sound of a door sliding open. Diane hopped out and Bardos pointed in my direction.

I passed more houses and saw, unhappily because it made me feel like I was barely going anywhere, that I was back in Dave and Ruth's neighborhood. I wasn't going to outrun Diane with my bad leg, so I stopped in the middle of the street and turned. I didn't have another choice.

I stood in the street and raised my fists as Diane emerged.

She looked at me, cocked her head, and exploded in laughter.

More headlights, and I lowered my fists, expecting to see the van, but instead it was some sedan. For a horrible moment, I thought Dave and Ruth had returned home with Julie, but it wasn't them. Instead, someone drove in front of me and pulled to a stop. A window lowered.

"Do you live around here?" a woman asked me.

Thank God for Homeland's neighborhood watch.

"Yes," I said, "but that woman across the street doesn't. Can you call the police?"

"It would be my pleasure," the woman declared. I saw her lean over to look in Diane's direction, then she looked back at me. "What woman?"

I peered into the space where Diane had been and didn't see anyone. "She must have been spooked and left," I said. "But she was with a van, a white van, and a man was driving it. I've never seen it here before. Can you call the cops?"

"And where do you live?" the woman asked.

"I'm Ruth Wilson's brother-in-law," I said. "I'm watching their house while they're away."

"Can I have your name?"

"Tom Starks."

"Well, I don't have my mobile phone with me, but I will call immediately when I get home. And I plan on telling Ruth about this encounter."

"Sure, sure," I said, already backing away from the car. I didn't want to be left standing alone in the street after she pulled away. "Just make sure you call the cops."

I turned and passed Ruth's house, heading between two backyard fences. Another street was before me and, beyond that, the main road leading into Homeland. I waited a few moments to cross the street, and then got into my old sprinter's stance and rushed across it. Half-way through, my leg gave out and I fell, but I clambered to my feet and kept running. I stopped when I reached the houses across from me and waited, but didn't see anyone following me.

I finally reached a main road, Northern Parkway, and walked along the sidewalk, deep in the shadows. I waited in a store's inlet near a bus stop and, when the bus rolled up, climbed on board and collapsed into a seat near the back door. I slumped down so that I couldn't be seen through the windows and tried to catch my breath. A distant thought came to me and made me feel better, if only a little bit.

Julie was safe.

CHAPTER 14

Crooked Wood Grown Full of Knots –
The Book of Wisdom, *13:15*

I rode the bus until I thought Diane and Bardos might guess that I took this bus and could be waiting for me at one of the stops. I immediately got off and found myself in Little Italy. I stayed in the shadows, self-conscious about my missing shoe, and walked through dark streets and past the small squares of light thrown from restaurant windows. A man stood in a doorway, rubbing his arms unhappily in the cold.

"Can you tell me what time it is?" I asked. The smells of Italian food, thick garlic bread and meat sauce, floated out. My stomach felt like it was being wrung.

The man glanced disdainfully at me and pulled a small phone out of his pocket. "Eleven," he said and looked in the other direction.

"One other thing," I asked. "Can I use your phone? Please?"

"Fuck off."

"It's an emergency. My car broke down and I need to call Triple A and I left my phone inside."

"Yeah? Hey, still, fuck off."

"That's not helpful."

"Where's your shoe?"

I looked down at my sock. "Can I just use your phone?"

He shook his head, slowly, deliberately. I kept walking.

I spotted an older couple across the street and hurried over to them. "Hey," I called out, waving my arms, "do you have a phone I could borrow?" But they gave me frightened looks, ducked into their car, and sped away.

Well, damn.

But even if I could use their phone, I didn't know who I could call.

I tried to remember if there was anybody I knew in this part of town, an old friend or even a former student, but I couldn't think of anyone. I left Little Italy and passed through long streets of aged buildings, walking toward Fells Point. My foot felt like it was going to freeze but I kept walking doggedly, determined to find a safe place. My row house was in the other direction, but it wasn't remotely safe.

I finally reached Fells Point's cobblestoned streets and made my way to the Fells Gate Tavern. I headed to the bar and waved over the bartender.

"Can I borrow your phone?" I asked. "I just need to make one phone call."

I was ready to make up some story, but to my surprise the bartender lifted a phone out from behind the counter and placed it in front of me. I reached for it but he covered it with his hand.

"Got to buy a drink," he told me.

"No problem," I said. "I'll do you one better. A Guiness and a burger."

The bartender hit the phone. The handset flew into the air. He caught it and handed it to me. "Coming up."

I dialed and listened to the line ring twice.

"Hello?"

"Richard? This is Tom. Tom Starks."

"Tomás?" Richard James asked.

"Listen, this is probably a bad time, but I need some help. Can you meet me?"

"It's past midnight!"

"Richard, please. I'm desperate."

A pause. "Where are you?"

"I'm at Fell's Gate Tavern."

"In Fells Point?" Another pause. "Can you wait twenty minutes?"

"Yeah, that's no problem. Thank you. Thank you so much."

"Certainly."

"Oh, and Richard—what size shoe do you wear?"

❦❦❦

I saw him walk into the bar and I stood up from my booth near the back. A burger and beer were sitting uncomfortably in my nervous stomach, but I felt a little better. Richard walked toward me, holding a shopping bag, slid into the seat across from me and I pushed a glass of white wine toward him. He took the wine, held out the shopping bag, and I grabbed it and looked inside. An old pair of sneakers. I reached under the table and gratefully slipped them on. They were loose, but I didn't care.

"So," Richard asked, eyeing me warily. "What's this about? What kind of trouble are you in?"

"It's a long story."

"I did come all the way out here."

"No, I know. Here's the thing," I began, glancing over him to see if anyone was in earshot. The booths around us were empty but, even so, I leaned forward and lowered my voice. "Uh," I said.

Richard looked at me skeptically. "I'm sorry?"

I couldn't tell him.

For one thing, I would put another person in danger. What if Diane and Bardos somehow knew that I had come here, or that I met with Richard? The only thing that would save him was if he knew absolutely nothing about tonight. And even if they didn't know I met with Richard, he might decide to go to the police and inadvertently get me arrested, and then what would happen when Dave and Ruth returned with Julie?

What if Diane and Bardos killed her as a way to send a message to me? Or what if Richard went to the cops and Diane and Bardos had a connection there, and they found out? My mind rushed into possibility after possibility, and I knew that there wasn't a strong chance any of these may happen…but there was still a chance.

"Tomás?"

"Listen," I said, leaning forward again. "I can't tell you what happened. I think what I need is…advice."

"How can I give you advice when I don't know the problem?"

"That's a pretty good point," I acknowledged. "Okay, I guess…" For some reason, I felt like squirming, or acting childish. Richard had that effect on me. Once, during a faculty meeting, I accidentally called him *Dad*.

"Can we make this hypothetical?" I asked. "That would help."

He spread his hands. "Whatever you want."

"If a family member of yours committed a crime, would you turn them in, regardless of what it was?"

"But I think it depends on what it was. If, in the classic example, they stole a loaf of bread to feed their children. Then no, I would not. If they murdered someone in cold blood, then I would."

"And what if that cold-blooded murder was deserved?"

Richard looked at me for a long moment. "Why would it be deserved?"

"I'm just saying, what if it was?"

"It's hard for me to imagine any instance where I could forgive, much less excuse, murder."

I detected a shift in his tone, something harder in his voice.

"What if the person…what if they killed someone in your family?"

"Tomás," Richard asked, and he leaned in across the table, closely to me. "Did you visit Chris Taylor? Have you killed him?"

"Who?" For a moment, I had no idea who he was talking about. "No! No, I'm just...no one was killed. I'm thinking of a hypothetical situation."

"I see. Well, I don't think I can give you an answer, quite honestly, with which I feel comfortable. I don't want to inadvertently excuse or inhibit something. So, instead of that, can I tell you a story?"

"Huh?"

"Actually, I want to tell you about a story. Are you familiar with Nelson Algren?"

I shook my head.

"You should be. I'm asking that he's taught next semester. He wrote the novel, *The Man with the Golden Arm*, made into a movie with Frank Sinatra."

"Right," I said, nodding, although I hadn't seen the movie.

"Algren also wrote a number of terrific short stories, including the one I wish to reference, *The Face on the Barroom Floor*."

That actually sounded familiar. I kept nodding.

"The story is about a bar in Chicago that's known for fights and tended by a young attractive man named Fancy. At some point, Fancy unfortunately gets in a dispute with a legless man named Railroad Shorty, and the two fight. Fancy is winning the fight and has Shorty stunned, but lacks the willingness to finish him off. And then Shorty grabs him and beats Fancy's face into a pulp. I believe Algren describes it as 'Fancy's single eye looking out, the only thing that is discernible from the mess his face has become.'"

I felt a little ill.

"After the fight, the owner of the bar serves a last round of drinks and closes the door of the bar forever. And, to me, that is what violence and crime beget, a final damning end, in a cell or a grave. Or in the case of Fancy, and perhaps even to those who witnessed what happened to him, somewhere even worse."

We were silent.

"What if Fancy had won the fight?" I asked. "How would the story have ended?"

"Tomás, you know there's no answer to that."

"Sometimes I wonder, though. Life's not a book, Richard. Like me: I didn't recover after Renee died. I didn't meet someone else who made everything better. Julie's future isn't promised for her. The lessons we learn in stories don't apply to life. It's all fiction, forced to end in a way that we can understand. But life just ends."

"So fiction is not reality," Richard argued. "But could it be illuminating reality?"

"I'm not sure it matters," I said, and frowned. "Look, I'm sorry, but I don't think I can have this conversation right now."

"Then what conversation do you want to have? Are you sure there isn't something you should tell me?"

I nodded, suddenly grateful, overwhelmingly so. "Yes, and I'm sorry about that. I asked you to come all the way down here, and I'm sure this was a huge waste of your time. Really, I'm sorry. I just—"

Richard lifted a hand, stopping me. "You have absolutely no need to apologize. If you need to talk, then I'm here."

"I appreciate that."

"I know you'll do the right thing."

He couldn't have been more wrong, but I thanked him and we slid out of the booth. I walked him to the exit, my feet loose in his sneakers. We shook hands and I watched him leave. Then I walked down the street and climbed into a taxi.

"Where to?" the driver asked.

"I'm not sure," I said. "Give me a minute."

Nowhere was safe. Diane already knew where I lived, she knew my phone number—she had access to my bank account.

"Harbor Court Hotel."

"Where?"

"Harbor Court Hotel. It's in Virginia."

"Do you know how much it costs to go from here to Virginia?"

I handed him the cash I had taken from my house, a couple of hundred dollar bills. "This should cover it, right?"

We left Baltimore. I watched its lights recede as the tall buildings bordering the harbor passed out of view, and I thought about Diane and Bardos, somewhere in that city in their white van, cruising corners, looking for me. Fear nipped at my mind. I tried to control it, tried to think about how I could change this situation. Nothing helped. What I told Richard was true. There was no easy solution in life, no guarantee, no safety net. We could not set the book down.

The world was clay, fashioned by an insane potter.

It was almost two in the morning when we arrived in Virginia, and the hotel bar and lounge were empty. I walked over to the desk clerk and asked for a room.

He asked for a credit card.

"Can you do me a favor? Can you just use that credit card to hold the reservation, and don't run it until I check out?"

He frowned.

I lowered my voice. "I don't want my wife to find out I'm here." I didn't really know what I was saying, or if what I said made an effective excuse. It just came out. I thought about Julie and felt like I was going to collapse, that my knees would suddenly give out, and I held onto the counter to steady myself.

"Well," the desk clerk said, eyeing me suspiciously, "I'll have to ask my manager in the morning. And I'll have to call and make sure that the card is good."

"That's fine."

He checked me in, gave me a keycard, and I took the elevator upstairs. I walked down the hall and into my room and, once the door closed behind me, sank to the floor, overwhelmed.

CHAPTER 15

Peace Is Impossible

I didn't leave the hotel room for the next three days. I hopelessly chased sleep through the first night and, as the cold dawn rose like a heavy cover lifted from the sky, I stayed huddled by the door. I finally rose, grabbed the phone, and called BCC to tell them I would be out for a few days. And then I sat on the edge of the bed, in view of the door—I always made sure I was in view of the door—and watched a lot of television, waiting for news about James Carr's murder.

The murder was never mentioned.

My guilt and fear kept passing each other, runners in an endless race. I went through periods where I desperately wanted to call the police and confess, to throw myself into prison and free myself from guilt. But I couldn't. I even tried confessing to myself. The words wouldn't emerge from my throat.

I jumped the first time there a knock on the door. I peered through the peephole and saw an older maid with a light blue uniform and gray hair. I imagined Diane standing behind her and called out a hoarse "no thanks." After that, I was too nervous to do anything but stare at the door for an hour or so.

I didn't leave the room and, as a weak sun swung it-self over me and dragged along the night, I realized how hungry I was. Nerves constantly had me near nausea, but I needed to eat something. I called room service, ordered a soup, and fretted about how I was going to answer the door when it was delivered. I couldn't shake a vision of Diane staying out of sight from the door's peephole and charging in when the door opened. I told room service to call when my food was on its way and, when they did, I headed into the hall and hid in the small room with the ice machine. I stayed out of sight until I heard someone knock on my room door, then peered around the corner, and saw a tall skinny male hotel attendant. I looked care-fully down the hall, didn't see anyone else, and walked out.

"Hey," I told him. "Sorry. That's for me."

I signed for the soup, took it into my room, and locked the door behind me. I sipped it while I watched the news, still waiting for a report about the murder, and lay down, my stomach queasy.

I finally slept that night, but fitfully, constantly wak-ing. I locked the door and shoved a chair against it, so I wasn't worried about someone breaking in, but my nerves were too sharp. Peace was impossible.

I woke around noon. I thought about going down-stairs, but the idea of leaving my room scared me too much. I kept the TV on throughout the day, slept on and off, and ordered soup for dinner again, this time with a sandwich.

I sat on bed, the television low and my stomach warm from the food, reached for the room phone, and dialed.

"Hello?"

"Hey, Mom," I said. "It's me."

"Tomás! Hi, honey. How are you? How's Julie?" It was nice to hear my mother's voice, her Spanish accent thickly filling words.

"I'm fine. She's fine. We're doing good."

"I haven't heard from you in a while. Is everything okay? I thought something was wrong."

"We talked last week, right?"

"We did not," she said sharply.

Much of me was happy that, no matter how many things in life abruptly changed, one thing was always consistent: a reproachful mother.

"I'm sorry," I said. "I thought we talked. I should do a better job of keeping in touch."

"And Julie is doing good?"

"Oh yeah. She's been…she's been okay."

"What's wrong?"

"She's having problems in school. Her grades could be better. But I think they'll improve. Ruth and Dave are working with her."

"So she still goes back and forth between you two?" She sounded dismayed. "Tomás, that's not how you raise a child."

"Well, she's not going back and forth as much now. She's staying with them while I get some things sorted out."

Silence for a moment. "So you gave her up?"

"No. I mean, temporarily. I have a lot of stuff going on."

"What kind of stuff?" Suspicion.

"Things at school have been really busy, now at the end of the semester. And I had some depression about Renee that I was dealing with…" That last part didn't feel true as I said it, but it was true enough. I wanted sympathy.

"And so you punish your child?"

"Julie's not being punished, Mom. Ruth and Dave give her a good home."

"But you're her father. And to deprive her of her father, after her mother is gone, is punishment. After your father died, I never stopped being your mother."

"You don't know—"

"I'm disappointed in you," my mother interrupted tersely. "I really am."

"You don't know what I'm dealing with right now." Any happiness from talking with my mother was gone.

"I only hope you stop to think about what Julie is dealing with."

"Yeah, okay."

"How are you?" she asked.

"Mom, seriously? Have you been listening? Things are bad. And I can't talk now. Listen, I'll talk to you later."

"Okay."

I hung up the phone.

After that night, the morning of the third day, my thoughts finally started to slow.

What happened wasn't my fault. I hadn't expected James Carr to die. I imagined confessing to the police, a judge, Dave and Ruth, even Julie, telling them all that this wasn't what I wanted. Chris Taylor was supposed to die, and I never expected any of this to happen. It wasn't what I wanted.

I was lying in bed that third afternoon and watching some television judge yell at a divorcing couple, each fighting not to retain custody of their child. The phone rang.

I stayed in bed, stiff.

"But your honor," one of the people before the judge complained, "I *work*, and I just don't have the time to…"

The phone rang again.

I slowly pushed myself up, leaned across the thick pillows and lifted the receiver. "Hello?"

"Mr. Starks?"

It took me a few moments to respond, and came out as a whisper when I did. "Yes."

"This is Paul, down at the front?"

"Okay."

"I have to apologize. I was unable to hold the charges on your credit card any longer, and my manager made me push them through."

I was already standing. "When did the charges go through?"

"This morning."

I hung up the phone and hurried around the room, making sure nothing was left behind. I rushed to the door, peered through the peephole, and slowly stepped into the hall.

I closed the door quietly and walked quickly toward the elevator, reached it, and was about to press the call button when I imagined the doors sliding open and Diane stepping out.

I slipped into the stairwell and raced down the steps, grimacing as my footsteps echoed. I finally reached a door marked *LOBBY* and slowly pushed it open, a little out of breath from rushing down six flights of stairs. Only a couple of people were lounging in the lobby, a man and a woman in dress clothes and a pair of clerks behind the desk. There was a straight path to the hotel entrance. I stepped out of the stairwell.

My body felt unnatural as I walked. I couldn't stop thinking that the people in the lobby or the group in the bar were all watching me.

I reached the tall glass doors and pushed them open.

I stepped outside and hurried to the street. The day was both colder and brighter than I thought. Someone was walking toward me but, blinded by sunlight, I couldn't make out who it was. Everything in me wanted to turn around, to step aside, to run, but I forced myself to walk normally. The person passed.

I reached a cab, opened the door, and climbed inside.

"Where are you going?" the driver asked.

∽∾∽

The cab pulled to a stop outside of the Rivers' house in Bethesda. I told the driver to wait, hurried to the doorbell and rang it twice.

Michael Rivers opened the door. "Tom?" he asked, and leaned out of the doorway, looking beyond me, as if he expected someone else.

"Is Robin here?" I asked.

Michael shook his head. "Did you need to talk to her?"

I felt vulnerable standing in the doorway. "Do you know when she'll be back?"

Michael studied me skeptically. "I'm not sure. She's shopping at Tyson's. Do you have her cell phone number?"

"No."

"Come in," he said.

I looked behind me. "I can't."

Michael cleared his throat. "Listen, Tom," he told me. "I know why you're upset."

"You do?"

"Ruth told me about the fight you two are having, about Julie. I know how painful all this must be."

"That's okay. It's better if Julie stays with Ruth and Dave."

"They'll give her a good home."

"Look, I need you to do me a favor. If someone comes looking for me, you never saw me. Please."

"Why not?"

"I can't explain it now."

"Does this have anything to do with a woman named Diane? She called yesterday, looking for you."

I couldn't breathe for a few moments.

"What did you tell her?"

"That I didn't know where you were," Michael told me. "She said that she needed to talk to you. What's wrong?"

"If she calls back, you never saw me. Do you understand? *Never*. Don't tell her I'm your family. I'm not your family. Do you understand?"

"Tom—" Michael started to say.

"Can I use your phone?"

He hesitated then let me inside. I walked into the kitchen and dialed my own cell phone, which had been left in my truck outside of Levees. I knew who would answer.

"Hello?"

It was Diane.

"I'm going to my house. Meet me there. We need to talk."

つぐつ

There were other places I wanted to go.

I wanted to see Julie again. I wanted that more than anything.

I wanted to visit Renee's grave. I wanted to return to the spot in the harbor where I had thrown her ashes, and mourn her.

I wanted to see Alison. I wanted to visit her in secrecy and lose myself in the darkness with her.

I wanted to return to school, to stand in front of a class of students in a warm, brightly-lit room, and talk about literature and the problems characters faced. I wanted that distance from any real concerns or crisis, the artificial world of the classroom.

But instead I asked the cab driver to take me home.

Federal Hill was quiet as we drove up Light Street. The stores on either side were locked and shuttered and a few people were on the sidewalk, but not many.

I didn't know what I was going to tell her. I thought about some sort of apology, or an offer of money if she would spare my life, but the speech in my head always ended with her cold stare and gun.

I could probably get her to spare Julie's life. There was no reason for Diane to go after Julie if I was dead. Killing Julie would just draw more attention to herself. Once Diane had me, she would have everything she wanted.

At least, that's what I hoped.

I asked the cab driver to stop a block away from my house, paid him, and stepped outside.

The cold air rushed into my clothes and over my body, but I barely noticed it. I was staring up the block, looking for the van or Diane's hulking figure. I didn't see either.

I walked toward my house, trying to think of something else, but there were no other options. All I could do was bargain for my life with Diane, try and find something—money, secrecy, anything—that would appease her.

And if nothing did, then all I could do was ask her not to hurt anyone else. Julie needed to be safe. Although, the thought that I was never going to see her again literally stopped me.

I had to see Julie again.

There was one other option left. But I couldn't kill Diane. I wasn't a killer, not before, not now, and I never would be.

I climbed the marble steps to my porch. The front door was unlocked.

I pushed it open and entered the main hall. I looked into the living room and family room, then the kitchen. No Diane.

I headed upstairs, my legs heavy. The hall bathroom was empty. I turned on the light in Julie's room and Bananas ran to the front of the cage.

"Oh, shit," I said. "You haven't eaten, have you?"

I went back down to the kitchen, opened the fridge, and took out a handful of lettuce and mini-carrots. I headed back upstairs and dropped the food in his cage. Bananas rushed to it and ate hungrily.

His water bowl was empty, so I took it to the bathroom, filled it, and brought it back to the room. Then I sat on Julie's bed and watched Bananas eat.

He sat up and rubbed his nose with his paws after he finished.

I walked to Bananas, leaned over and picked him up, then sat back down on Julie's bed. I held him in my lap and petted his ears while he lay still. I kicked off Richard's shoes and closed my eyes.

"Most villains hold a cat in their lap," Diane said.

My eyes opened. She was standing in the doorway, a giant in an open flannel over a black T-shirt and jeans and a black baseball cap pulled low over her blonde hair. A gun was in her left hand.

"I'm not a villain."

"No, you're not," she replied. "You clearly don't have a clue what you're doing. Although, I gotta admit, you are pretty crafty."

"What do you want to end all this? More money?"

Diane nodded. "I do, but not right now. Now, I want you."

Relief thudded into me. She didn't want to kill me, at least not right away. "For what?"

"I need you for another job."

"Another job?" I asked, weakly. "In this economy?"

Diane didn't smile. "Turns out Bailey and Carr were related," she said, "and a little more connected than we thought. And Bailey…well, he's not taking what I did to his cousin too well. Somehow he found out what happened, and he found out that we're the ones responsible. He told our contact that he wants to talk to us, and he wants to talk to the guy that hired us. So we're going to see him and we're bringing you along."

"Can I hide forever instead?"

"Bardos and I aren't big on hiding. If Bailey wants to meet you, then he's going to meet you. But he's going to think Bardos and I hightailed it out of town."

"He just wants to kill me."

"We'll kill him first. All you have to do is walk in, distract him, and wait for us to make our move."

"I can't do that."

"Sure you can. If you don't, then I'll kill Julie."

Everything in my body tensed. "You don't know where she is."

Diane gave me a condescending look. "How long do you think that will last?"

"Why would you…" I asked, my voice small, "why would you threaten her? She's just a girl…"

Diane walked over to me, one hand keeping the gun trained on me, and scooped Bananas off my lap with the other. She set him down in his cage. He was still for a few moments, then briskly shook and hopped into his cardboard box.

Diane was staring down at him. "Not exactly an attack dog you have here, is it?"

"Why would you threaten Julie?" I asked again. "Why not go after someone else," I thought for a moment, "like Ruth?"

Diane walked over to the bed and sat next to me. "I don't want to stick a twelve-year old girl in the morgue. Hell, Starks, I don't want to kill you, much, even after all the trouble you've caused. But this Bailey is asking to see my hand, and I need you. I'm desperate."

"Maybe you should try another vice, other than killing. Like me. I eat too much when I get desperate."

"Shut up."

"I didn't know any of this would happen."

"You wanted someone dead," she told me.

"Yeah, but I didn't think he was innocent! These other people definitely are."

"No one's ever innocent."

I didn't know what to say.

"You do this for me," Diane said, "and I let her live. Your choice."

"There aren't any choices," I said, bitterly.

Diane nodded. "No, there aren't."

CHAPTER 16

We Fuck and We Kill

I packed a duffle then followed Diane from my row house to her van.

"I can't believe you found parking here," I told her.

Diane didn't respond. She watched me climb into the passenger seat then closed my door and walked around the front of the vehicle. She slid into the driver's seat and started the engine.

"Where are we going?" Asking a question, just speaking out loud, made me nervous, but I had to learn more about what was happening.

"South."

"How far south?"

Diane didn't answer.

"Can I ask you something? Why did you...cut up Carr? Did you know I was there? Were you sending me a message?"

"She did it because she didn't need to be pulled over with a dead body in back. Easier to hide parts." The answer came from behind me. I turned and saw Bardos sprawled between the two benches in the back.

His ear was bandaged, and I could see a white wrap peeking out from under his shirt, over his shoulder.

I turned back halfway, facing both of them. "What happens when we get where we're going?"

"Well," Diane said, letting the word drawl, "you'll find out. Now put this on." She was holding something out to me. A black hood.

"Put it on," Diane said, "or I'll put it on you. And slide down in your seat."

I did as she told me.

I couldn't see anything. Diane and Bardos drove in silence. The hood smelled like sweat. I wondered if Carr had been the last person to wear it.

"Listen," I said, blinded, "I don't want to kill anyone, or even be part of anyone killing someone. Not anymore."

Silence.

I wondered if I should say something else or ask more questions, but speaking scared me. Instead, I stayed quiet, unsure of how much time passed until I felt the van slow and the hood was pulled off. I looked out the window and saw the dark silhouettes of trees.

"There's a house to our right," Diane told me. "We're going to wait there till tomorrow night."

Bardos slid open the door in the back, stepped out, and grunted in pain as he lifted a large flashlight. The house appeared in the beam of light, a sad two-story structure that looked like it had died years ago. Weeds sprang from the lawn, pointing in different directions, and a long wooden porch wrapped around the side with dark windows spaced equally apart on each of the two floors. There were no other houses in sight, and the air felt colder here, as if we had moved forward in time, past November.

I took the duffel bag Diane had made me pack and slung it over my shoulder. It only held a change of clothes that she'd picked out of my closet, black jeans and a black sweater. Bardos walked to the door. I followed him, and Diane followed me.

"Where are we?" I asked.

"South," Diane said and pulled open the front door.

"Is this your house?"

"Only when we need it," Bardos replied.

I was a little worried that they didn't seem to mind answering my questions anymore, but I needed to keep asking. I needed to know more about what was happening. "What do you use it for?"

"Whatever we need."

I felt Diane's hand on my back. She pushed me inside.

The door revealed a long, narrow hall that ran to my right and left and opened to rooms on either side. A staircase led up directly in front of us to someplace dark. We headed to our right, passed through an empty room and into a kitchen with a chipped wooden table and four chairs around it and nothing else.

"You come here to hide?" I asked.

"We don't need to hide," Diane said carelessly. "We come here to plan."

She turned on a light switch, but the light only made things look worse. Now I could see the broken floor and the faded paint on the walls. Diane pointed to one of the chairs and I sat in it. Bardos opened his bag and handed me a sandwich, white bread with thin slices of ham and hard American cheese.

I ate silently. Diane and Bardos acted as if my escaping wasn't even a possibility. They spread out a small, wrinkled, handmade map and huddled over it, planning tomorrow night.

"It's just Bailey at the cabin," Bardos said.

"Mackie tell you who Bailey's working for? Bailey can't be independent, not if he found out about us."

Bardos shook his head.

Diane tapped her fingers on the table. "What does Mack always say? Better the enemies, you know…"

"Otherwise enemies are everywhere."

"Right," Diane said, and her fingers stopped. "We got the rifle and scope, right?"

"And shotguns, yeah. All in the van."

"Shotguns aren't going to work unless we get into the house," Diane said, and she turned to me. "That means you don't mess around and don't try anything cute. We'll get you out alive, if you do what we tell you. Otherwise, I'll kill you myself."

I nodded, but I knew there wasn't any way Diane and Bardos would let me live after tomorrow night.

I had to escape.

౿౧౿౧

They never left me alone. One of them was always near me. Diane even went with me when I had to use the bathroom, standing outside a door that she made me leave open. There was only one window in the bathroom, and it was painted black, sealed shut, and too small for me to slide through. I touched the glass to see if I could break it, but the glass was thick against my finger.

I flushed the toilet and ran the sink. Diane was waiting outside, leaning against the wall.

She led me back to the kitchen table and I watched them clean and load their guns. Neither of them said anything until, finally, Diane stretched.

"I'm heading up to the attic, and then to bed," she told Bardos. "You got him?"

He nodded.

"Good." Diane took a pistol and slid it into a holster on her hip. "Get some sleep."

"Here?" I asked.

She shrugged. "At the table or the floor. We only got one bed here and I'm in it. And trust me, you don't want to spend the night in the attic."

Bardos laughed at that as Diane went upstairs. He turned toward a long rifle lying on the table and began to disassemble it.

"Can I ask you something?"

Bardos grunted.

"What was going on in the bathroom, that night at the motel? When I was in the bedroom talking to Diane, I heard thumps."

"Fixing the toilet."

"Really? That's it? You were fixing the toilet?"

"It was clogged."

"Oh." I felt relieved until I asked, "What was clogging it?"

Bardos was using a small screwdriver on the handle of the gun. "Parts of a woman. She was from Bethesda."

My sense of relief left. "This wasn't how I thought I'd spend my last night alive," I said, miserably.

He picked the rifle back up and cocked it. "How'd you figure to spend it?"

So much for hoping Bardos would contradict my "last night alive" statement. "I don't know. It wasn't something I've had to think about until now. Why? Have you thought about it? Probably not, right?"

"Why'd you say that?"

"Because you do this all the time."

Bardos picked up a scope and peered through it. "Doesn't mean you don't think about dying."

"Are you ready for it?"

"Everyone fights dying when it comes."

"You mean the people you've killed?"

He set down the scope. "I'm talking about some people I killed, sure."

I wondered if I was making any headway. "Why do you do this?" I asked, trying to go a little deeper.

Bardos started screwing the scope onto the rifle. "I have nothing else."

"I couldn't do it," I said.

"Probably not."

"When was the first time...how did you know this was what you wanted?" I asked.

"I'm going outside," Bardos said instead and stood. "Stay in here." He walked out of the kitchen. I heard the front door open and close moments later.

I was alone.

My mind raced, and I wondered if this was my chance to escape. Unfortunately, the house seemed built to contain prisoners, and maybe it was. There were no doors leading into the house other than the front one, and I didn't dare walk out to Bardos and his gun. The kitchen windows were high and narrow and too small for me to fit through. And Diane was here, somewhere upstairs. I knew that the sound of breaking glass would send her and her gun running down.

I stood and slowly walked through the kitchen, my heart beating so hard it hurt. I walked into the dark empty dining room and toward the front.

I stopped halfway through the room. I couldn't do it. I couldn't risk getting caught. If I stayed innocent, if I did what they wanted, then maybe I had a chance. But if Bardos caught me…

I sat down in my chair back in the kitchen, suddenly exhausted, like a fist had knocked the wind out of me. I put my head down and the next thing I knew, Diane was shaking my shoulder.

"Was I asleep?"

"For a couple of hours," she said. She pulled out the chair across from me. I saw, as she bent and her shirt lifted, a gun resting in her hip holster. "My turn to babysit you."

I rubbed my eyes. My neck hurt.

"Not comfortable?" Diane asked. "Has to do. Just for the night, anyway. You'll be back in your bed after tomorrow. Or dead." She shrugged. "And then it won't matter."

"You're okay with that? Me dying?"

Diane winked at me. "I'm okay with you dying."

I looked away and, for some reason, thought about Alison.

"Have you ever been married?" I asked.

Diane reached down into a bag next to her chair, pulled out a bottle of water, and twisted off the top. She drank and offered it to me but, thirsty as I was, I turned it down. She grinned and set the bottle on the table.

"I was," she said.

"Did you kill him?"

That drew a sharp bark of laughter from her. "You got a low opinion of us, don't you? He's living somewhere up north. I don't know...it's been maybe twenty years since we split."

"Twenty years?"

Diane shrugged. "Got married young. We all did. Small towns."

"What happened?"

She took another sip of water. "This really what you want to talk about? My marriage?"

"Sure." I wanted to form some type of bridge with Diane, some emotional connection that would convince her to keep me alive.

"No," Diane said. "Let's talk about something else. Like how come you're not terrified?"

"What do you mean?"

Diane leaned close to me, so close that I could see small scars on her face, white lines around her eyes, like tiny dead worms. People often write about someone having "dead eyes" or a "cold, empty gaze," but Diane had *something* in her eyes. It was something bleak and lost years ago, beyond the point of rescue. "A man is going to die tomorrow night," she said, "and probably more than one since Bailey doesn't travel alone. You understand that? Because of what you've done."

"It's not because of me," I said defiantly. "I'm not going to be the one killing them."

"Why aren't you more scared?" Diane asked again. "I've seen men crap themselves the night before they fought. I've seen grown men, hard men, that had to be dragged or carried into a gunfight, and they were crying and screaming up until they died. People are going to die tomorrow night, and you seem too smart to kid yourself about it. So why aren't you scared?"

"You know I don't want to do this," I told her. "You know I don't want any of this to happen. This isn't my choice."

Diane leaned back in her chair. "Nothing matters as much when it isn't your choice. That's true."

"Is that how you feel?"

"Pretty much."

"Because you're just the messenger, right?"

She nodded.

"And that's how you live with yourself? With what you do?"

"Tom," Diane said, surprising me by saying my name, by the softness in her voice, "don't you understand what I am?"

"You're a killer."

"We're all killers."

"What are you talking about?"

"You pay taxes for war, for deaths, for an American or an Iraqi or Afghani or a Vietcong or someone somewhere to get killed. Every man and woman of every nation has done the same. You're a killer, Starks, and so is everyone else you know, and so am I. You just buy the bullets instead of pulling the trigger."

"You can't blame everybody in the world. You can't blame everyone for what a few people do. Most people wouldn't do that if the choice was theirs. That's why we're different from you."

"I'm part of them, part of you, part of everybody in this country, everybody in this world. Bardos and I both, he and I are just weapons." Diane leaned back in her chair. "Mack told me something, back when we first got into this work. We're what you see, he told me, when you look away from the shadow on the cave wall." Diane grinned. "I don't know what it means, but it sounds nice. Did you know Bardos started writing poetry?"

"I don't want to hear his poetry."

"Really?"

"Actually, I sort of do, but not right now. Look, you can tell me that we're all in this system, and we're all guilty, but you're forgetting about choice. You don't have to be like this. You don't have to make me do this thing tomorrow night. You can do whatever you want."

"There isn't a choice," Diane said. "There are two things people do, and they're the two things we've always been told *not* to do, but we do them anyway. We fuck, we kill, we do both to save our own lives. We've never chosen otherwise. We can't."

Diane took another swig of water, and I thought about the third thing we do to save our lives, the thing I would do as soon as I had a chance.

Run.

⁋ʘ⁋

Diane never gave me an opportunity to escape. I stayed awake and played gin rummy with her, even though she was a blatant cheater. Then, finally, I heard Bardos coming down the stairs.

Diane waited until he walked into the kitchen, then she pushed back her chair and stood. "You got him till dawn?" she asked.

Bardos rubbed his eyes and yawned. "I got him."

He looked moments from falling asleep, but Diane didn't seem concerned. She left the kitchen without giving either of us a glance.

Bardos sat heavily in her chair, lifted the cards she had left on the table and squinted at them. "Diane cheating?"

"Yeah."

"All right," he said. "Get some sleep. You'll need it for tomorrow."

"Where are we going tomorrow? You can tell me that, right?"

"Nope."

By now I knew when Bardos was going to offer more information and when he wasn't, and *nope* was the most information I was going to get. "Aren't you tired?" I asked.

"Nope."

"So," I said, "Diane tells me you write poetry. Is that true?"

"Yep."

"Well, you know that I teach English at BCC," I said brightly. "Do you want to read me some of it? I'd like to hear it."

"Isn't BCC a community college?"

"I don't see what that—"

"I didn't bring any, but I have some of it memorized," Bardos told me, and he set the gun on the table. "Want to hear it?"

"Sure."

Bardos leaned back in his chair.

> "My father was a drunk who
> always smelled like beer,
> He'd come home from the bar
> and threaten his wife,
> I'd watch my dad, hiding from him in fear,
> And lock the door to my bedroom,
> fearing for my life.
> One day, the cops came and took him to jail,
> Because he killed my mom
> and I never saw him again.
> As I grew up, I realized I was going to fail,
> Because even without him,
> I'd be like him when I became a man."

Bardos was quiet.

I asked, timidly, "Is that the end?"

He nodded.

"Thank you," I said.

"What'd you think?"

"What'd I think of what? The poem?"

"Yeah."

"I mean…it needs work."

Bardos picked up the gun again and examined it. "Needs work?"

"It sounds very honest," I said, eyeing the gun. "It's very brave to talk about your childhood so honestly. A lot of writers have problems with that."

"You didn't like it."

It was hard to take my eyes off of the gun. "Not really, no. The rhyme scheme is pretty simple, and off, and it needs to be more subtle. Or more raw. One of the two."

Bardos and I looked at each other for a long moment, then he grunted and went back to cleaning his gun.

"Thank you for sharing it," I said, mildly.

No response. I didn't want to risk aggravating him any further, so I said, "Well, good night," then pushed my chair back, leaned on the table, and rested my head over my arms. I could watch Bardos by peeking over my elbow, but I kept my eyes closed because I didn't want him to realize I was awake. He finished with the gun, picked up a deck of cards, and played some game, scrutinizing the cards on the table, a plastic bottle of water next to him.

I waited for about an hour but Bardos didn't seem to grow more tired. I was beginning to worry that I would never have the chance to escape, but he finally stood, stretched, holstered his pistol, and left the kitchen. I heard the front door open.

I stood and looked for something I could use as a weapon. All of the guns they had cleaned earlier were gone, and I didn't have the courage to search the house. There were drawers in the kitchen, and I thought a knife might be in one of them, but I worried someone would hear a drawer slide open. I saw a heavy dirty glass in the sink and took that instead.

I crept out of the kitchen and through the dining room, and this time I didn't stop. I walked to the front door and peered outside.

Bardos was there, his back to me, standing on the porch and staring into the night.

I knew that I could head back to that kitchen table and sit back down and stay safe, but the idea of being safe was only an idea.

I stepped onto the porch. My plan was to sneak behind Bardos, around the house, and escape into the woods before he knew I was gone. And then, as soon as I was far enough away, I'd run until I found help.

Bardos turned toward me.

He didn't seem surprised. He just looked at me with his hands in his pockets.

"You want to talk about the poem?" he asked.

I swung the glass as hard as I could into his bandaged ear. The glass shattered in my hand. My palm burst with pain then went numb, like electricity had struck it.

Bardos shouted, stepped back, slipped and fell, reaching toward the holster on his hip even as he hit the ground. I turned to run, but he had already pulled the gun out, so I stepped toward him and brought the remainder of the glass down again over the bandage. He cried out and the gun dropped.

I picked up his gun and turned. Something struck my face.

I was sitting on the ground as Bardos writhed next to me, pain echoing through my face. Diane breathed hard in front of me. I still held the gun, Diane and I both seeming to notice it at the same moment. I lifted my hand just in time to see her fist.

Nothing had ever hit me that hard. My body fell back to the ground like it was flattened against it, the back of my head smacking against the dirt then bouncing back up. Diane knelt over me, lifted my chin and punched me again. All I saw was red and I tasted blood. I rolled to my side, nauseous. The gun was pulled out of my limp hand.

Diane lifted me to my feet. I stood unsteadily in front of her, my legs wobbling.

"You just made this hard on yourself," Diane told me.

I punched her in the face.

Diane frowned and backhanded me. I fell to the ground and rolled over, trying to rise to my knees, trying to crawl into the woods.

Diane grabbed me by my throat and pulled me back toward the house. I had no choice but to follow her. Bardos walked behind us, his hand pressed against his ear.

Diane dragged me upstairs and into a room that had nothing in it but a staircase leading up to the attic. I saw a dim light shining through the small square opening.

"What's up there?" I asked. My lips were already swollen.

"Initiation," Diane said.

The attic was small, with sloped brick walls and no windows. A small tub was on the other end of the room with a metal bar over the top of it. Diane pushed me toward the tub. The smell of disinfectant was strong.

Diane stopped me when I reached the tub's edge. She handcuffed one of my wrists to the bar above the tub, then pushed a rag into my mouth.

She reached into her pocket and pulled out a thick elastic strap. She placed the strap around my head then over my lips. It was tight, so tight that it seemed like my teeth were being shoved inward.

Diane turned me toward the tub and made me grab the bar over it. When I did, she handcuffed my other wrist to the bar.

"Keep your head out of the water," she advised me and walked off. I could see her, only out of the corner of my eye, pull down the latch of the attic door. I heard it lock.

I turned toward the tub, and the aroma from it burned my eyes. There was a thick soapy layer of foam over the top, but something nudged through the surface.

An arm. It floated away and I screamed into the rag and tried to force myself away but the handcuffs stopped me. My movements forced the water to slosh around the tub.

It splashed up and I felt heat rise from the chemicals. More body parts rose to the surface, a bloodied foot, a long piece of torn flesh, fingers, Carr's eyeless head. I struggled violently, until my wrists were limp, until I tasted blood. I couldn't move away.

CHAPTER 17

Goodbye, Beautiful

Someone touched my shoulder.

The handcuffs were taken off. I was pulled away from the tub and the rag was removed from my mouth. I sat on the cold attic floor.

"You ready?" Diane asked. I didn't answer and she touched my shoulder again. "Come on."

I stood, sluggish because of my sore knees, and followed Diane through the attic. She stood to the side of the ladder and I went down first.

Bardos waited on the landing. He wore all black, jeans and a sweater, under a long open coat. A rifle was slung behind his back. Behind him, through the bedroom window, it was dark outside.

"What time is it?" I asked. My voice was thick and slurred, almost like the rag was still inside of my mouth.

"Nine o'clock at night," Diane said, as she pushed the staircase to the attic back up. "You hungry?"

She was wearing a similar outfit to Bardos, two guns on her waist but without the rifle.

I shook my head.

"Really?" she continued, surprised. "You should be. You were up there an entire day. Christ, you didn't eat Carr, did you?"

"Does he have a change of clothes?" Bardos asked Diane.

Diane blinked. "I made him pack it when we left his place. Come on." She led me to the bedroom, watched as I changed, then we headed downstairs and out into the cold. The white van was parked in the driveway. Bardos climbed into the driver seat and Diane and I sat in the back, across from each other.

"How you feeling?" Diane asked.

The van began to move. I still felt chained above that tub, with body parts slowly bumping into each other in the red water below me. I could almost taste whatever chemicals they had used to dissolve Carr's skin and bones; a smell that reminded me of detergent or cleaner, an acidic scent of poison and death.

"Rough night, rough day, right?" Diane asked me.

I had looked into Carr's empty eyes after his head drifted to the surface until I eventually felt nothing. No guilt, no sadness, no relief. My mind was a grave waiting to be filled.

"I ever tell you about the time I almost died?" Diane went on. "It was kind of like tonight. We were meeting someone about a job that had gone wrong—someone ended up killing the guy we were hired to kill. So we're heading to this apartment, and we get out of the elevator and see nothing but men with guns pointed at us. Bardos closed the doors right away, but I got hit in the side. We had a third person with us but, well, he wasn't as lucky as we were.

"Anyway, we're heading down to the lobby, but we stop on the second floor. Bardos has to practically carry me to the stairwell, and he leaves me by the door and creeps out. I start to hear shots firing and bodies dropping and then some guy comes sprinting through the stairway door. He sees me lying there and pulls out his gun, leans over me, and I drive my knife right under his jaw. It goes up into the roof of his mouth and he falls on top of me, dead in a second.

"So I'm lying there, and I don't have the strength to push him away with this bullet sitting in me, and I hear someone walking toward me. All I have is my knife, and I'm trying to work it out of this guy's throat, and it's making his head move back and forth, and the footsteps are right around the corner. And I can't hear Bardos anywhere. I can't get my knife out of this guy's throat, but I'm trying and his head is moving all everywhere.

"And then I hear some girl say 'Get a room.' And she walks off." Diane laughed, loudly. "Jesus, that was a wild night."

No one said anything else the rest of the drive. The van stopped maybe an hour later. I leaned forward to look through the window and saw a group of lights, a ring reflecting around a small lake.

"All right," Diane said. "Here's the plan. I would have told you earlier but I didn't want you to spend all day figuring out how to escape. Better to tell you right before. And believe me, if you do something to screw me and Bardos over, your body will end up melting next to Carr. You hear me?"

She looked closely at me before she continued.

"This Bailey lives a few cabins down, number five. He's expecting all three of us to come walking through his door, but you're going in alone. And if you break out and run in another direction before that, or you try and get away, then Bardos is going to end your night really quick. His rifle has a night scope and he doesn't miss."

I didn't respond.

"You're going to go to this Bailey's house and tell him that you haven't heard from us since we killed Carr. And then you're going to tell him that you went back to Mack and he told you that we left town. Got that?"

"Okay."

"Now, you're probably thinking he's going to shoot you right then and there. And he might. But Bardos and I will be coming in. We'll stop him, and we have our own questions for him. And then you're free to go."

"Okay."

Diane looked at me closely. "Good," she said. She stood and slid open the side door of the van and cold air rushed inside.

"Stay alive till we get there," she advised me.

I stepped outside the van. Diane followed me. Bardos came around the front, the rifle in his hands.

"Last house on the left," he said.

I started walking toward the cabin and they followed me through the trees. I didn't know where we were other than Maryland. The area was dark. Street lamps were spaced too far apart to be useful, and the only other lights came from one or two of the cabins around the lake. They looked empty, abandoned for winter.

I reached the cabin Bardos had indicated, stopped, and looked around. I couldn't see Diane or Bardos anywhere. The woods and lake were as quiet as a held breath.

The cabin was lit by a long narrow light that hung on the side of the door. A sidewalk made of gravel led to the entrance. I walked up to it and knocked twice.

No answer.

I tried the knob and it turned, but the door was heavier than I expected. I pressed my shoulder against it. It suddenly swung open and I fell inside.

A hand grabbed me, held me up, and the door slammed shut. I heard a lock click and the hand quickly patted me down then disappeared.

A flashlight clicked on and illuminated a single wooden chair in the middle of the room.

"Sit down." A man's voice.

I walked to the chair and sat in it, facing the light. I looked into the beam. It was all I could see.

"More are coming, right?"

"Yes," I said.

"How long?"

"They're right behind me."

"You're Tom Starks."

I squinted. I could see a silhouette behind the light, but barely. "Are you Bailey?"

"Robert Bailey."

"You knew they were coming," I asked, "and you're just waiting here for them?"

"I'm not alone."

I turned to look behind me. All I saw was a dark hallway, too dark for me to see into.

"My friends are outside." He paused. "With your friends."

"They're not my friends."

"So they forced you to come." Nothing Bailey said came out like a question. Everything was a statement.

I nodded. "Why did you want to see me?"

"You were responsible for the death of my cousin. I had to see you, face to face, after what happened to Jimmy."

There was a sudden explosion outside. My body jerked so hard that I fell off the chair. I heard shouts and small popping sounds.

"Sounds like our friends are getting to know each other," Bailey remarked.

I pulled myself back up and sat on the chair. "They're not my friends."

He was silent for a long moment. "Listen."

Someone near the cabin was moaning, just on the other side of the wall, sounding like slow wind.

"I have about five trained killers out there," Bailey said. "The people who brought you here will never survive."

I thought briefly about Diane and Bardos. "No, I don't think they will."

"So we have time for some questions."

"Why did you kill my wife?" I asked.

Bailey laughed. I was starting to see his silhouette better, but all I could make out was that he was tall and thin. "I meant my questions," he said, "but I'll let you start. Jimmy and I were paid to kill her."

"Paid by who?"

"A lawyer in Boston."

"Are you telling me the truth?"

"There's no reason to lie to you."

"Why would a lawyer in Boston want her dead? Renee didn't even know anyone in Boston."

"It had something to do with the affair they were having."

"What?"

There was a moment's pause. "I told you that I have no reason to lie to you."

"But what about…" My voice was high, desperate. "You're thinking of the wrong person. What about Chris Taylor?"

"I'm thinking of the right person. Taylor was nothing. A scapegoat."

Something thudded against the wall, like a bird had flown into it, then I heard loud shouts and men running.

"Renee wouldn't have—she wouldn't have cheated on me," I said, my voice low, dull. "He killed her because of—because of that?"

"She was going to tell his wife and then tell you. Apparently, that worried him. He had married into money, from what I remember."

I was gripping the chair. I saw Bailey's silhouette approach the light, almost as if he was going to walk around it. I could see that he was thin and tall with blond hair and glasses.

"You only came with two people? And they're still alive?"

He left the light. The door to the cabin suddenly burst open. Bardos. His face and chest were covered in blood, and he stopped when he saw me. I didn't have time to do anything but open my mouth as a knife plunged into his neck. Bardos staggered forward and fell to his knees, his hands scrabbling at the blade. He pitched forward and rolled to his back.

Bailey was suddenly over him, and I saw the shine of another knife, this one longer. He drove it into Bardos's stomach as Bardos tried to push himself away. And then the knife lifted and was shoved into Bardos again as his body frantically, helplessly arched.

Bailey stabbed Bardos over and over and, every time he did, Bardos's body rose a little, and then a little less, until finally he lay still as the knife gutted him, the sound like a wet foot slapping down on tiles.

It seemed like hours, but probably no more than a minute passed when Bailey climbed off Bardos, used his sleeve to clean his glasses, and looked at me. "There's another, right?"

And again, I didn't have time for a response. I heard an explosion. Blood burst from Bailey's shoulder and his body pitched forward.

Diane was in the doorway.

Bardos had been covered in blood and exhausted, but Diane looked clean. She had a small gun in her hand and stared at me, then looked down at Bardos. "Is that—"

Bailey suddenly sprang at her and Diane lifted the gun, but she lifted it too late. Bailey's knife was in her side. Diane stepped forward and fell heavily to one knee. He lifted the knife above her head, but she swatted his legs with one hand and knocked him over. He fell backward clumsily, almost hitting me. Then Diane was on him.

They were sitting up, facing each other. I heard each of them crying out and saw flashes, like light, between their bodies.

They were stabbing each other.

"Please!" Bailey begged her, even as he kept pulling his knife out and plunging it into her, even as his voice thickened to a gurgle. "Please! *Please!*"

I stayed sitting in my chair until they were both lying on the ground, barely moving. I could hear them breathe, Bailey, slowly, every few seconds and Diane, hoarsely, loudly.

I rose and picked up Bardos's gun.

"Tom," Bailey rasped, his words thick, "please."

"What?"

"Help me—"

He tried to sit up, but only lifted his shoulders a few inches off the ground. He lay back down, his eyes wide, panicked. He looked like he had fallen into a deep red pool.

I knelt by Diane. Bailey's long knife was buried in her stomach up to its handle.

"That Bardos?" she asked, her voice low, nearly a mumble. "Over by the door?"

"Yes."

"Oh, no," Diane said. She looked to the side, and her eyes seemed to widen. She seemed, at that moment, intensely beautiful. Small tears rolled down her cheeks. "All this, for one dead woman."

I looked outside the cabin. Shadows of bodies littered the ground.

Diane tried to sit up, but her arm collapsed underneath her, and she cried out as she fell back to the floor.

I knelt over her.

"What are you doing?" she asked.

I didn't answer.

"I'll leave you alone," Diane rasped. "You'll be free. You and your family."

"I need to be sure," I said, and my hands wrapped around her neck.

I squeezed until Diane's eyes bulged, until it looked like her eyes were going to burst. Her tongue stuck out of her mouth as she tried to pull my hands off her. Mucous ran clear from her nose, shiny against her skin, and her body pushed up underneath mine.

Finally we both stopped.

I used Bardos's gun to shoot Robert Bailey twice in the face after Diane was dead.

Then I left.

CHAPTER 18

The Inner Harbor

J ulie and I had slept late but Renee was always up first thing in the morning, opening cupboards, emptying the dishwasher, watching television with the volume low. Those sounds would come into my dreams, the world whispering me awake.

One day I woke, walked down the hall, and saw Renee standing outside of Julie's bedroom.

"I like watching her sleep," Renee told me as I stood behind her, my arms around her stomach, my chin against the back of her head, the fragrance from her still-wet hair filling me.

Spring was starting then, the end of winter, and morning sunlight from the window rose up our legs. Outside, a bird chirped curiously. Cars passed. Renee was warm in my arms as we leaned against the doorframe.

☙❧

I parked the van at a gas station in Towson, wiped off fingerprints anywhere I thought they might be, found my cell phone in the glove box, and took a cab back to Baltimore. I had about two hundred dollars in cash from Bardos's pocket, and I still had his gun.

I told the cab to drop me off in the inner harbor and walked to my row house. I kept a spare key hidden under a loose cobblestone on the side of my house, and I used it to let myself in. The first thing I did was head to the kitchen, grabbed handfuls of thick leafy lettuce, and took them upstairs to Bananas. He was standing on his hind legs, leaning against the cage, and he raced over to the lettuce after I dropped it inside. I took his water bowl to the bathroom, washed it out, then filled it with fresh water. I changed his litter, watched him eat for a few minutes, then went to the bathroom and showered.

I emerged ten minutes later, changed in the bedroom, and checked online to see if there was any news about the night before. Nothing.

I was waiting for something, some horrible guilt or epiphany about the night at the cabin, but nothing happened. I had been through shock before, and this wasn't it. I remember that day in basic training when a misfired explosive detonated near me and my entire body suddenly lifted into the air, yanked by an unseen hand. I remember shouts, colors, then the sky. I remember thinking it was funny how concerned everyone sounded as they raced toward me, as I sat up to look at them. They were pointing at my leg and I looked down and saw something white glint in the sun until a thin layer of blood ran over it and pain screamed through me.

But now pain didn't come. I watched television for a bit, then flipped it off, and walked outside.

A police car was waiting at the top of the street.

The car slowly cruised toward me. I stepped off my porch and headed down the sidewalk, aware that the cop car was slowly following.

I didn't see anyone else on the street, but there was no telling who was watching from their windows, or who would hear a gunshot and spot me before I could hide. And odds were, if that cop was here as a result of last night, then he wasn't alone. I heard the car pulling closer and I wanted to reach for the gun, but I knew that any movement, from this angle, would be hopeless. Nothing to do but keep walking, and wait for him to draw near. Wait for him to lower his window, find out what he wanted, and shoot him to make my escape.

A sudden siren startled me, and I flinched as the car suddenly roared past and rushed around the corner.

My breathing calmed. I turned and headed back into my row house. I needed to pack a getaway bag, and find out where I could buy more bullets, and say goodbye to...

Julie.

I closed the front door behind me, leaned against it, and closed my eyes. After a moment, I headed upstairs.

"So," I said to Renee, as I sat on the bed. "It's over."

She didn't appear.

"Turns out Chris Taylor wasn't involved, after all. And you were right. I probably wasn't going to kill him earlier, but it's a good thing I didn't. Only one person could have told me for sure that he didn't do it. Only one person I would have believed.

"I'm a little mad at you, you know. Meeting you just completely upended my life, from day one to now. Nothing was ever normal after that point. It wasn't just the love, although that was part of it. I guess I didn't know how to handle love, and it was too much for me. I always thought that I never really loved anyone until I met you. No one echoed in me like you did.

"I know you're here. I can feel you, your presence. I can feel you holding your breath. And I know what you're worried about. You're worried because I know the truth.

"So who was he?"

I heard the thumps of a helicopter's blades passing overhead.

"Some guy in Boston. I remember those trips you took to visit your girlfriend out there. I found that lawyer's office's address on a slip of paper and I knew, I *knew*, something wasn't right about it. The way you acted. I still have that slip of paper, Renee. I found it after you died, when I was going through your things. I found it crumpled in the corner of the nightstand and kept it because it had your handwriting on it. I can find it again. And maybe I will.

"I *knew* something wasn't right when I asked you about it. But I didn't worry because I didn't think you were the type. Now I know there are no types. Anyone is the type. For anything."

I lay down, tired.

"So maybe I will go to Boston. But I'm going to come back. I'm not going to run, Renee. I'm going to stay here…"

Sleep.

⌇⌇⌇

Something woke me, but I didn't know what. I lay in bed and stared at the ceiling, at the smooth white paint, and noticed a pen mark in the corner. I wondered how it got there. It couldn't have been left without a ladder. The pen mark didn't any have purpose. It was too high for a picture or painting. But, somehow, the blemish was there.

I glanced over at the alarm clock, and my entire body hurt when my head turned. Ten o'clock stared back at me in small green lines. I climbed out of bed and looked out the window at the gray night, then stuffed my black Orioles baseball cap on my head and wandered downstairs. Hungry.

I stopped by the front door. I could see a silhouette of someone through the frosted glass.

I opened the door.

"Hi, Tom."

I knew the voice.

Alison.

I had no idea what to say.

Alison frowned. "You look different than I thought."

⌇⌇⌇

We walked into the den. I turned on the light and noticed how disheveled the room was. Alison stood behind me, still in the hallway, as if she wasn't sure she should follow me farther.

"I thought you were dead," she said.

This surprised me. "What?"

"It's just been so long since I heard from you."

Alison had long dark hair, deep brown eyes, and dark skin.

"Something seems different about you," she said. "Now that I can finally see you."

She didn't have on earrings or any other jewelry.

"How did you find me?" I asked.

Alison smiled. "I know, it's weird. I used the phone book. Why? You didn't want me to come?" Her tone wasn't accusatory.

She had pink paint on her fingernails. Her eyebrows were thin, and a shade lighter than her dark hair.

"No," I said. "I'm glad you did." Even to me, my voice sounded unconvincing.

"Don't you have a daughter?" she asked.

"I did. I mean, I do. But Julie isn't here right now."

"Did she end up with her Aunt?"

"Yeah. I gave her up."

Alison had a small mole on the side of her left eye.

"So that's what's bothering you," she said. "Tom, I'm so sorry."

We were quiet for a few moments.

I shrugged. "I'll be okay."

"Do you mind if I sit down?"

She settled on the couch, near the edge. I sat in the armchair across from her. Alison crossed her legs and wrapped her arms around her stomach. "You look older than I thought you would," she said.

"Thank you?"

She smiled. "But in a good-looking way."

"I'm sorry that I'm so distant," I told her. "I've been...I..."

I killed two people, I didn't tell Alison.

But I could. Their deaths didn't raise any emotions in me.

"When I lost Julie," I said instead, "I kind of lost everything."

"It's okay," Alison told me. "We can talk, or we don't have to talk. Whatever you want."

"Want a tour of the house?"

"Sure," she said. "Might as well see where I'm sleeping tonight."

Despite everything, that almost made me smile. "You think you're staying here?"

"You don't want me to?" she asked, and there was something flirtatious about her face that, for the moment, I fell overwhelmingly in love with.

Then, suddenly, memories of Renee invaded, like an army...

ᏜᏜᏜ

Renee decorated the house with pictures she had taken of the city, black-and-white photographs of Baltimore's bay, its streets, Canton, Fells, her sitting on a cannon when we visited Fort McHenry, smiling into the distance. Renee used to have a long old wooden dresser with a long old mirror, the dresser covered with more pictures, brushes, watches, a carved ornamental box, tiny stuffed animals, old books, a lamp, and a glass flower jar in which she collected change. She kept an empty hope chest in front of the bed. She kept a rosary among the books on her nightstand.

Renee would wear my T-shirts to bed, and in the morning she would sit up, yawn, stretch in the sunlight in our warm room, and pull the shirt off—the graceful way women remove their shirts, with two hands from behind. She would turn and see me looking up at her, and she would bend over to me, smiling. One hand would hold herself up, and her other would be below, on me. Her eyes watched me mischievously, her hips turned toward me, and then I was lost in her. Before I knew it years had passed. Before I knew it over a thousand nights had passed, like words slipping after each other in a romantic sentence, and then the sentence ended.

 espes

I led Alison to the guest bedroom. "So," I said, "here's where you'll stay."

Alison looked around the small room and asked, "You sleep in here?"

"No. I sleep in another bedroom."

"Oh." Alison walked into the room, her arms wrapped around her as if she was cold.

espes

"Do you want waffles?" I asked, after I got out of the shower the next morning and knocked on her door.

"Don't you have to go to work?"

"I've been off work for a while."

"You lost your daughter and your job?"

"I haven't lost my job yet. Probably will soon."

We were quiet for a moment.

"I'm going to go downstairs."

I headed into the kitchen and opened the freezer. I pulled out a box of Eggos, dropped two in the toaster, and set some plates on the table. The table didn't look particularly nice—in fact, nothing in my house did—but it would do. Besides, I didn't think Alison would care.

Alison came downstairs wearing the same clothes she wore last night. She glanced at a plate with waffles heaped on it. "You're really into waffles, aren't you?"

"You're not?"

She ignored me. "So...I went to your bedroom. I thought you'd be there. Is that Renee? In the picture on the nightstand next to the bed?"

"Yeah."

"She was pretty."

"I found out she was sleeping with someone else. She was having an affair before she died. And do you really like waffles, or were you just saying that?"

Alison looked at me. "Are you serious?"

"Yup."

"Wow. That's terrible."

"Yup."

"How'd you find out?"

"Long story. And not one I want to tell right now."

Alison suddenly screamed. "What's that?!"

"What's what?" I asked, then looked to where she was pointing. "Oh, that's Bananas."

"Why is a rabbit on your kitchen floor? Is it a pet?"

I nodded. "I like having him around. He doesn't do anything, really."

"He's chewing the bottom of one of your cabinets."

"He likes eating wood."

"Okay," Alison said. Her expression was worried then faded to something like defeat.

I decided to go for a walk after breakfast. Alison wanted to come, but then said she didn't feel like going.

"No problem," I told her.

"On second thought," Alison said, "I want to go." She ran upstairs and came down with her purse and wearing one of my hooded sweaters. She pulled the hood over her head when we stepped outside.

"I don't really know Baltimore very well," Alison told me. She looked like she expected the cast of *The Wire* to pop out from behind the corner. "Where do you want to go?"

"How about we go to Fells Point, or maybe Highlandtown? There's a hill there where—" I stopped speaking. I was just about to tell Alison about Patterson Park. "Maybe we could just go to the harbor," I told her instead. "We can walk there from here."

Five minutes later we were on the harbor's wide pathway, passing people heading in the other direction. It was about three in the afternoon and cold, but there were still a lot of people out. And there was holiday festivity in the air. Green wreaths and red bows were strung over the streetlights, and most people carried two or three shopping bags.

"I was never really into Christmas," Alison said, and she pointed to a bench. "Can we sit down over there, away from the crowd?"

"Sure."

We walked over to the bench and Alison sat next to me. She leaned in so close that I thought she was going to kiss my neck, but instead she said, "You're really sad."

Her statement startled me. "You think I'm pathetic?"

"No. I mean sad as in, not happy."

"I don't feel unhappy."

"You barely said anything when I showed up on your doorstep last night. You had me stay in a different room. You haven't even tried to kiss me or touch me." Alison sounded like she was going through a checklist. "That's not how you were when we got together before. Is this all because of what you learned about Renee?"

Anger flared in me, sudden and surprising. I took a moment before I spoke. "You want to know what happened to me?" I asked, looking straight ahead. "You really want to know?"

"Okay."

I kept my gaze forward as I spoke. "Alison, I hired people to kill the man who killed Renee."

"I thought she died in a car accident."

"She didn't. And things ended up going...really wrong. And I had to kill them to protect myself and my daughter."

"Are you going to go to the police?"

"No."

She looked around and lowered her voice. I was taken aback by her lack of surprise and I wondered if she believed me. "But they'll find you."

I shook my head. "They won't find bodies. Someone must have cleaned up the mess. Nothing in the papers or TV about it."

"But you don't want to go to the cops for protection?"

"They won't protect me."

"If you killed someone, then shouldn't you tell them?"

"No."

"Don't you feel guilty?"

I didn't respond.

"They'll find you eventually," she warned me. "Someone will tell them."

"You're the only person I've told. You're the only person who even knows I was involved."

"So, why did you tell me?"

"You asked. And kept asking."

"And how do you know I won't go to the cops?"

"I don't," I told Alison, and opened my coat to show her the gun tucked in a holster under my arm. "But it's not the cops you should be worried about."

People in the harbor walked by us, talking, laughing, going on about their lives. No one noticed Alison and me, or the gun hidden between us.

"You're going to shoot me?" she asked.

"I want you to know that I will shoot you. Do you understand that?"

"I believe you." Her voice was strained in a whisper. If she hadn't believed me before, she did now.

I closed my coat. "You can't tell anyone about me, Alison. Ever. Do you understand that?"

She nodded.

"Get out of here."

She stood and hurried away. I watched Alison walk and stayed on the bench until she was out of sight.

Then I stood and started off in the other direction. I didn't let myself look back.

CHAPTER 19

Winter, Spring, Summer, Fall

Chris Taylor's mother answered the door.

"Can I help you?" she asked, squinting at me.

"Is your son home?"

"No, he's not," she told me, peering through the crack between the doorframe and the door. "What is this about?"

"I'm with the Virginia prison system, and we're doing research on the employment prospects for former inmates." It was amazing how easily lying came to me now. Effortless. Sometimes you sink, sometimes you dive.

"You look familiar to me," she said.

"I get that a lot."

The door opened wider. "Well, you can talk to me. I'll answer any questions you have."

She let me in and led me to the living room. The living room was antiquated, with floral prints over the couch, arm chair, and drapes, and dusty dark hardwood floors. She sat on an armchair and motioned for me to take a seat on the couch. The cushion was hard beneath me, as if this was the first time it had been sat on.

"Can I have your name?" she asked. "Chris always tells me not to let people I don't know in, but I just..." She let the sentence trail away and smiled.

"Bardos."

"I'm Christine." Christine Taylor was wearing large eyeglasses with a chain, dark pants and a light blue sweater.

"Was Chris named after you?"

She nodded.

"How has his search for work been?"

"No one will hire him," she complained. "He can't find a job. And I keep this place on my husband's life insurance. If Chris doesn't find work soon, then..." She looked away. "I'm sorry."

"It's all right."

Silence for a moment.

"On a personal note," I said, "I reviewed his case, and it doesn't look like they ever had enough evidence against your son. But they still convicted him."

"You're right."

"Do you believe he was guilty?"

"He's my son," Christine said, as if that answered the question. "They never caught the right man."

"You seem...you don't seem angry, then, about what happened to Chris."

Christine leaned forward, her hands clasped over her knees.

"God has everything happen for a reason. I do believe that."

"Do you mind me asking what reason was there for Chris to be in jail, if he was innocent?"

She spread her arms. "I don't know."

"What reason was there for Renee Starks to die?"

"I don't know," she said again. "I don't presume to understand how the Lord works."

"You just know He works, and that's it?"

Christine adjusted her glasses. "You had some questions for me about employment?"

"I'm sorry," I said, suddenly reminded of what I had told her. "I do. I got caught up in the conversation. This has been on my mind a lot lately."

Christine nodded. "People ask me how I was able to keep my faith, after Chris was taken away. And I told them that I believed in a just God, and the men who were responsible would be punished for what they had done. The Lord would find a way to reach them." Christine closed her eyes before she spoke again. "Punish them, O God, let them fall by their own devices, cast them out for their many sins, because they have rebelled against you." She opened her eyes. "Sooner or later, those men will pay for what they have done. He'll send someone to avenge her."

"If these men suffer and die, do you think that's the will of God?"

"I told you I don't know the will of God."

"But...you seem to think God is going to do something, even if you're not going to understand it. That doesn't make a lot of sense to me."

Christine adjusted her glasses again. "Faith is belief in what you can't see."

"Your son was in jail for three years for a crime he had nothing to do with. That doesn't sound like a just God."

"It does if Chris wasn't innocent."

"What?"

Her voice lowered. "He was not uninvolved with that woman's death."

I stared at Christine.

"He served three years for a crime he committed," she said. "The law said so. My heart says so. He was guilty, and he was punished."

Moments, maybe even minutes, of silence passed between us. I could hear a clock tick from somewhere in the room, and I smelled the cherry red candles.

"He confessed to you," I asked, "about killing Renee Starks?"

Christine looked at me for a long time then she slowly shook her head. "No. He did not. But I believe he was involved. I believe it deeply."

An urge suddenly overcame me. "I should probably go," I said.

She stayed seated. "Didn't you need more information about Chris?"

"I have enough."

Christine rose, slowly. "I'll walk you out."

When we reached the front door, she told me, "Please, Mr. Bardos, don't tell anyone what I believe. It doesn't matter to anyone at this point, but it does matter to me, and it does matter to Chris."

"I won't tell anyone."

She squinted at me. "Are you sure I don't know you?"

"I'm sure."

The night was cold, but the chill in the air, the occasional passing car, and the darkness seemed to distance themselves from me as I walked to my truck. Stars dotted the night, burning so brightly that they gave the illusion they would last forever.

☙☙☙

I surveyed the parking lot outside of Mack's Guns and Gifts to make sure it was empty. Then, after checking my Glock, I shoved open the door and thought, distantly, how strange it was that just a couple of weeks earlier I had been hesitant about even stepping inside this store.

The three small aisles were empty. Mack was standing behind the counter. He saw me and started to lift his hand from under the counter. I fired a shot that spun Mack around, and he cried out as he crashed into the wall behind him and crumpled to the floor.

I locked the door behind me and walked over to him. Mack was lying on the floor, clutching his arm. Blood covered his fingers.

I knelt next to him and examined his wound. "Just grazed you," I said.

"You're a son of a bitch," Mack told me, his raspy voice trembling with anger. "You got my friends killed."

I shook my head. "Just one of them. And she would have killed me if I hadn't."

"What happened that night?"

"Diane and Bardos killed everyone that Bailey brought. Then Bardos was killed. I killed Bailey and Diane."

"You liar. You couldn't have...*you*, a green..."

"I just finished what they had started."

"So now you're some sort of assassin."

"No. I just have one more job to do, then I'm retiring."

"Me, right?"

"That's right."

Mack looked so angry that I thought he was going to curse at me again, but the fire left his eyes and he slumped down, so that only the back of his head was resting against the wall. "Diane and Frank are gone," he said.

"Who's Frank?"

"You called him Bardos."

"Frank? No wonder he went for Bardos."

"Tom ain't much better."

"Well, technically, it's Tomás."

"Look," Mack said, and he touched the wound on his arm and winced. "If you're going to do it, then just do it. I don't want to waste time talking to you. You piss me the hell off."

I obliged by holding my gun to his head.

"Shoot me, and then go on and keep killing," Mack grumbled. "Till someone comes up and ends you, you little—"

"I told you," I said. "After you, I'm done."

"There's more," Mack said. "There's always more. You got, what, the people who got your wife, and you got me and Diane and Frank? You think that's it? You think I don't know people who will find you?"

Something in my face must have changed, because Mack sounded encouraged as he kept talking. "You think they won't look for you?"

I stayed silent.

"You can get the drop on me, a seventy-five year old man, but even you told me that you only took out Bailey and Diane after they were almost dead."

I rubbed my forehead with my free hand.

"You don't have the stomach for this, do you?" Mack sneered.

"Well," I said. "I could probably kill you, but that's it."

"That isn't it," Mack said. "You're in, and you ain't leaving."

I lowered my gun. "Is there any way out?"

Mack smiled and used one arm to push himself back up to a sitting position.

"Look," I said, "this isn't just for me. There are other people involved, other people in my life."

"You're a widower. No family. A mom almost as old as me in Florida. Daughter ain't yours. Nobody here."

"I have people that I care about. Give me an option. Please." It felt strange to be the one asking, begging, when I was holding the gun and he had the wound, but I didn't know what else to do.

Mack studied me. "You're scared."

"Yes. Because it won't just be me who gets hurt."

"I can tell everyone to leave you alone," Mack said, "tell them that the situation with you is over, but you got to do a lot for me."

"What?"

"You owed Diane and Frank five thousand for Carr and Bailey. You paid them some. I want the rest of it."

"Fine."

"And I lost my friends."

"What do you want me to do about that?"

Mack touched his wound again and grimaced. "You can't put a price on a friend."

"How about five thousand?"

"Ten."

"So you want fifteen thousand total? Right now?"

"You can pay me over time. Not too much time, because I want to be here to get it all."

"You know I'm a teacher, right? It would take me...five years, fifteen thousand...to pay you, after bills and everything else."

"You can have three."

"Four."

"Fine," Mack assented.

"Is that it?"

Mack grinned. "One last thing."

"What?"

"I want to shoot you in the arm."

"Absolutely not."

The grin grew. "Just like you got me. I ain't going to stick a bullet in you, just have it graze you. That's what I want."

"You expect me to give you a gun and let you shoot me?"

Mack nodded.

"Why?"

"Because," Mack said, "you shot me. And because I still don't like you. And because I think, somewhere up in heaven, it would make Diane and Frank real happy."

"You're being optimistic about heaven."

"Enough of that. Help me up and give me your gun."

I placed my gun on the counter, bent down, lifted Mack by the waist and stood him up. He seemed a little wobbly as he reached for my gun.

"Wait," I said, taking the gun before he could. "How do I know you're not just going to kill me?"

Mack considered it. "That's a good point," he admitted.

We were silent for a few moments.

"You could point a gun at me at the same time," he said.

"But what if you do shoot me in the arm, and then I accidentally pull the trigger and kill you?"

He grunted. "Fair enough."

Again, we lapsed into thought.

"Well, here's the thing," he said. "If I shoot you, then I'm out fifteen grand."

"Yeah, but Diane was able to get into my account. I'm sure you could too, or you could find someone to do it for you."

"That's true," Mack acknowledged. "I probably could."

"How about this?" I said. "I shoot myself in the arm?"

"But I want to do it," Mack whined.

"Then how about you do it, but I get to hold your hand, to make sure that the gun stays pointed at my arm?"

Mack brightened. "Yes!"

"Okay," I said, grimly. "I need to hold your arm because you're all wobbly and unsteady right now, and I don't trust your aim."

"Well, I wonder why that is."

"Let's just do this," I said, and gave him the gun and grabbed his hand.

Together, we slowly pointed it at my arm.

"Wait," I said, jerking the gun away. "That's too high. That's my shoulder."

"Got to aim for the meat," Mack said. "And you ain't exactly a body builder."

"Can we do it a little lower, between the bicep and the shoulder?"

Mack shrugged and winced. "Your arm."

We aimed the gun, but I pushed it away again.

"How much is this going to hurt?" I asked.

"Oh," Mack nodded. "It'll hurt. Ever had a tattoo?"

"No."

"It's worse than that."

"You have a tattoo? What of?"

"Stop stalling," Mack said, and he brought the gun back to my arm.

We aimed the gun at the spot just under my shoulder, on the outside of my arm.

"Wait!" I cried out, again, but Mack just said, "Horsedick," and pulled the trigger.

❦❦❦

I was on the floor, writhing in pain. My arm felt like it had been seared with a branding iron.

"What the hell was that?" I shrieked.

Mack looked down at me, grinning, the gun smoking in his hand. I could smell gunpowder everywhere.

"Hurts don't it?" he asked, and he tossed my gun on the counter.

"That was terrible!" I held the wound with my free hand and curled in a ball.

Mack bent down and looked closely at me. "Did you piss yourself a little?"

"I don't know, Mack! I'm not sure what happened after I *got shot in the arm*!"

"I think you pissed yourself," Mack said, and he straightened. "Come on. It ain't that bad."

I breathed deeply and rose to my knees, still clutching my arm. After a few more moments, I was able to stand. "This is bullshit," I told him. "You should only make me pay ten thousand after that."

"Nope."

"Well, is that it? Are we done here? Am I free to go?"

Mack shook his head, hobbled over to the counter, opened a drawer, and laid a bottle of rubbing alcohol, a sewing kit and a pack of bandages on the countertop. "Let me patch you up."

"I have one thing I need to do," I told him, as he doused a rag in alcohol. "But I need help. From you."

"Yeah? What's that?"

"I need to find one last person."

CHAPTER 20

The Last Person Left

I didn't plan on staying in Boston longer than the three days I had already been here. I left my hotel and slipped into a cab. It was a quiet ride. The cab driver didn't say anything to me the entire way as I read *The Count of Monte Cristo.*

The driver stopped in the financial district and I placed *The Count* in my satchel, paid, and stepped outside. A blast of cold air struck my face. I hadn't realized how windy it was. My shoulder ached from the wound, but not enough to stop me.

I walked inside a building with a marble-floored lobby crowded with people. It was almost five o'clock in the afternoon, and it seemed like everybody was leaving. More people than I expected. I thought lawyers worked until late in the evening, except for the man I was here to see. I knew when he left the office. He had left at the exact same time the past three days.

I took an elevator to the parking garage. When the doors opened, I walked to the wall on my left, slid behind a BMW with dark tinted windows, and waited.

About twenty minutes later, I saw the elevator doors open and he walked toward me. I ducked down, lower than the car windows. He unlocked the doors and climbed inside as I took my gun out of my satchel.

I entered the backseat and pressed Bardos's gun against the side of his head before he could turn around.

"Look forward and don't make any quick movements. You're Phillip Stone?" I already knew he was.

"Do I know you?" His voice was shaking.

"Do you remember Renee Starks?"

Phillip started. "You're her husband?" he asked, hoarsely.

"I was."

His voice was still a rasp. "There were other people involved. It wasn't just me."

"I know. I've met them."

"It was a mistake. The whole thing was a mistake. I regret it everyday."

"Drive to the other side of the garage. No one's parked over there. I want you to pull into a space in the corner, head first. Do you understand me?"

Phillip did, driving us to the dark, isolated corner of the garage, where I told him to shut off the engine.

"Okay, listen," Phillip said, after the car was silent. He slowly reached toward a small picture hanging from his rear view mirror and turned on the interior light. "Do you see that?" he asked, his voice earnest. "If they find out what I did, I'll lose them. I don't care about my job or anything else. I can't lose my family."

"I know what that's like."

"Is that what you want? You want me to confess what I did?"

I briefly looked at the picture. A pretty smiling wife, two squinting kids in Sunday church clothes, Phillip standing behind them, overshadowing everybody.

"They can't find out," he said. "If they did, I'd—"

"I'm not going to tell them anything," I said, and I flipped off the interior light with my free hand. "That's the reason I came here to kill you, instead of doing it at your home."

It was obvious Phillip was afraid, but there also seemed to be something inside him that refused to give into panic, some natural inclination to turn to bargaining. I could see why he had become a lawyer. "What do you want?"

I reached back for the door and made sure it was locked. "Tell me about her."

"About who? My wife?"

"Renee."

"What do you—what do you want to know?"

"I want to know about the affair."

"Renee and I met—we met in, um, just after college—" Phillip's voice wavered, and whatever control he had left. He started crying.

"Come on, Phil. Calm down. I'm not going to kill you."

"You're not?"

I tapped my gun against his head. "Not until you're done telling the story. So it's in your interest to tell me everything you can. Make your time last."

"Is there—is there any way you won't kill me?"

"No."

Phillip still sounded terrified. "We met after college and dated for, like a year. But it didn't work out, and—"

"Why didn't it work out?"

"I don't remember! Oh God, I'm sorry, I don't remember."

"Think, Phil."

"It's because I moved here. That's it. It's because I moved to Boston. That's why!"

"Keep going."

"But we kept in touch. I came here because I thought I wanted to be a musician, because I play the piano, or played back then, and I was in a band and we thought moving here would help. But the band broke up, because we weren't very good. I mean, we were okay, but it was so hard to get gigs, and we had a stupid name. I think it was the High Tides, but I'm not sure."

"Stick to the parts about Renee, Phil."

"She came up here to see us play a couple of times, but then I met my wife, and I stopped seeing her. We kept in touch, but we stopped—we stopped sleeping together. And she started seeing someone else, who got her pregnant."

"Who was the guy who got her pregnant? Do you know his name?"

"No."

"Keep talking."

"My wife's father was—after the band broke up, I thought that maybe I wanted to be a lawyer, and my wife's father, and his father, were all lawyers, and it seemed to be a good way to get her family to like me. I mean, they weren't thrilled that she was dating a musician. So they got me into a good law school here and helped me out. I mean, I'm not an idiot, but I couldn't have gotten into that school without their help."

"You're saying *I mean* a lot, Phil."

"Is that a bad thing?"

"Pet peeve of mine. Kind of like when people say *like* too much."

"I'm sorry," Phillip said, his voice raised, "but it's hard to talk well when a gun is pressing against your head."

"You're a lawyer. I thought you'd be better under pressure."

"I'm not a trial attorney! I mainly do research and—"

"Phil."

"Yes?"

"Back to the story."

I heard him take a deep breath then he asked, "What was I saying?"

"Your father-in-law got you into law school. So your wife comes from money?"

He nodded. "Yes."

"That why you married her?"

He shook his head. "I loved her. I mean—I'm sorry, I shouldn't have said *I mean*."

"I'll let it slide."

"I meant that I do love her."

"Don't start crying again, Phil. So her family got you into law school and probably paid for it, right?"

"Yeah. Law school, our house, our kids' schools, they've helped with everything."

"And you were still keeping in touch with Renee."

"Yeah, I was."

"Why?"

Phillip shrugged, helplessly. "Renee and I always had—we always had this sort of relationship that, we just sort of always turned to each other, and—"

"Phillip."

"What?"

"You're Julie's father, aren't you?"

"What? No," Phillip said, and he turned and looked back toward me, cautiously.

I sank into the back seat. The gun was limply at my side.

My mind felt like it had fallen into a deep ditch.

"You're Julie's father," I said again, slowly.

"How—how do you know?"

"You were married, but still seeing Renee." I was still speaking slowly, spelling everything out. "You didn't stop seeing her. You slept with Renee, and she got pregnant, and you never told your wife. Have you ever met Julie?"

He shook his head. "I saw her once. I went to Baltimore and saw her, but I didn't talk to her."

"Julie doesn't know who you are."

"Has she—has she asked about me?"

"No." I lifted the gun and he started to speak, but I interrupted him. "You're not done with your story." I pushed the gun against the side of his head again until he was looking away from me and out the windshield. "Keep talking."

It took a few moments for Phillip to start. "After Renee had Julie, she was just—Renee was just shattered. I would spend a lot of nights on the phone with her, trying to comfort her. She was alone, and she had *nothing* going for her. And I was pretty much the only person she had to turn to."

"Did your wife know you were having these conversations?"

"No. She had no idea. I would talk to Renee from campus. My wife thought I was studying."

"Your grades must have been terrific."

He let out a little laugh. "No kidding."

I shoved the gun against him until his head bumped against the window. "Don't get comfortable," I told him. "You're not making any headway with me. I don't care who you are. Do you understand?"

I barely heard his, "Yes."

"Then keep talking."

He took a breath. "I was under a lot of pressure, with school and with my engagement and the marriage, and I took a couple of trips to Baltimore to visit my family. I told Jen—"

"Jen?"

"My wife. I told Jen that I wanted to go alone. I told her that because I needed to get away from everything. And I did see Renee, but she wouldn't let me see Julie. Renee came to my hotel room and we fought. I think we both felt so desperate and scared about everything we were going through that we kind of fell into each other. Again."

A strange feeling was welling in me, strange because emotions had been distant from me for a while now. Pity. Not for Phillip, but for this image of Renee, by herself in Baltimore with a small baby, terrified of being alone and turning to someone from her past out of depression, out of desperation.

And anger, that I never knew any of this.

"That happened a few times," Phillip continued. "It wasn't like an affair, at least, I didn't think it was, but we did see each other before and after I got married. Sometimes I think even a year would pass between visits, but we always stayed in touch, and then we'd meet up in Chicago, or something—"

"Wait, Chicago?"

"No, I'm sorry, not Chicago. That wasn't her."

"There was someone else you were sleeping with?"

Again, a barely audible, "Yes."

"Phil, I don't know whether to be impressed or disgusted. You're still sleeping with someone other than your wife, aren't you?"

He nodded.

"Eh, I don't really care. I'm not here to judge you."

"Then why are you here?"

"I'm not the judge or jury, Phil."

I heard him swallow before he spoke. "Renee and I kept seeing each other until she met you, to be honest. She told me about you, and I could tell that it was going to end with us. I could tell by her voice."

"Then what?"

"So I didn't hear from her for a long time. I mean, I always thought about her, and I sent her e-mails once in a while, but I stopped hearing from her. Then, one day, I'm traveling to L.A. for business, and I see her. In my hotel."

"You and she ended up in the same hotel, across the country, by accident?"

"I swear it! I swear it. She was visiting her friend in L.A., and we ended up at the same hotel for the week. She couldn't stay with her friend because she'd just had a kid or something. It felt like—it felt like fate."

I remembered the trip, just a month or two before her death. "What happened?"

His voice faltered as he spoke. "With Renee and I, there was always something there."

My finger was curled so tightly around the trigger that it ached. If the safety hadn't been on, Phillip's brain would have been spread over the car and on the wall outside.

"It was just a coincidence, but it seemed like more, you know, like I said, fate. Nothing happened for the first few days, or most of the week, but we spent a lot of dinners together, called and texted during the day, had breakfast at the hotel before we went to work, but nothing happened. Until the last night."

"Don't tell me those details."

"Really?"

"No. I don't want to know them."

"She hated herself, afterward."

"I don't need to know."

"Everything with her seemed like it was really—intense, afterward. I told her I was in love with her again. She said she couldn't do it anymore."

"So you had her killed because she wouldn't go back to you?"

"No! Her guilt about everything was too much. She wanted to tell you, to tell my wife, to practically tell *The Globe* about everything that had happened with us in L.A. We used to talk on Skype and she looked like death. She said it was eating at her. I mean, you must have seen it in her. The change?"

"No."

"Yeah, so she kept threatening me, and I thought that even if she just told you, word could get back to my wife and—look, I know I'm not the greatest husband, right? But I can't lose my wife or my kids."

"What did you do?"

"One of my uncles is connected—he knows some people. So I told him everything, and asked him if he knew a way to keep her quiet."

"Did you know he was going to kill her?"

"Everything was so surreal right then. I didn't know what was happening. I just couldn't lose my family, everything I had—"

"What did you think was going to happen?"

"I promise you, I didn't think he was going to kill her! I was sick when I found out! I just—I just ended up getting dragged into some mess and got dragged in deeper than I thought."

"I see."

"At the end, I wanted out," he whimpered. "I just wanted out."

Silence.

"When I found out Renee was dead," Phillip said, "I didn't know what to do. I honestly thought about going to the police, but I didn't have the courage to turn myself in. And I couldn't cross my uncle, or the people who had done it. I didn't want them after me either."

"I understand that."

"But I always figured this day would come. I knew I wouldn't go unpunished."

"So that's everything, then?"

He nodded. "Can I say one more thing?"

"Sure."

"I always—I always thought that, with Renee, I was honest. And I'm sorry. I'm so sorry for everything I did."

"I'm sorry, too."

"Please don't—"

"I'm sorry, too," I said again, robotically.

"Please don't kill—"

"I'm sorry. I'm so sorry." I took the gun away from his head and dropped it into the seat next to me, and I covered my face with my hands. Pain shot through my wound, but I ignored it. "Everything that—I'm sorry, too."

I heard rustling. I grabbed the gun and pointed it at Phillip in one motion. He froze in the front seat, his body half-turned to the door.

"Calm down," I said. "Hand off the door, Phillip. Hand off."

He settled back into his seat.

"There's one other thing I need you to do," I told him.

"What?"

"I need you to forgive me."

"What?" he asked again.

"Forgive me."

ം

A few days later I was subbing for Richard James's Advanced Literature class—my bandaged arm still hurt but it was no longer throbbing—waiting for his students to finish filing in. It wasn't a large class. There were only about seven students total, but they all showed up.

"So I see that you were in the process of finishing up Faulkner's *The Wild Palms*," I said. "Did you like it?"

"It's okay," one of the women in class offered. "Kind of confusing."

"It is a confusing book," I admitted. "Honestly, how many of you have skipped parts in your reading?"

No one replied.

"Come on, it's the last day of class. Grades are in. You can go ahead and be honest."

"I did, but just a page or two," someone said.

"Me, too," another student offered.

Gradually, all of the students admitted that they had skipped pages or sections—or, in one case, all—of *The Wild Palms*.

"Well," I said, "that's really terrible. Honestly. You're robbing yourself of one of the greatest American love stories ever written."

"What about Romeo and Juliet?" a student asked.

"Listen," I said, ignoring the question, "take my advice. If you didn't read the book now, or if you feel at a loss at some of the parts, read it later in life. You'll appreciate it."

Silence. This late in the semester it was impossible to get students motivated to do anything.

"All right," I said. "Let's go right to the end. What's happening here?"

The students opened their books.

"Willbourne tells Rittenmeyer that he's going to kill himself," someone said, "but then he refuses to do it and ends up staying a prisoner instead."

"Why does Willbourne refuse suicide?"

"Because it's the only way to keep his memory of Charlotte alive, sort of, after she died. In his mind. Anyway, Willbourne says that if he dies, then his memory of Charlotte will also die."

"Where does it say that?"

"Here," a student said. "At the end. 'So when she became not then half of memory became not and if I become not then all of remembering will cease to be.'"

"Right." I nodded. "And that's followed by the last line in the book, which I think is the most beautiful line in all of literature, 'Yes, he thought, between grief and nothing I will take grief.'"

It took me a moment before I could look up to the class.

"What do you," I asked, "think of his decision?"

"I didn't like it," a student named Mark admitted. "He's going to spend his life living in his past, remembering her."

"I think it's romantic," another student, a woman named Tisha, argued.

"It's romantic in a book," Mark replied. "In life, you would never want someone to live like that."

"What do you mean?" Tisha asked.

"Imagine if you were Willbourne's friend, and he couldn't get over some chick. Would you tell him to remember her forever?"

"Well, first off," Tisha said, "it's different than a choice of remembering her or forgetting about her. It's a choice between life and death. He can be free in death, or he can be alive and in pain. And he chooses to be alive."

"I don't think his choice mattered," a quiet student in the back of class named Eric said. "I just loved how it was written."

"Professor," Mark asked me. "What do you think?"

I had been listening to their comments absent-mindedly, something on my mind, but I wasn't sure what. "Well, I think you're all right."

Someone laughed. "Cop out."

"I think Willbourne made the right choice, especially given how easy it was for him to make it. When Rittenmeyer gives him the cyanide, Willbourne only takes a few seconds to crumble it up and rub it away. That first choice was easy for him. But Willbourne's real sacrifice isn't at that moment. His real sacrifice will happen later, after the book ends, when he'll have to make that same choice again and again. This is the type of choice that will only be made when he is finally over Charlotte. And

I don't think, for Willbourne, that will ever happen. He's alive and damned."

The class was quiet.

"Okay," I told them. "Last assignment. I want you to write down your thoughts about those last pages. Leave it for me and you can leave class whenever you're done. Make it at least a page."

The students started writing as fast as they could. I opened my laptop and turned it on. I checked my e-mail and saw one from Alison.

I stared at the monitor for a moment then opened the message.

> *Tom,*
>
> *I've thought a lot about what happened last week. Honestly, I haven't been able to think of anything else. It keeps me up at night, and I'm constantly crying, and afraid. I went to see a therapist but I can't tell him anything because you told me not to say what really happened. And I don't know what to do.*
>
> *I don't know if I can believe what you told me, but even if you lied, you're still crazy. I've never had a gun pointed at me before, and I've never had my life threatened. You seemed totally different from the man I was with in the hotel room, and I don't get what happened. You told me, and I guess I believe you.*

I wish I didn't, though. I wish I had never gone to see you, or met you, or responded to you in that stupid chat room. I wish my life was the way it had been a month ago. I was lonely, but I didn't know that I wasn't unhappy, if that makes sense.

One of the students brought me her paper, and I lowered the laptop before I took her assignment. She gave me a curious glance. After she left, I lifted the laptop back up and kept reading.

I'll never tell anyone what happened. Just please, please, *promise me that you'll never contact me again. Please tell me that you'll forget about me. Please tell me that we can pretend the last three weeks never happened. You said you'd kill me. Please pretend that you already have.*
Alison

I read the e-mail a few times, unable to identify the feeling rising in me. Students brought their papers to me and said their goodbyes, but I don't remember responding. All I felt was a vague sense of terror, like something in me had come unmoored, and was threatening to overwhelm me. But I didn't know what.

I hit *Reply* and wrote a few responses that I kept deleting. My nervousness was so strong that my fingers were almost to the point of trembling, and I went with:

> *Alison, I'm so sorry for what I said and did. You have my word that I'll never contact you again, and I would never hurt you in any way. I'm so sorry.*
>
> *Tom*

I sent it and, the moment I did, I realized that nothing I wrote to her would matter. Alison would never feel safe or comforted. Nothing I could say would help.

And I did miss her. For a brief moment, I imagined life with Alison and Julie. I had no idea if Alison would have made a good mother, but she had said she wanted children.

She needed a child, Julie needed a mother, and I needed love. I'd had a chance at all three and lost it.

I suddenly desperately wanted to send Alison another e-mail, to beg her to give me another chance, to let me relive the excitement of our anonymous meetings and make them into more, but I didn't. I couldn't.

The last student left and, alone, the feeling floating beneath my surface rose and was so terrible that I pushed my chair back, stood, and ran to the men's restroom. I found an empty stall, rushed inside, and closed the door behind me.

More than I ever had, more than I ever thought possible, I missed Renee.

Grief overtook me like a brightly flared match. I curled up and wrapped my arms around myself, the bullet wound throbbing with the contact but I barely noticed. A sob broke from me, and I realized, distantly, that I was saying her name, over and over.

Renee was gone. And there was nothing I could do about that.

CHAPTER 21

Nothing But You

One should wait for death there, where one has found happiness." I stopped reading and looked up at the class. "All right, any thoughts on this line, in the last chapters of the book?"

No takers for a few moments then Marcia hesitantly raised her hand.

I nodded in her direction.

"When Mercedes says it," Marcia said, "she's thanking the Count for bringing her back to where she used to live, because she feels like she's going to die soon. And she wants to die where she was happiest."

"All right. Anything else?"

I didn't expect an answer and didn't receive one. Grades were decided and I was pretty sure they considered attending this final class largely as a favor to me.

"Here's what I think Dumas is saying," I told them. "Death is all around us, and unpredictable, and we should live our lives in a way that ensures happiness when it comes." I thought for a moment. "But that's too easy. Look at Edmond. He's spent the entire book, his entire life, trying to ruin the happiness of the people who wronged him. But he never found happiness. He almost found death a few times and, in every instance, he would have died unhappily. So his vengeance failed him, and his quest failed him. Does anyone here think that Edmond might have been happier if he had never become the Count?"

"I dunno," Sam said, slowly, thinking as he spoke. "He kind of had to go through all this stuff to get to where he is. Like, he would have regretted never doing anything."

"So he was going to be unhappy no matter what?"

"I think so."

"But he's not unhappy," Song argued, tossing her hair over her opposite shoulder. "He tells Mercedes and Morrel that his work was God's work and God's retribution. So he thinks he did something good. He never says he wouldn't have done it."

"But he's not, like, guilt-free," Sam countered. "What does he tell Mercedes?" He frowned into his book and turned the pages. "Here!" he said triumphantly. "He tells Mercedes, 'I made myself into a vindictive, treacherous and wicked man.' That doesn't sound happy."

"Okay," Song said. "He's not at peace yet. He even tells Morrel that a few pages later. But he also tells Morrel, when he takes him to the island of Monte Cristo in the final chapter, that he has suffered enough to finally have happiness. And that's when he shows him that Valentine really is alive."

"And what's the process Morrel goes through before he learns that Valentine is alive?" I asked.

"He has to die," Song answered. "Or commit suicide. Or he thinks he commits suicide, anyway."

"So again," I said, "someone has to die to be reborn. That theme continues all the way to the end of the book. And Edmond has gone from the person that dies and is reborn, to the person that administers death for someone else. He has moved from patient to doctor, or from student to teacher. But back to what you were discussing. Is Edmond happy?"

"It's hard to tell," Song said. "He seems happy. I mean, the book ends with him sailing off into the sunset, right? That's kind of the ultimate ending."

"But when someone sails off into the sunset," Sam replied, "like in a movie, it's hard to tell how they're feeling, because you're never with them. All you can do is guess. And try and figure things out from what other people are saying."

"Well," Tamara, who rarely spoke, offered, "it seems like his happiness is in making other people happy. He keeps Haydee with him, because she told him that she'd die of unhappiness without him. He spent the whole book breaking people down, and now it seems like he's going to spend the rest of his life trying to do the opposite."

"But he's making other people happy," Song argued. "What about himself?"

"What do you think, professor?" Marcia asked. "Do you think Edmond ever found peace?"

എരുഷ

"Can I come in?"

Dave stood in his doorway, regarding me with suspicion, then he stepped back. "Here to see Julie?"

"Yeah."

Ruth appeared behind Dave. "Hey, Tom. What do you want?"

"I wanted to talk with both of you." I headed inside and went to the living room. "Julie's upstairs?"

Dave and Ruth stood next to each other in the arched entrance to the living room. "Yes," Ruth said.

"Don't tell her I'm here yet." I took a seat in a leather recliner and directed them to their sectional. When I sat down, the cushions let out a leather scent that wrapped around me. I had noticed the smell before, but never placed it until now. It smelled like wealth.

Dave had a perplexed smile on his face. "Well," he said, speaking slowly, "I was just making some iced tea, so I'm going to finish that, but I'll be right back." He walked out of the living room and Ruth sat on their couch, close to the chair I was in.

She leaned toward me. "What are you doing here?" she asked, her voice a high whisper. "And why are you acting this way?"

"What way?"

"Manly. It's a weird look for you."

"I want Julie back. Today."

She shook her head. "That's not going to happen."

"You give her to me, or I tell Dave everything that happened between us."

Ruth's eyes widened, and she was about to speak when Dave came back. "Tom, do you want any tea? Or anything else? Beer, soda?"

"Just a glass of water."

Ruth leaned toward me again once Dave left. "You wouldn't dare."

"Try me."

"He'll kill you."

"I doubt that."

Dave reappeared, holding a tray with three glasses on it. He set it down on the table between us. "Crap," he said. "Forgot the sugar. Be right back."

"Tom, please," Ruth said, as soon as Dave left. Her eyes were filled with tears. "Please. You know how much I want a child. Please—don't do this. I'm begging you."

I shook my head. "Give her to me or I tell him everything."

"Tom—she's all I have left of Renee."

I looked away from her, but Ruth stared at me until Dave walked back in the room, holding a small canister.

"All right," he told me, as he sat down next to Ruth. "What can we do you for?"

"I'm taking Julie back home."

Dave nodded then used a small spoon to pour sugar into his tea. He stirred as he spoke. "Tom, Ruth and I talked about it, and we think it's a good idea that Julie stay with us from now on."

"I think Ruth changed her mind."

Dave looked quickly at Ruth. "It may be better for Julie," she said, quietly, looking into her lap.

Dave seemed stunned. "What?"

"I'm sorry," she whispered.

He stared at her. "We talked about this—we talked about this last night!"

"Dave," Ruth said, and her voice broke. "I'm sorry. I just feel differently about it now." Her face stayed down.

"Julie will still be around," I told them. "You'll still see her all the time. I want her to be around you. But I'm her dad, and she needs to live with me."

Ruth abruptly stood and left the room.

Dave stared after her for a few moments then he turned to me. He clasped his hands together and rested his chin over his fingers. "Tom," he said, and his voice was as hard as stone, "I don't know what wild hair you have up your ass, but you're not taking Julie away from us. Especially after your last visit here."

"That's been settled."

Dave eyed me carefully. He seemed very methodical and deliberate in everything he did. "Really?"

"Really."

"Are you going to tell me about it?"

"No. But there's nothing to worry about. You know I wouldn't take her back if I thought she was in any danger."

"I think you need to tell me what happened."

I shook my head. "I promise you, everything is safe now. Like I said, I wouldn't want Julie to live with me if I had doubts about her safety."

"Fair enough," Dave agreed, surprising me. "But I don't think you're fit to be her father."

"Nothing I can say would make you change your mind. But, legally, you can't stop me from taking her."

Dave smiled a slight smile. "You really think you could win a court case against me?"

"Well, there is this attorney in Boston who owes me a favor…"

"Actually, you're right," he said, surprising me again. "Legally, there's not much I can do. I could try to prove that you're unfit, but I don't actually believe that. What I do believe is that Julie has a better home here, as well as a better future. The simple facts are that two parents are better than one, and we have more money, time, and resources to dedicate to her. We can give her more than you can, and living with us is better for her. Her grades have already improved."

"I don't disagree with you," I told him. "I'm not saying I was the best father, or that I even gave her the best home. But I want to try again."

"And so do we," Dave said reasonably. "The difference is, when things get too hard, unlike you, we won't give her up." He raised a hand, stopping me before I could speak. "And you did give her up. Say whatever you want, that's what happened."

I didn't know how to respond.

"If you were her," Dave said, "who do you think would be better to stay with? For her best interests? Do you think it's wise to give her a life with less potential?"

"It is, if I love her. That doesn't make sense, but you know what I mean." I thought for a moment. "Look, Dave. You're right. You and Ruth can offer her more. But I realized something—Julie is the only thing in the world I care about. And I've missed her. I miss the stupid stuff, like her little hands and feet, or the way she lumbers up stairs. I miss her awkward questions, and I miss cooking for her. I like when she's eating and I say something to her and she stops with the spoon in her mouth and just looks at me. I like the way she blinks twice when she puts on her glasses, and how she wraps her hair in a towel after a shower, like Renee used to. I like how intensely she stares at the television, as if the characters in a show were real people she had relationships with, and how excited she gets when she gossips on the phone with her girlfriends. I love how she holds her stomach when she laughs too hard. She's going to grow up, and there's no way I'm missing any more of it. I want to be her father."

Dave unclasped his fingers and rested his fists on his knees. "Julie leaves this house over my dead body." His voice was softer, but somehow louder, like a whisper played through a speaker.

I stared at Dave's hand, at the onyx wedding band on his ring finger. His fists seemed much larger than I remembered.

"You want to fight me for her?" I asked.

"I want to do whatever it takes."

"You'll win," I lied. "We both know that."

His fists relaxed. "Okay, then."

"But I'll still fight. And even when you beat me, I'll come back and fight you again. And again. I'll do it until I can't walk anymore."

He leaned close to me. "That's fine with me."

"Dave!" Ruth's voice. We both turned and saw her standing in the doorway to the living room. "Stop it."

"I'm not letting her leave," Dave said.

Ruth shook her head. Tears marked her cheeks. "Tom's right. If we want any part of her life, we have to let her go. Otherwise, he can take her and we'll never see her again."

"We talked about this," Dave said. His voice was hoarse.

"And we don't have a choice," Ruth told him.

I stood up, and Dave looked at me quickly, surprised, like he was about to jump up and stop me, but he just slumped into the couch. Ruth walked with me to the stairs, but grabbed my arm before I headed up.

"I want to be able to see her," she told me, her voice low, angry.

"I know," I told her. "It'll be just like before."

"If you mess up again, if things get too hard and you quit on her again, you're not getting her back. Do you understand?"

"I'll never give her up again," I said, and I walked upstairs. Julie's door was at the end of a long hall. I walked to it and knocked. "Julie, it's me."

"Come in."

I did. Julie didn't look up. She stayed sitting on her bed, Indian-style, a large book spread open in front of her. Her long brown hair was tied in a pony tail.

"I made a mistake," I told her. "I never should have said what I said. And I never should have given you up. I've made a terrible mistake, and I'm sorry."

No response.

"Julie, I miss you. I know I wasn't that great before, but I want another chance. I promise it'll be different. *I'll* be different."

She looked up at me but her expression told me nothing. Her eyes behind her glasses were blank. She said, almost like an observation, "You're just lonely."

"Well, yeah, I am. But that's because you're not there."

Julie looked back down, pushed her glasses back up her nose, and slowly closed her book. She was staying in one of their guest bedrooms, but it didn't have her small furniture or pictures. The room was too adult for her. "You don't miss me. You miss Mom."

"I miss both of you."

"You miss her more."

I wasn't sure what to say. "I do miss her a lot," I admitted. "But I miss you, too."

Julie didn't say anything.

"Listen," I told her. "I had a moment, and you only have this kind of moment once or twice in your whole life, when I realized exactly what I wanted. I knew without a doubt. I want you."

"But you told me you didn't want to be my dad."

"Honey, I was *kidding.*"

Her eyes flashed up at me. "It's not funny!"

I sat on the edge of her bed and Julie stood and stalked to the window. "You're right. It's not funny," I said, somberly. "Look, I want another chance. I do miss your Mom. I love her a lot. But the worst mistake you can make in your life is not to love somebody when you should. Or know them as well as you should." I paused.

"I don't know how good a dad I can be, but I want to try."

Julie's eyes were hooded, suspicious. "You can't hurt me again, if I do come back."

I didn't tell her how urgently, painfully, the way she quickly glanced at me reminded me of Renee. Instead, I shook my head. "When you're a teenager, I'm probably going to make you really mad. Often. And neither you nor I will be able to help it. But I'll never hurt you the way I did. I can promise you that. No matter what, you'll always know I love you. Always."

"Aunt Ruth and Dave take really good care of me."

"Aunt Ruth and *Uncle* Dave will still be around. You'll see them all the time, whenever you want. All I want is what we had, but better."

Julie waved her hand in front of her eyes to dry away her tears, the way women do. "You'd better not screw this up," she said.

Something in me felt like it was going to break, but warmly. "Are you coming home?"

"Yes, but you have to promise me something."

"What's that?"

"I want to get a tattoo of a star next to my eye. You have to let me."

"No."

She shrugged. "Okay."

"But I do have a surprise for you in the car. A lonely rabbit is sitting in the backseat, waiting for you."

Julie squealed and ran downstairs. I packed her stuff, just what she'd need for the night since I could pick up the rest tomorrow. Then I let her say goodbye to Ruth and Dave while I waited in the car.

It took us about twenty minutes to drive back to our neighborhood, but I parked at the top of Federal Hill instead of driving to our house.

"What's up?" Julie asked.

"I don't know," I said, and I honestly didn't. "I just wanted to stop here instead. Want to walk around?"

"What about Bananas?"

"Let's take him."

Outside, the sun shined even as a chilly wind rushed over us. Julie fastened a harness around Bananas and I looked out over the city, out over the distant buildings of Highlandtown and Hampden, like postcards documenting the major moments of my life. I thought about Renee and a sudden rush of sadness hit me, still strong, but less. Finally, it was less. I glanced over at Julie and she was sitting on the ground, Bananas chewing grass in front of her.

"I remember when we were down there," Julie said and gestured toward the harbor, "for Mom's funeral. When we threw her ashes into the water."

"Me, too."

"I wished we'd picked somewhere else," Julie said. "Now every time I come here I think about her, and I think about how sad I was that day."

"Sometimes when I get sad," I started to tell her, "what helps me is to—"

"And I think about that day." Julie kept on talking. "And I know it's going to happen again and I get really scared. Like, *really* scared. I'd never felt that awful before." She wouldn't look at me, but I heard a shadowy panic moving behind her words.

"I know."

"I don't want to lose anyone else."

I nodded.

"Sometimes I feel like if I wait long enough, and hope hard enough, she'll come back." Julie's voice lowered. "I've never told anyone that." She took off her glasses and rubbed her eyes, then put the glasses back on and looked at me. "What helps you when you're sad?"

"Nothing but you."

Julie scooped Bananas up and we stood. She reached for my hand, held it, and her hand was soft and small in mine, like an empty mitten waiting to be filled. Families and couples dotted the hill, looking out over Baltimore, watching the night whisper down. Lights winked on. A dog barked in the distance. The wind picked up.

We walked away from the water.

The End

About the Author

E.A. Aymar studied creative writing under some terrific professors at George Mason University (2006 Final Four!) and earned a Masters in Literature from some equally terrific professors at Marymount. He has lived throughout the United States and in Europe and was born in Panama, the country with the canal or bridge or something. In addition to writing, and his beloved GMU basketball team, he's also into crafting third-person bios that run no longer than five sentences. He and his wife, and a relatively benign animal menagerie, live just outside of Washington, D.C.

You can find more information about E.A. Aymar's upcoming work and read his weekly blog at www.eaymar.com.

CPSIA information can be obtained
at www.ICGtesting.com
Printed in the USA
LVOW01s2258050117
519946LV00006B/75/P